Praise for book one:
The Ten Riddles of Eartha Quicksmith

'Deeply hilarious and highly intelligent…'
Children's Books Ireland

'An incredibly inventive, fabulously funny book … one of the best children's fantasy books I've read so far this year. Do not miss it!' **Dan Walker, *The Light Hunters***

'Inventive first fantasy novel.'
***The Observer* Best Children's Books of the Month**

The Guardian best books of 2020, chosen by Booksellers

'Brimming with interest and detail ... a thoroughly enjoyable book.' **NSTBA longlist**

'It's exciting, it's funny, and it's very clever … an absolute wonder and a joy.' **@notsotweets / BookWormHole**

'A fast-paced adventure imbued with the true magic of science and all the limitless possibilities of the world.'
Gavin Hetherington

'An amazing story of strange happenings and adventure, skilfully interwoven with messages of friendship and resilience. A fantastic read for anyone young or old, and an ideal choice for whole class reading.'
Sam Phillips, @ReadingZone

Selected for the Summer Reading Challenge working with the Science Museum. Shortlisted for the Leicestershire Libraries children's book award.

Loris Owen likes mysteries, enigmas, conundrums, puzzles and synonyms. She roamed around the world a bit before moving to Kent where she runs a mowl sanctuary and spends her days hunting for interesting combinations of words.

Other books in this series:
The Ten Riddles of Eartha Quicksmith

The Myriad Mysteries of Eartha Quicksmith

LORIS OWEN

First published in 2022
by Firefly Press
25 Gabalfa Road, Llandaff North, Cardiff, CF14 2JJ
www.fireflypress.co.uk

A CIP catalogue record of this book is available from the British Library.

1 3 5 7 9 8 6 4 2

ISBN 978-1-913102-87-6
This book has been published with the support of the Books Council of Wales.

Typeset by Elaine Sharples

Printed by CPI Group (UK) Ltd, Croydon, Surrey, CR0 4YY

To Mum & Dad

All *that we see or seem*
Is but a dream within a dream.
Edgar Allan Poe

INSIDE ATLAS HOUSE:
- HALL OF MAPS (GREAT GLOBE)
PLAYING FIELDS
OLD BOATHOUSE
SIXTH YEAR BLOCK
SKYCRACKLE TOWER
MUSIC ROOMS
BOTANICAL GARDENS
ATLAS HOUSE
CLOCK TOWER
FIFTH YEAR BLOCK
FOURTH YEAR BLOCK
CELESTIAL HALL
SECOND YEAR BLOCK
QUICKSMITHS
COLLEGE OF STRANGE ENERGY
SECURITY CENTRE
BUNKER
GARDEN OF GIANT LEAPFROGS
INSIDE CELESTIAL HALL
- THE BUTTERY
- MISS TWISS'S OFFICE
- COUNCIL ROOM

INSIDE THE LABS:

- PROFESSOR STEAMPUNK'S LAB

SKIMMIDROME

ARISTOTLE'S THEATRE

LIBRARY

SKIMMI REPAIRS

LABS

SINGING MILL

WORKSHOPS

STORAGE ROOMS

PROFESSORS' BLOCK

QUANTUM QUARTER

THE HIVE

PORTERHOUSE

QUICKSMITHS

COLLEGE OF STRANGE ENERGY

FIRST YEAR BLOCK

THIRD YEAR BLOCK

INSIDE THE SINGING MILL:

- PROFESSOR KORIOLIS'S STUDY
- MILL ROOM
- ALBERT AND LEELA'S WORKSHOP

Chapter One

The Ark Hospital

Violet vapour seeped through the keyhole. Seconds later, the vapour solidified, cracked and fell tinkling to the ground in jagged shards. Kip and Albert leapt aside as a burst of light-flecked froth surged through the inch of space under the door and washed away the lavender splinters.

Kip faced the door, his hand ready to knock below the sign.

PROFESSOR STEAMPUNK'S
PYROTECHNIC ARK HOSPITAL
DO NOT DISTURB
(unless you have biscuits)

'Got them ready?' he asked Albert.

Albert grinned and held up his cupped hands, scattering an assortment of crumbs. There was a rustle in Kip's pocket and a small, furry face with soft brown eyes poked out. Pinky yawned, licked her lips, snuffled the pink smudge of her nose, and looked up at Albert hopefully.

'Cannot. Resist. Tiny mind control,' said Albert, lowering the biscuits robotically.

'Nope,' said Kip. 'Professors get professor snacks. Flying squirrels get flying squirrel snacks.'

Pinky looked at the biscuits longingly but took the slice of carrot Kip offered before retreating inside her comfy campsite in the pocket of his cargo shorts.

A faint sound whined out from behind the closed door, and Albert pressed his ear against the wood.

'Sounds like a giant mosquito riding a squeaky unicycle,' he said.

Itching to see what was happening inside, Kip knocked and pushed down the handle at the same time.

The laboratory behind the door was as big as the entire floor of the building and filled with honey-tinted light. An assortment of drones drifted along the gently curving contours of the room, exchanging quiet clicks whenever they met. Winged shadows of varying sizes had been burned into a section of one wall, and the opposite wall was covered in blue splatter marks.

Somewhere near the centre of the mostly empty lab, a black parrot was suspended in mid-air by golden spotlights shining out from some unseen source. Each wingtip pointed to one of two tall spirals that rose up from the floor like gnarled trees.

'The Ark of Ideas,' said Kip, in the kind of hushed voice you might use in the overgrown ruin of a temple.

The Ark of Ideas. The ancient black parrot that had once belonged to Eartha Quicksmith. Everyone at the college knew her story – how an Elizabethan girl from the hardest of beginnings had grown up to be the greatest thinker of all time. And now, four centuries later, Kip and Albert stood before the mechanical bird that had kept the secrets of her forgotten discoveries to itself all this time. Almost to itself.

'It still hasn't quite sunk in,' said Albert. 'Gorvak fooled everyone in the entire college. How could someone as evil as him be related to someone as good as Eartha?'

'Distant relation,' Kip replied. 'Suppose a lot can change in four hundred years.'

'*We* solved Eartha's ten riddles,' said Albert. 'He never should have got to the Ark first and stolen all her ideas. He never should have got away. It's so unfair – that sneaky slimeball slimed up to us and tricked us into thinking he was on our side. I'll never get tricked like that again.'

Kip felt a brief anger flush his face as a memory rose up from that day on the cliff – the day the Ark had been found. The sound Gorvak's boot had made as it connected with the parrot's ribcage.

It didn't need to get broken, Kip thought. *It shouldn't be broken.*

'At least it managed to fly back to us,' he said.

They both stared up at the black parrot.

'I wonder if it's said anything else yet,' Kip murmured.

He felt an urge to stroke the parrot's wing. It looked so fragile. Kip reached out, but then thought better of it. This was a lab, and bursting into the middle of Professor Steampunk's experiment might not be wise.

Instantly proving him right, a ticking sound came from the gnarled spirals and they each released a beam of Strange Energy. A midnight-blue sparkler trail and a stream of orange ripples met in the middle, exactly where the Ark of Ideas was. The two beams skirmished and sputtered, the Ark glowed for a moment, and a downfall of twinkling flakes cascaded to the floor.

'Watch out!' cried Albert.

The glittery residue formed an ankle-high wave which surged towards them with a sound like rattling marbles. They jumped to one side and watched it go past. Kip had been at Quicksmiths for long enough now not to be surprised by the wave of unknown Strange Energy that flowed up the wall, and across the ceiling.

'Looks like my little sis decorated your face,' said Albert cheerily.

Running a hand over his eyes and cheeks, Kip dislodged a rain of sparkles. He looked over at Albert to see lingering glitter melting down over the black starburst that crowned his head.

'Hah!' Kip replied. 'Well, it looks like my face decorated your hair.'

Overhead, the energy beams disappeared and a voice foghorned in their direction from the other side of the lab.

'Try the wingpit switch again will you please, Dennis?'

An Oddjob Drone approached from the left. Drifting at about chest height, it looked like a small, floating, many-trunked elephant. One of these thin trunks reached into the yellow spotlights and flicked a switch concealed under the parrot's wing. Its beak opened and one eye fluttered.

'The Crazy Paving,' rasped the parrot, mechanically. 'The Crazy Paving. The Crazy Paving…'

It went on like that for a while until a second flick of the switch returned the Ark to its silent repose and the drone descended from the spotlights. It turned towards Kip and Albert and regarded them serenely.

'You have guests, Professor Steampunk,' the drone said loudly.

'Thank you, Dennis,' a voice echoed in reply. 'Over here! Follow the path.'

An Ember of Energy

A tarmac-grey pathway curved around the research area at the centre of the lab. When Kip and Albert stepped on it, it sprang into motion, sweeping them past the spiral energy conductors, and towards the far side of the room. As the pathway brought them closer, Kip saw that Professor Steampunk was upside-down, standing on all four of his hands.

Only the best kind of professor blows up their arms in an experiment and then builds themself four new ones, Kip thought, with a smile.

Arms bending at the elbow like short, bow-kneed legs, the professor scuttled over to meet them.

'I'm not always good at thinking on my feet,' explained Steampunk as he sprang lightly the right way up.

His spray of white hair was ruffled from being upside-down, and his face flushed. All in all, he looked not so much like a professor but more like a thin yeti in a lab coat recovering from a recent electric shock.

'Albert, Kip,' he said, 'welcome to the Ark Hospital!'

Albert offered up the handful of slightly squashed biscuits.

'Don't mind if I do, thank you,' said Steampunk, taking four at once, shaking off some glitter, and cramming an entire jaffa cake into his mouth. It was demolished in a few chews, as the professor considered the remaining three. 'Wouldn't it be excellent to have four mouths?' His head twitched as if he'd startled himself with the idea, he scribbled a hasty line in a notebook he took from his pocket, and looked up at the two boys. 'I expect you're here to see how our patient's doing?'

Kip nodded.

'Has the Ark said anything else yet?' he asked, hopefully. 'Except "the crazy paving".'

'The Ark has not squawked,' Professor Steampunk said. 'Not yet. But there is something interesting.'

Steampunk's four arms blurred into motion. He dusted biscuit crumbs off his lab coat and gave his college-issue Candle badge a firm double tap. A carousel of symbols appeared in a ring of hazy light around him, and he began to swipe through them.

Kip leaned in for a closer look. He had a Candle badge himself of course, but he was still learning about everything this powerful little device could do. His class had only been taught how to use the Carousel a few weeks ago. Made of a type of light you could touch, the on-demand console allowed each user to tap into the marvellous functions of GENI's Strange Reality Drive. Like all the First Years, he and Albert were still becoming familiar with the different apps, and Steampunk narrated helpfully as he flicked through the stacks of icons.

'That's the Wingmirror symbol – handy if you need eyes in the back of your head ... Translator ....

Magnifier … Speech Bubble … Wormhole Positioning System … Scratchpad … Camera … Quicket Market. Ah, here we are … Wave Sensor!'

The professor stopped at a symbol formed of a magnifying glass and wavy lines, and ticked it flamboyantly with one finger. A veil of energy readouts appeared all around them.

'The issue has been focusing in on the Ark, which has been a bit challenging because it's such an unusual device, as well as being so oldfangled. But with GENI's help – I really can't imagine how we managed before Strange Supercomputers – and our measuring oojamaflips and a few tricks of my own – well, it looks as if there is an ember of energy left inside…'

'A battery?' Albert said.

'It could be the spark from some form of battery, yes. Or something else. Eartha was a genius after all. And there are many hundreds of combinations of Strange Energies that do gabberflasting things. It's a bit too early to tell you much more. Why don't you come back on Saturday morning – that gives me a couple of days.'

Kip and Albert stepped on the travelator path which began to propel them back towards the exit.

'Fear not!' proclaimed Steampunk as they slipped away. 'I have at least four more tricks left up my sleeves.' He waggled his quadruple hands above his head. 'If there's anything left in that mighty bird brain, I shall do my best to set it free.'

Chapter Two

Skimmies

Kip unshouldered his Skimmi and flicked it out. It floated flat in the air in front of him like a circular flying carpet, about the length of his arm. When he smoothed a palm over the surface, it became as rigid as a plank, and the feel of it was rough on his skin, almost gripping his fingertips like the lick of a cat's tongue. He pushed it down lightly so it was a foot off the ground, and Albert's Skimmi sank down to hover loyally next to it.

They stepped back together and admired their handiwork. Kip's was cookie-brown on top, and popcorn-beige beneath, just like Pinky. Albert's had turtle-green scales, each with a red trim.

'Two-and-a-half months' hard work, plus Slipstream, multiplied by Thoughtwaves, equals Tah-dah!' said Albert.

'Every second in that workshop was worth it,' said Kip. 'I wanted a ready-made one at first – it seemed really harsh that we had to build our own. But this way we got to customise our rides.'

'Take them for a spin?' said Albert. 'Might spot the girls from higher up – they should be back from their field trip round about now.'

Kip stepped on to his Skimmi. The diamond-shaped connectors that joined mind and body to machine dissolved and reformed under his feet, adapting to his stance. A carefully guided thought sent him lifting upwards, following Albert into the sky. They gained height and distance quickly, only stopping when a floating traffic light abruptly turned red. A surge of Skimmis flowed across their path, followed by a slightly confused pigeon.

'Remember how rubbish we were at flying the girls' Skimmies at the start of term?'

'Speak for yourself,' said Kip. 'You spent a lot of time going backwards into walls.'

'Well, maybe I like walls,' retorted Albert, pretending to be offended. 'Maybe I was a wall in a past life. And I had a family of little bricks and worked in a maze.'

'You know, we totally lucked in when they were handing out Befrienders. Just imagine how different things might have been if we hadn't got Leela and Timmi.'

'Yeah, they turned out OK, didn't they? Much more than OK.'

'Can't imagine Team Glowflyer without them now.'

'And the mowl. Don't forget the mowl,' added Albert. 'Or Pinky – we wouldn't be Glowflyers without our ultraviolet-ultraglowy flying squirrel!'

The traffic light turned green and they rose even higher over the top of Quantum Quarter, one of the four main halls of the college. It was probably the strangest building on the campus, which was saying something at Quicksmiths. Kip hadn't realised what was so special about it at first. But it wasn't too long before he and Albert had figured it out: every time they passed by, it looked different. Right now, it was made of some kind of hard magenta foam with spiky balconies.

'I'll never, ever get bored of all this,' Kip murmured.

The four halls – Quantum Quarter, Celestial Hall, Atlas House and Singing Mill – surrounded a neat green square at the heart of everything – Clock Tower Courtyard. From there, a patchwork of avenues, terraces and buildings – both modern and ancient – spread out towards the playing fields in the north and the gardens in the south.

Kip's gaze skipped from roof to roof – it was something you never got to set eyes on much in the outside world unless you lived at the top of a tower block, and his flat back home on the Eelstowe Estate was an uninspiring three floors up. Here at Quicksmiths the rooftops seemed alive with twisted turrets and parapets, unexpected stairways, and chimney stacks which sometimes let out a burst of coloured sparks.

Ahead, Albert was making a wide turn at the white-pillared Library. Circling around more tightly, Kip took a shortcut across the professors' quarters to cut Albert off above the Hive – the enormous, mirrored colony of hexagonal classrooms.

'Did you forget to take your Vitamin F this morning?' Kip shouted, urging his Skimmi forward with Albert gnashing at his heels.

'F?' Albert yelled back.

'Fast!' yelled Kip, pulling ahead.

Catching the sunlight in the distance was an iron gateway. Kip set his thoughts on it and his Skimmi sliced through the air, whipping a cool wind against his sunburned face. Sprawled out beyond the gate were the tranquil lawns and whimsical pathways of the Garden of Giant Leapfrogs – the travel hub that connected Quicksmiths to the outside world. Kip found himself recalling his first wormhole trip and his arrival in the garden, how bemused he'd been and slightly sneezesick.

As the world and Kip's memories streaked by, Albert zipped ahead with a stealthy power move and took first place, hooting with victory. Kip sent him an air fistbump and slowed down to scud over the Touchlight sign of tall, pearly letters above the gateway:

'We're baaaaaa-aaaaaack,' Leela's voice called out.

A few metres below, the edge of a peacock-patterned disc nudged into view and a wurbling noise floated up.

Kip looked down to see the mowl standing to attention at the edge of Leela's Skimmi. He was about twice the height of Pinky, and twice as fat. The chubby fingers of his little ottery hands tickled the air, and a glimpse of orange scales flashed under his black wings as they lifted in excitement. Underneath the fleecy balloon of his body, curved talons clenched and unclenched eagerly.

With another joyous wurble, the mowl glanced up at Kip and Albert's faces and then turned back to his main objective – to find Pinky – who surprised him by leaping from Kip's Skimmi and gliding down in a sneak attack from behind. They rolled around in a ball of flying squirrel fur and mowl feathers, lirriping and squeaking.

'Did you miss us?' said Leela.

'*Somebody* definitely missed you,' said Albert. 'How was the field trip?'

'I know a lot about forcefields now,' said Leela, drawing up level, 'and different kinds of power crops. They wouldn't let me drive the combine energy harvester though.'

'Where's Timmi?' asked Kip.

'Her Skimmi's in the repair shop. She basically burned it out at the SkimmiDrome – that girl is definitely going to get Speed Trials gold this year – like she doesn't have enough medals already – anyway she's just been to the Quicket Market, I'm on my way to pick her up. You coming?'

Kip slipped comfortably into auto-pilot mode, and began to cruise effortlessly after Leela.

'Does the Quicket Market ever have a sale?' Albert asked.

'Yup,' said Leela. She swished her hair and a dozen peacock eyespots rippled against a background of black silk. 'I got my look on "Truckloads-Of-Discounts-Do-You-Really-Need-To-Buy-It-Before-Now" Friday last summer – that's TODDYRNTBIBN Friday for short.'

'Snappy,' said Kip.

'There's an all-year bargain bin too, if you're really short of Quickets. Anyway, why do you need a sale? You're loaded. We all got a big, fat payout for solving the ten riddles.'

'Oh yeah, I keep forgetting I'm rich now,' said Albert.

'Aw, I knew it wouldn't change you.'

Listening to his friends, Kip filled up with a mellow sense of wellbeing. It took both good work and good deeds to earn currency at Quicksmiths, and the four of them had racked up a small fortune after finding the Ark. He felt like the king of the world to be earning his own way – here at least, if not in the outside world.

'By the way, did you speak to Professor Steampunk while we were gone?'

'Good news, I think,' said Albert. 'He showed us some energy readings today.'

'He thinks there's some sort of spark inside the parrot,' Kip added. 'It might even be a battery.'

'That sounds *very* promising,' said Leela. 'Maybe we can get it jump-started?'

Pinky scrambled her way up Leela's torso. After a quick stop to test the wind, she scrambled up a bit more and launched herself from Leela's shoulder. Her wrists and ankles spread wide, transforming her into a furry, flat square of sky sail. Kip sped up to meet her and she landed neatly on his open hand, wrapping herself around his outstretched fingers.

'Pinky definitely thinks your Skimmi is a jumbo flying squirrel,' said Leela. 'You even made it the same colours.'

'I'll have to be careful she doesn't take it out for a joyride…'

'Pssst. Kip,' interrupted Albert. 'Your not-so-secret admirer…'

The new girl, Iris, strode alongside Celestial Hall, thin pale arms swinging purposefully. From this distance, the curved cocoon of black hair on her head looked like a tight crash helmet – something you might wear if you spent your time power-smashing your way through walls and anyone who got in your way.

'…must be Kip-hunting season.'

Iris was a latecomer to the summer term, having only arrived a few weeks ago, and had latched on to Kip like a lovestruck locust. Luckily, she wasn't in Professor Mo's form class with Kip and Albert, but she did keep popping up at random times; when they were having meals in the Buttery for example, or when they were walking past a hedge she conveniently happened to be inspecting.

Leela patted her knee to tempt back Pinky, who was easily persuaded to leap from Skimmi to Skimmi.

'Hmmm,' she said. 'Without sounding too cruel, something about that girl makes me think of a piranha in a goldfish bowl. Given half a chance she'd eat you for breakfast…'

Not really listening, Kip watched Iris turn a corner and inwardly breathed a sigh of relief. He just didn't know what to make of her – she was a strange mix of over-confident and lonely.

'I know she's a bit *out there*,' he said. 'But we are too. And we really shouldn't be unfriendly to her. It's not fair, especially when you're new.'

'There's our girl!' said Leela. 'Antimony! Antimoneeeeeeee!'

Timmi waved up at them from the middle of the lawn. On her head was a pig-pink baseball cap, pulled down firmly over long hair the colour of churned butter. She always wore a hat. No matter how many times her friends told her it didn't matter, those sticky-out ears still bothered her. Kip wondered for a moment if there was a Strange Invention that might whisk away her embarrassment.

Thoughtwave Lenses

'We struck gold!' Timmi shouted up, as Leela began to descend.

When Leela was within arm's length, Timmi handed over some thin round lenses, milky white and run through with melted colour.

'The Quicket Market was packed,' she said. 'But I managed to get the last ones on the shelf.'

'TREASURE!' yelled Leela.

The mowl jumped up and down and tugged at Leela's leggings, trying to see what she was talking about, before flapping up to her mowl-proof shoulder pad to get a better view.

The lenses in Leela's hands reminded Kip a little of the seaside riches he and his mum and sister, Suzanna, used to find when they went beachcombing. He smiled, thinking of the display case his dad had built for them at the old house, which they'd filled with seaglass, shells, worn coral pieces and the occasional ammonite. It was all in a box under Kip's bed in their poky new flat now.

I should take one of them to show Mum, he thought, reaching for the leather cord around his neck. *Maybe it would do something, wake her up again somehow, like this did.*

Kip didn't talk about it much. About how a long-ago lightning strike had left Rose Bramley locked in her mind. How she was snagged somewhere among decaying memories in a confusing, twilight world that he and his dad, Theo, could only rarely reach. How a few months back there had been that strange moment at St Antony's care home when she seemed to be startled awake from her stupor.

The feeling was still raw, from when his mum had spoken directly to him, as if nothing had happened, and reached out for the pendant he wore around his neck. When he'd told his dad, Theo's face had lit up, mirroring the disbelief and joy that Kip had felt himself.

'Mum might even be back home for the holidays,' Theo had said.

But the excitement had been short-lived. She had spoken only twice to Kip after that, to ask him to pass her tea and find a jigsaw piece, and had quickly receded back into the mists of her condition. Kip's dad had managed to persuade the doctors to take her out of the care home and run some more tests. But there was no good news. They were back to square one…

He pulled the pendant out from under his shirt, where he always kept it safely tucked away. It was made from the fragment of quartz that Rose Bramley had given him when she had first been taken ill. Kip had kept it safe now for more than half his lifetime. Faint curls of amber lapped at the heart of the blue crystal, like the fossilised waves of a prehistoric sea.

He stared at it for a moment, then tucked the pendant under his shirt again and caught up with what the others were saying.

The mowl was trying to grab one of the lenses off Leela and she pulled it back protectively.

'Not for mowls.'

'Hey, can you drop me off at the Skimmi repair shop?' said Timmi. She hopped on the back of Leela's Skimmi. Sensing the extra weight on board, the disc widened out a little to provide more standing space. They rose up over the domes and greenhouses of the Botanical Gardens and cruised past the Skycrackle Tower.

'Not so fast!' said Albert. 'You haven't told us what those things are yet.'

'Thoughtwave Lenses.' Leela held one up to the light. 'And if they work in the Dreambomber then we are going to have more fun than a mowl on a mowlercoaster.

No...' she held up her forefinger, '...more fun than a porcupine at a balloon shop.' She cradled the glassy lenses and cackled. 'More fun than a fundraising fungus on a funky funicular.'

'What does a Dreambomber do, exactly?' Kip asked quickly, before she could think of something else it would be more fun than.

'You know photobombing? When you hijack someone else's photo? Well, this lets you do the same in someone else's dream. It's a bit like when you wake up inside your dream and work out it's not real. Like a lucid dream – only better – except you're inside someone else's head, not your own.'

'How come this is the first we're hearing of it?' asked Kip.

'I've been working on it for a while and wanted to get it right before I showed anyone. Now it's nearly finished...'

'I'm sold,' said Albert. 'Where do we sign up?'

'Well, it's not quite there yet. At the moment, I don't seem to be able to make it last more than a second at a time – on people, anyway. It seems to work on the mowl OK – which has been hugely useful because he's a galaxy-class napper. By the way, we were close to guessing right – what he dreams about. Lost cities of mowls. Shiny, shiny things. Melty cheese baths. Anywaaaay – while I'm still figuring out how the Dreambomber can join up dreams between people, we could try it on Pinky if you like.'

Pinky was now over on Albert's Skimmi, scurrying round and round his feet. Hearing her name, she stopped and looked over at Leela.

'Isn't this the middle of the night for her?' said Timmi. 'Have you been feeding her coffee beans?'

'She sleeps the whole day at home,' Kip called over, 'but it's too exciting here for her to sleep through. And she's waking up even more now there's a Skimmi to play with.'

'She's not the only one,' Albert said. 'Have I mentioned how much I love Skimmies?'

'Not once,' said Leela.

'They've been around since, what, 17-something-something,' Albert continued, 'even though the first ones were big clunky things. That was how many years ago? And right here and now, outside of Quicksmiths, no one even suspects Slipstream exists.'

'Well, no one suspects Quicksmiths exists either,' said Leela. 'And if they did, they'd never find it. I mean, even we don't know *exactly* where Quicksmiths is, not really.'

'You know what I mean,' said Albert. 'All of this. No one knows.'

'Well, sure, but that's because most people get unfriended by Strange Energy as they grow up,' said Timmi. 'But our quixars keep on quixing.'

'True,' said Albert. 'I was always being told by adults that I was over-imaginative. And all along it was just quixars in here,' he pointed at his own forehead, 'trying to connect with all the Timeyarn and stuff out there.'

The first term was only just drawing to a close but Kip felt like he'd known about the Strange Energies all his life. And in truth they had always been there, whispering to the quixar cells under his skin, waiting for him to come and find them. Their names still felt like delicious secrets when he said them aloud. Thoughtwaves. Timeyarn. Slipstream. Wormholes. Aeon Light. Especially Aeon Light. Only the strange plasma, Skycrackle, still made Kip feel uneasy. The impossibly high Skycrackle Tower was always there in the background, and the flashing in its cloud-filled spire looked like veins of lightning sometimes. It was similar enough to remind Kip of that electric sky split in two, that frozen-in-time moment when his mum had been struck on the clifftop by their old house. He looked back at the tower fiercely and gave his head a sharp shake.

'Can't believe you Firsties have got the next-gen Skimmies that roll up,' said Leela. 'While Timmi and I and all the poor Second Years have still got Stone-Age folding ones.'

'You've done a really good job, both of you,' said Timmi. 'I like yours, Albert – the green and red go well together.'

'Why thank you,' said Albert. 'Green's my favourite colour. Red's a close second.'

'Peacock's mine,' said Leela, running a hand through the blue-and-green eyespots in her hair.

'Peacock's not really a colour, is it?' said Albert.

'Isn't it?' said Leela. 'Are you sure? Absolutely-ootly sure?'

'Mine's fruit salad,' said Timmi, before Albert could reply.

'That is an excellent favourite colour,' said Kip. 'Mine is flying squirrel.'

'Fine,' said Albert. 'You lot win. My favourite colour is Godzilla in red wellies.'

'That's more of a state of mind,' said Leela with a giggle, swooping out of Albert's reach.

Chapter Three

Gravity Foam

Leela started to descend near to a fountain built out of the discs of old Skimmies.

'So what did GENI say about selling your thing?' she asked. 'In the Quicket Market.'

'She loved it!' Timmi replied.

'I think this is your best invention yet,' said Leela. 'Bet you're going to break the record for most Quickets ever earned. As well as all the other records you keep breaking. Actually, I think you should leave some records for us other feeble flea-brained people – maybe I want to break a record some day – you're just hogging them all – no one needs *that* many records...'

'Dunno,' said Timmi. 'I just like inventing stuff. Anyway, you already have a record. Most words said without taking a breath.'

'What's your invention?' said Kip and Albert together.

Timmi pulled up the sleeve of her shirt. Around her wrist was a silver bracelet from which eight animal charms dangled on short chains.

'Jewellery?' said Albert. 'Thanks, it's nice, but pass.'

'Ah, but is it really just any old boring jewellery?' said Timmi, fiddling with a bat charm. 'Perhaps *this* will change your mind…'

The talisman began to pulse rhythmically in a soft, silvery heartbeat.

Above and below them, the sky and ground began to tilt, and Kip's insides turned slowly. It was as if the whole earth were losing its balance.

'It's gone all earthquakey!' said Albert.

Despite being only a few metres off the ground, Kip flinched and put his hands out. It all came flooding back. Thag Grittleshank's cruel, wide sneer. Being baited and lured into the no-fly zone around Skycrackle Tower. That lurching sensation in his stomach. The near-death fall. Then, feeling a little foolish, he recalled that Professor Kvörk had insisted on safety mechanisms being built in to all Skimmies after that, so it was impossible to come off now. And Thag was long gone.

Trying to work out what was going on, he found that somehow the lawn had flipped, or he had, so it was about a metre above his head, like a sweet-smelling, green ceiling. And it wasn't just him. Next to him, Albert was reaching up to touch the grass with his fingertips.

Leela and Timmi were smelling some roses that trailed down from a flower bed.

'Spot the difference,' said Timmi, obviously relishing the looks on their faces.

'Explain please?' said Albert.

'Gravity Bracelet,' Timmi replied.

She unclipped the silver circlet from her wrist and the charm stopped beating. The earth lost its balance again, Kip's stomach fluttered, and just like that everything was the right way up. He landed his Skimmi a bit unsteadily, and the others followed.

'How does it work? Gravity Waves?' Kip guessed.

'Sort of,' said Timmi. 'Although Gravity Waves are thousands of kilometres long so they wouldn't have much of an effect on little things like you and me. My bracelet works using Gravity Foam.'

'Gravity Foam? Sounds like something you get at the seaside on Jupiter.'

'Is it a Strange Energy?' Albert asked.

'It's like a Strange Energy in disguise. You'll get to it in the Second Year,' said Leela.

'So were we upside-down just now, or was the world the wrong way up?'

'Upside-down depends on where you're looking from. You were actually falling feet-first towards the sky really, really, REALLY slowly.'

'Just us, or the whole college?' Albert asked.

'Just us. The area of influence is only a few

metres. But this little bracelet can do all sorts of neat tricks.'

She held it up so Kip and Albert could see the animal charms.

'Each one does something different,' she said.

Squirls

'Where there's a will there's a wave,' crowed Leela. 'And where there's a wave, there's foam!'

She grabbed the bracelet and pulled the seahorse charm. The fountain's watery contents were slingshot into the air, forming a twisting tide of droplets above her that caught the afternoon sunshine like a skydrift of tiny disco balls.

'Hey, is that what squirls are like?' Albert asked thoughtfully.

Kip smiled. There was no feeling on earth like having friends who wanted to understand you.

'Kind of,' he said. 'They can be bright like that, and they flow and ripple too. But sometimes they're more like an infinite tunnel.'

Timmi closed her eyes and rubbed them gently.

'Wish I could see Aeon Light,' she said. 'The strangest of all the Strange Energies.'

'Wish I could show you,' said Kip, a little wistfully.

But the swirling lights he had always seen when he shut his eyes, lights he now knew to be mysterious reflections of the future, had only ever revealed themselves to two humans: himself and Eartha Quicksmith. These days, he was seeing the squirls more and more with his eyes open, and he wondered what that could mean. If only he could have asked Eartha about it, but there were four hundred years between them. Even with all the Strange Inventions to be found at Quicksmiths there were still some things that were impossible.

On the other side of the fountain, Leela launched into a cartwheel that whipped the water around, sending a spray of droplets raining over the group. The mowl and Pinky shook themselves and rolled about in the sparkling shower like tickled ferrets.

'But how can a teeny bit of jewellery create gravity?' asked Albert. 'The technology…'

'Well see – that's the beauty of it. It's actually a gravity factory the size of a city that has been shrunk down to a nice, convenient bracelet size.'

'When did you find the time to build a great big factory?' Kip asked.

'GENI lent me some of her drones, and I programmed them to make me one over the holidays. I didn't invent the factory – someone else did that. I just found a neat application for it.'

'Wait a minute! Shouldn't the bracelet weigh as much as a city, then?' Albert said. 'The mass of the factory won't change surely, even when it's been shrunk?'

'Well, I could tell you that when it shrinks, some of the mass is converted into Strange Energy, which doesn't weigh anything. But that would make your head fall off, so I won't.'

She unclipped the bracelet from Leela's wrist.

'There you go. Back to normal.'

'Normal?' said Albert incredulously. 'At Quick-smiths?'

Four Ballmoths bipped into the air between them.

'I mean, is it "normal" to have little pet glowing balls of energy that lead you where you need to go? That turn into camouflagey moth-shaped tracking devices when you tell them to?'

'Yup,' said Leela, with a shrug.

'Better get going. See you later for a Dreambomb then?' said Timmi, and jogged away towards the Skimmi repair shop.

'Oh crabs!' said Albert. He took a hasty look at the words above the Ballmoth spelling out the destination for their next lesson. 'Is it Quixology now? I forgot my puzzle homework...'

'This reminds me of that proverb, you know the one?' said Leela.

'No?' said Albert.

'What?' said Kip.

'A mowl with many hands,' she said, holding up her finger wisely, 'needs a big handbag.'

Chapter Four

Deep Thinking

Leela headed off, chattering to the mowl.

'What happened to all the would-you-rathers?' Albert called after her.

'The mowl and I are into proverbs now,' Leela replied airily, and carried on her way.

Albert and Kip launched their Skimmies, following the Ballmoths' guiding lights.

'Wonder if she ran out?' said Albert.

'Leela Lee *never* runs out of words, especially not would-you-rathers,' Kip replied.

When they had landed neatly on the lawn, he rolled up his Skimmi like a huge pancake and slung it over one shoulder with the carrying strap. As they reached the path, he glimpsed a shadow waving over to his left. Before he had glanced over, he knew whose shadow it was, because Albert was already groaning under his breath.

'Hi Kip,' Iris said sparklingly, ignoring Albert. 'Can I walk you to class?'

'Actually,' said Albert. 'Kip has extra lazy legs. I was just thinking we could do with another person to help him move them.'

Iris double-ignored Albert and gave Kip a radioactive smile.

'Sure, we're all going the same way,' he said, giving Albert a don't-be-mean look.

The many mirrored surfaces of The Hive reflected the early July heatwave, sending white-hot twinkles in all directions. It was a relief to step out of the sunshine and into its cool interior. At the entrance Iris turned aside, promised to find Kip later, and marched away.

The honeycomb network of corridors buzzed with students and teachers heading to their lessons, and the Ballmoths weaved among them, leading Kip and Albert to the right door.

'Hey! Slackers!' called out a friendly voice. 'Why so slow?'

Kip looked up to see the base of a sky-blue chair rushing past over their heads and grinned.

Not long after the start of term, Badger had swapped his wheelchair for an Airchair, which he had wired to be faster and more flexible than the speed-restricted classroom ones. Albert and Kip raced him on their Skimmies every few days, and Badger regularly won by at least the length of a mowl.

The classroom was already full when they arrived and Kip sat hastily in an Airchair of his own, the velvet welcomingly soft on the sunburnt backs of his knees. Pressing the buttons on the side of the chair, he thought upward thoughts. It began to rise just as Professor Mo stumbled into the room, his arms stretched out like a zombie. He wore a floppy cricket hat, and there were at least five pairs of spectacles hanging on cords around his neck. A Māori *tā moko* tattoo twined around the lower half of his face in curlicues of dark ink.

'You'll have to give me a second,' he said, blinking hard behind a pair of red-framed, triangular spectacles. 'Ever since the Fourth Years' Phantasmagorical Frost experiment, all my glasses stay freezing cold and won't stop steaming up.'

Albert's hand shot up and the professor nodded amiably in his direction.

'We could add some windscreen wipers?' said Albert helpfully. 'They'd come in handy when it rains too? Or micro-drones with sponges?'

The professor laughed heartily and nodded at Badger, who also had his hand up. Albert and Badger liked to compete for the unofficial title of class comedian, and this week Badger was the frontrunner. He folded both hands over his cropped black hair and leaned back in his Airchair for effect.

'Professor Mo – you know how your glasses help

you to see a different perspective on everything? Well, now solutions should appear before your very *ice*.'

Professor Mo groaned so hard he had to sit down.

'Well, I suppose having supercool lenses does have its *froze* and cons,' he replied, and then it was the class's turn to groan.

The professor wiped the lenses of his triangular glasses with a square of green silk and then tried to untangle the spectacle cords around his neck.

'I'll just need a moment to sort these all out,' he said. 'Could someone jog my memory – where did we get to in the last lesson?'

Seeing an opportunity to be teacher, Maya jumped in. The tight bun of brown hair on her head seemed to have grown bigger during the term, as if it had been secretly feeding on smaller buns.

'Mindfulness,' she said. 'Deep Thinking. It's been around for thousands of years – the Ancient Egyptians and Greeks used it.'

Penny, who was sitting in the top row of Airchairs, looked down and curled one of the many ribbons in her hair around a finger. Like Kip she'd caught the sun, and there were pale circles around her eyes where her shades had kept the rays out.

'Isn't that what the oracles did before they delivered their messages at the temple of Apollo?' she said.

Maya copied the professor, taking off her glasses to wipe them on her T-shirt.

‘They did,’ she said. ‘There was also this olden-day monastery of Buddhist monks in Tibet who were highly advanced, like the Quicksmiths of their time. They understood that there are lots of types of Thoughtwaves – like Alpha and Beta and Delta – and they all mean different things. And they discovered that we produce special Thoughtwaves when we dream.’

Professor Mo held up his glasses to the light.

‘That’s right,’ he said. ‘From our earliest beginnings, philosophers from around the world have explored Deep Thinking. With it, they could practise lucid dreaming and meditate in their sleep. They learned how to move the dream sun in the sky with a single finger, or turn into a dream eagle with a clap of their hands.’

The professor squinted through another pair of glasses, and put them away in a case.

‘Did everyone get a chance to practise some Deep Thinking after dinner?’

Kip nodded with the others. Last night, with the Candlelight at a gentle flicker, he had felt as relaxed as a potato at a couch convention. Even Pinky had joined in, curling up sedately in her coconut cradle. Albert had fidgeted and tutted a lot, but Kip had sunk into himself effortlessly. With eyes closed, he had recalled Professor Mo’s instructions.

Imagine all the thoughts in your head are smoke

billowing out of a smoke machine. Take a deep breath, allowing in the cool, fresh air. When you breathe out, you're breathing out all that smoke. Soon you might start to feel that your head is clearing.

It was easy to imagine that his thoughts were cloudy loops of smoke and watch them blow away in unseen winds.

Now the smoke is disappearing, you can see that this is your space, only for you. Go forwards. Keep going. What sort of a place is at the end of the space inside your eyes? Is it a cave behind a waterfall? Is it a safe hollow in a deep-forest oak? Is it an oasis of soft sand under the stars?

The reddish blackness behind Kip's closed eyelids had seemed to push out and take on 3-D shapes and he had peered around inside.

Somewhere quiet, he'd thought. *Near the sea, maybe with rock pools.*

Back in the here and now, Professor Mo had finished cleaning his glasses and was putting on a large round pair that seemed to magnify his eyes.

'As you're finding out for yourselves, Deep Thinking can be used to clean the mind and activate quixars. This is an excellent preparation for observing the marvels of Strange Energy. Yes, Em?'

Kip looked over at Em, who was also on the top row. Reflecting the uncertainty in her brown eyes, the henna designs on her hands and forearms had begun to shift and waver, and were tying themselves into complicated knots. Em had been working hard since the very first day, and had recently spent all her saved-up Quickets on extrasensory body art.

'I've forgotten how Deep Thinking is different from Sideways Thinking,' she said.

'I'm glad you asked,' said the professor. 'Deep Thinking unclogs your mind to allow clear focus. Whereas Sideways Thinking looks at a problem from different angles.'

Em nodded, and the henna knots on her skin untangled themselves.

'I really should think about getting my tattoo animated,' said the professor, with a smile. 'So, where was I? Ah yes, Deep Thinking is a way of super-charging our quixars which, as you know, connect us to Strange Energy, and put us in a very small percentage of the population. And as it happens, quixar cells are especially numerous in the problem-solving regions of our brains, as well as being spread throughout our organs and limbs. That means Deep Thinking is a workout for both mind and body… yes, Badger?'

'Can I think with my belly button?'

The professor paused for a moment.

'Badger,' he replied, 'I believe YOU can.'

Professor Mo stood up and strolled alongside the the elevated rows of Airchairs as he spoke.

'I'd like each of you to take five minutes to write

down your experience with Deep Thinking last night…'

Albert breathed out heavily.

'If we were actually trying to be rubbish at it,' he whispered, 'I'd be at the top of the class.'

Dreambomber

They slowed down on the approach to the third storey of the Second Year Block.

'I do love me a good Skimmi,' said Albert. 'But remind me why we don't use wormholes to shortcut around Quicksmiths?'

'We do sometimes,' said Timmi, 'but using wormholes in residential areas was banned after someone got trapped in a feedback loop and ended up stuck between their wardrobe and Professor Steampunk's prize biscuit gallery.'

'It was several days until they were found,' Leela added. 'But obviously they didn't starve to death.'

She came to a hovering standstill next to a windowsill, and a walkway slid out smoothly from under its lip. Leela hopped on to the walkway and into the window. The others tied up their Skimmies too, and followed her into the girls' room.

Leela had scooped up the Thoughtwave Lenses and was cavorting around her desk like a maniacal optician. She spun on her heel and bent over a wooden chest about the size of a footstool. On its side were two sturdy wheels, one painted glossy green and one candy yellow. They were the metal kind, the sort that might open a valve on a gas pipe.

'Is that it?' asked Albert.

'Watch and learn,' Leela replied.

Jiggling with excitement, she turned the green wheel. The lid folded itself up and disappeared into the box. Then, a fat lime-coloured cylinder rose up and began to spin slowly.

'What's my nan's lampshade doing here?' said Albert.

The mowl lirriped and crept as close as he could, watching the cylinder turning. Kip watched too as the room went quiet. There was something soothing about the motion.

'Our cat does that with the tumbledryer,' murmured Timmi.

The box beeped softly and cut-out shapes appeared in the sides of the cylinder. They seemed familiar but, however hard he tried, Kip couldn't tell whether they were circles or triangles or squares. Twinkling lights projected out of them and flowed around the room, creating blurred shapes on everyone's faces as the cylinder turned.

The mowl lay on his back and scratched his tummy happily as he watched the projections wheeling around the walls and ceiling.

'Does mowly like the shinies?' said Timmi, stroking his head. 'It must be lonely being the only one of your kind. I'm so glad he has us.'

'Leela, are you ever tempted to try and make him a mowl friend?' Albert asked.

'Well, it *is* tempting. He does need some mowl-sized buddies to practise his mowl-sized Taekwondo with. But where would I even start? It was an accident, after all. I'd need an electromagnetic storm, and a Time Tagger, and some old bones…'

'Best bumble you ever bumbled,' said Timmi.

'So what now?' asked Kip. 'How do we bomb Pinky's dream?'

'First this,' said Leela.

She turned the second wheel and a yellow cylinder rose up around the first. Cut-outs appeared in this cylinder too, and it began to revolve in the opposite direction, throwing out starry lights among the green twinkles. There was a pleasant sound like the distant rustling of leaves.

'And then, this.'

Leela ducked under the desk. When she came back up, she was wearing what appeared to be a frilly shower cap decorated with bulging flowers. Front and centre was a large round clasp – it was empty as if the central jewel were missing from a mad mermaid's crown.

'You have got to be joking!' laughed Albert.

Leela glared at him.

'The Psychogenic Beret is a very powerful and sensitive piece of equipment! May I continue?'

Albert sucked in his giggles and looked serious.

'Please, please, continue your synchronised swimming.'

Leela's glare turned into a grin, and she swam pretend breaststroke to the other side of the desk where she finished with a pirouette. She bustled around an instrument panel at the back of the box, then, satisfied that everything was in order, she turned to the others.

'Do we have a volunteer?'

Kip gently unpocketed the sleeping Pinky, who snuffled and squeaked contentedly.

'You're sure it's safe?' he whispered, not wanting to wake her up.

'Absolutely,' said Leela. 'I would never have tried it on the mowl unless I'd already used it on myself...'

'And me,' Timmi piped up.

'...so we know it's totally harmless.'

Kip placed Pinky on the bottom bunk bed.

'Thoughtwaves can exist outside the body, right,' Leela said. 'But most are very weak and often can't be detected without special equipment. That's where the Thoughtwave Lens comes in...'

She picked up one of the milky lenses.

'When connected to the Dreambomber, they can

capture and translate the Thoughtwaves made when we dream.'

'Oh,' said Albert, 'we actually know what something is for a change! That came up in class today.'

'The lens focuses two or more minds together,' said Leela. 'Like tuning a walkie-talkie. Luckily the mowl also makes the same kind of Dreamwaves we do – although personally I think there might be Wurble Waves in there somewhere – anywaaaaay we can assume fairly safely that flying squirrels dream like us too. So, we connect our DreamMeister,' she paused and stage-whispered, '*that's me* – to the Dreambomber, thus...'

With a flourish, Leela slid the Thoughtwave Lens into the empty clasp at the front of her cap.

'I'm now fixing the subject in my mind.'

She stared keenly at Pinky. The fur of the little flying squirrel's soft white underbelly moved up and down gently as she breathed.

'Timmi, could you please check that the Dreamwave Gauge is responding.'

Kip and Albert leaned over to look at the instrument panel with Timmi. A needle flicked side to side like an old-fashioned metronome.

'Ready, steady, dream!' said Timmi with a thumbs-up.

Leela sat cross-legged on the bed and rested her hands in her lap. The yellow cylinder slowed and stopped and started to turn the same way as the green one. Gradually, all the chequered yellow and green lights coming out of the cylinders began to turn blue.

'Before I start,' she said, 'any ideas for catching her eye, Kip?'

'Try waving around some sweet potato?' he suggested. 'Or a slice of orange?'

'Easy, peasy, weasy,' she said.

Leela closed her eyes, and her face and neck relaxed.

'I'm inside Pinky's dream. We're in a forest. There are teeny bells and mirrors growing out of the trees. Piles of nuts on the floor. She's jumping around after a Ballmoth. Let's see if she'll come flying with me. Keep watching her!'

All eyes had been on Leela, but now the movement on the bed pulled Kip's gaze down. The sleeping Pinky had uncurled and was kicking her feet. She fell still again before squeaking and sleep-scratching her squirrel butt.

'She's learned that from you, mowl,' muttered Kip.

At their feet, the mowl clapped his little hands proudly and waggled his stumpy tail.

Nestled on the duvet, Pinky stretched out all four paws and pulled her wing membrane taut, just as she did when she was flying. Her head began to roll from side to side as if she were turning left and right. Not wanting to miss out on anything, the mowl crept on to the bed. He put his face close to Pinky's and spread his own feathery wings wide too, lirriping happily.

Without any warning Pinky leapt up, still with her furry wings stretched out, and latched on to the mowl's face. They fell off the bed together in surprise and then both crawled back up the duvet looking stunned. Pinky blinked the sleep away and yawned wide.

'Poor furball!' said Kip. 'What's going on?'

'Aw, did we play a mean ol' trick on you?' said Timmi, making a fuss of her.

'It worked like a dream,' said Leela, her eyes now open. 'The perfect subject. Really vivid.'

'She was sleep-flying!' said Kip. 'Don't think I've ever seen her do that before.'

'You know what they say,' said Leela in a wise-woman voice. 'One sleep-flying squirrel is worth a hundred sweet potatoes.'

Suddenly much more awake at the prospect of food, Pinky stared expectantly at Leela and then insistently at Kip.

'When you get to use it on people, won't you upset them?' Kip asked, giving Pinky a sunflower seed from his pocket. 'You know, for gatecrashing their dreams without asking?'

'That's the beauty of it,' said Leela. 'Everyone's subconscious mind has its own built-in security. So unless they like you and want you to join in, you'll be locked out.'

Careful not to dislodge the Thoughtwave Lens, she took off the Psychogenic Beret, ruffled a hand through her hair and packed the beret away in a crate under the desk.

'Once you've got it working, how close do you have to be to Dreambomb someone?' asked Albert. 'Do you have to stalk around people's bedrooms with your shower cap on?'

'*Actually* it's not a shower cap. And *actually* distance doesn't apply to Thoughtwaves. You can think about someone on the other side of the world, or even on the other side of the Universe, and they're instantly in your mind.'

'Well,' said Albert, tapping the outer case of the Dreambomber admiringly. 'For a couple of lamp-shades and a shower cap, that's quite impressive!'

Chapter Five

Iris

Iris was heading straight for them. She was wearing the sort of clothes adults wear to the office – a smart grey skirt and primrose-yellow blouse – and her stare was searingly focused.

A frown wrinkling up his forehead, Albert turned away.

'Oh molluscs! Don't look!'

Kip looked. Albert tsked under his breath.

'I said *don't* look. Quick, I don't think she's seen us yet! Let's retreat and go the long way.'

'Nope,' said Kip, staying on the path. 'I don't want to go the long way. We're already late.'

'Hi Kip,' said Iris, as she came within earshot. 'Where are you off to?'

'We're going to see Professor Steampunk,' said Kip, wishing immediately that he'd kept quiet.

'Professor Steampunk? Isn't he working on the Ark

of Ideas? It's amazing that you did all that by yourself, solving the riddles and beating Gorvak. I heard you got that Thag guy expelled too. I bet he was frothing at the mouth. And there was nothing he could do except pack his bags.'

'Well, I didn't really beat Gorvak,' said Kip uncomfortably. 'He won, technically. And honestly, Thag got himself thrown out – the whole college voted, not me. I was lucky to keep my own place here. Anyway, it wasn't just me solving the riddles – it was the others as well.'

'That's not what I've heard,' said Iris. 'You were really brave, and smart.'

'Er, hello?' said Albert. 'I'm right here.'

But Iris carried on as if Albert were inaudible and invisible.

'Can I come with you to see the Ark?'

When she turned her gaze on Kip it was like being speared with a harpoon. Even when she batted her eyelids, it wasn't softened in the slightest. Out of the corner of his eye, Kip saw Albert's grimace turn into a grimmerace.

'Sorry,' said Kip. 'Professor Steampunk only asked *us* to come, so I don't think we should take anyone else. But catch up with you at lunch?'

Iris didn't try to hide her disappointment.

'Well, OK,' she said, with a dramatic sniff. 'I'll save you a seat in the Buttery.'

This time, there were no surges of unexpected Strange Energy when they opened the door to Professor Steampunk's laboratory. The professor stood beneath the Ark, gazing up. He saw them approaching and waved absent-mindedly. An island of pink stain covered one side of the baggy white lab coat that he rarely took off.

They came to a stop beside him and followed his gaze. Kip couldn't begin to count all the hours of hoping that had been invested in this humble black bird. Despite himself, he clung to the idea that there might be some record of Eartha's lost inventions still jammed inside the broken Ark. Some scrap of knowledge that could help his mum get better…

'I know this means an awful lot to you,' Professor Steampunk was saying. 'But the last scans didn't reveal anything new. And, unfortunately, I've got to put things on hold for a while – Miss Twiss has asked me to look into something urgent. Between you and me it's rather puzzling. Holes. Holes that shouldn't be where they are. They're altogether in the wrong places.'

'It's OK,' Kip said, finding a smile from somewhere. 'I've waited this long.'

'Well, we've got more than just the Ark to be going on,' said Albert. 'There must still be some surprises in Eartha's secret study. All those books and maps and gadgety-widgets – who knows what might come from that? You and I should head over to the Great Globe and take a look inside.'

Professor Steampunk clapped two of his hands together, held up a fist and saluted with the last.

'You, Albert Masvingo, are a Nevergiverupperer!'

'It's true,' said Albert proudly. 'The Irish side of my family are Nevergiverupperers. And the Zimbabwean side are Neverevergiverupperers. Double whammy.'

'Ultimate whammy,' said Professor Steampunk in approval. 'As it happens, I was going to ask you to take the Ark to Eartha's study and put it in the birdcage. Miss Twiss requested that it be returned there, while I'm not working on it.'

After the half-term, Miss Twiss – the Professor-in-Charge of Quicksmiths – had announced that the Great Globe had been turned into an exhibition on the life and work of Eartha Quicksmith. The secret Africa door concealed in the side of the globe would be permanently kept open so that students could explore Eartha's study and find out more about her methods for manipulating Strange Energy.

'Dennis could take it, of course,' Steampunk said, 'but I'd rather it was you.'

The professor pressed a button on one of the gnarled spirals and the Ark sank down out of the air into his outstretched hands. Kip took it carefully, even though it was already broken.

'Come on then, pal,' he said. 'Let's take you home.'

The Flickering Gauge

On the way from the laboratories to Atlas House, Albert spotted Timmi and Leela walking through Clock Tower Courtyard and called after them. Hearing the shout, they looked around and changed direction.

Between the two girls, perched on Leela's opened Skimmi, was the wooden chest of the Dreambomber. They walked on either side of it, both holding its closed lid lightly to glide it forward.

'Is it heavy, do you need a hand getting it off the Skimmi?' asked Albert, looking at the makeshift airtrolley. 'Where are you taking it?'

'Going to see if it picks up stray Thoughtwaves from the Singing Mill,' said Leela. 'And thanks, but one person can easily lift it. We're just being lazy…'

'The Ark!' Timmi interrupted. 'Did it say anything?'

Kip shook his head, held up the black parrot and looked into its eyes.

'You'd think with all the Strange Technology around here, we'd have been able to fix it. But no. It's properly busted.'

'That's funny,' said Leela.

Kip looked around. She was tapping the panel on the side of Dreambomber.

'What's funny?' he asked.

'Well, it's just...'

She skimmied the box closer to the parrot and tapped the panel again.

'The Dreamwave Gauge is giving a reading.'

'What does that mean?' said Albert.

Leela looked up, her eyes wide.

'The Ark is dreaming,' she murmured.

Dumbstruck, Kip gazed at the motionless parrot and then at Leela.

'But why didn't we see anything on the Wave Sensor at Professor Steampunk's lab?'

'The Dreambomber has a different kind of detector,' said Leela. 'It's got a really narrow focus. I've been working on it for ages.'

They all stared down at the black parrot.

'I'm a million per cent sure,' Leela added.

Kip felt a lifting feeling in his chest, like a Skimmi swept skywards by a Slipstream updraft.

'But don't you need a brain to make Thought-waves?' Timmi asked. 'The Ark's mechanical, isn't it? And even if it had a brain, it wouldn't still be alive now after four hundred years.'

'What if,' said Leela, chewing her lip thoughtfully, 'I know this sounds crazy, but just hear me out – what if Eartha planted Dreamwaves somehow inside the parrot? I don't even know if that's possible...'

There was an electrifying pause, broken by the click of Albert's fingers.

‘Quick – to the Dreambomber! Oh wait, it’s right here. Quick – to the shower caps!’

A few minutes later, they were tumbling back into the girls’ room. Leela opened the crate under her desk and started handing out Psychogenic Berets. The beige material was soft and rubbery in Kip’s hands, and covered in clumps of fine pinkish antennae. He pulled it on and snapped the elasticated edge over his forehead.

Meanwhile, Albert was having a good moan in the background, flicking at the flowery frills in disgust.

‘Why couldn’t you make it look better? Even an upside-down pan with cat food in it would be an improvement.’

‘You have two options,’ said Leela, holding up two fingers at Albert the rude way round. ‘Look cool on the outside, or be cool on the inside.’

Albert grumbled some more but took the Psychogenic Beret meekly, jamming it over his hair and failing to get it all tucked in.

‘This ’fro don’t wanna go,’ he said.

‘Hmmm.’ Leela fussed around him. ‘What we need is a beret for big styles. I’ll get something sorted out if you can manage, just for now?’

She arranged the group into a circle, everyone facing inwards towards the black parrot which lay on its side on the floor. After a last look at the gauge, and some fiddling with switches on the Dreambomber,

Leela came to her place in the circle and handed everyone a Thoughtwave Lens.

Kip's clicked easily into the clasp at the front of his cap and there was a slight tingling in his scalp, like mint shampoo.

'What do we do now?' he asked.

'Focus on the Ark,' said Leela. 'You've learned Deep Thinking, haven't you? That'll make things a lot easier.'

Behind his closed eyes Kip watched ringlets of smoky red curl away into infinite glowing darkness. Somewhere far off, a milky-white circle appeared. He went towards it – or it came closer, he wasn't sure which – until he stood before an ethereal, misty-edged portal.

'There's a weird white blobby thing,' said Albert's voice.

'That's the Thoughtwave Lens. Just go through,' replied Leela's voice.

In his mind's eye, Kip stepped into the misty circle and the darkness around it cleared away like ink rubbed off a whiteboard.

Dreamwave Town

Kip was looking down at his feet, which were standing on a cobbled street. He lifted his head to see a ditch at the side of the road. Onion skins floated in some brown water at the bottom and he turned away from the fetid smell. A little way down the street, noisy marketeers were selling their wares.

It seemed the most natural thing in the world when a cabbage rolled between Kip's feet and began to trundle away. Two knobbles and a dent on its outer layer gave the impression of a delighted face. Whooping happily, Albert began to run after the cabbage which accelerated down the gently sloping street.

'Any idea what we do now?' asked Kip.

'Just wander around and think hard about the Ark and Eartha I guess,' said Timmi.

At the bottom of the cobblestone slope, a foot stopped the cabbage's progress and a hand reached down to pick it up. Albert stood enraptured as an old man picked up more things off the street – a paperweight, a hot-cross bun, a jewelled egg – and began to juggle.

Leela marched up to Albert and clapped her hands in front of his face. He jerked his head back and frowned.

'Whatcha do that for?' he said.

Even though they were some way off, Kip could hear everything and supposed the dream was responsible.

'Reality check,' said Leela. 'You're getting pulled away by the dream – dreams'll do that – they're constantly screaming "LOOK AT ME!" – try and keep your focus – Deep Thinking, remember? If you feel something dragging you in, stay detached, check all your senses, and ask yourself "is that what we're looking for?"'

'So what *are* we looking for?' said Albert. 'Other than "not cabbages"?'

'Anything to do with Eartha,' Leela replied. 'Puzzle boxes, mad inventions, secret studies, that sort of thing.'

'So let me get this straight,' said Albert, as he and Leela walked back to the others. 'We're inside Eartha's dream? From four hundred years ago? A dream she made in her laboratory from special sleepy Thoughtwaves? A dream with happy little cabbages in it? That she somehow put inside the mechanical parrot?'

'I don't see what's so difficult to understand,' said Leela, shrugging. 'It's crystal clear.'

'Correction,' said Albert. 'It's crystal *weird*.'

Clucking for its life, a chicken ran past them, pursued by a woman wearing a dirty skirt that billowed around her. They chased around an outdoor stage, where a town crier dressed in a red hat and gown began to shout out some garbled announcements. In one hand he held up a brown-paper poster with a blue buttercup on it and in the other hand was a kind of rattle, which he shook after every word.

'There!' roared Leela. 'A blue buttercup – Eartha's symbol!'

'Did that guy just say "follow the parrot"?' asked Timmi.

Kip was only half listening.

There's something strange about that chicken, he thought.

The woman was chasing it round and round, faster and faster, in circles. Making a break for it, the chicken swerved away from the woman's clutches, crossed the street (narrowly avoiding the hooves of a galloping horse), and dived into a basket of something white and fluffy.

Kip followed and looked into the basket. Wigs! A sharp, hooked beak poked out, and then a colourful, intelligent face; the attached body jumped out and swaggered jauntily back across the street.

'Please tell me you just saw that chicken turn into a parrot?' he asked.

'A parrot inside a parrot?' Albert said thoughtfully. 'Imagine if there were a tiny you inside of you … hang on … is *that* why I hear audio feedback when I'm thinking really hard?'

The parrot cleared its throat, looked right at Kip, and spoke in a woman's voice.

'You must find the Futurescope,' it declared. 'The path begins here.'

'Okaaaaaay,' said Albert.

Eartha's dream-bird flew up to a tree stump and preened its feathers. They weren't black like the Ark's, but all the colours of a rainforest rainbow. With an enchanting parroty flourish, it produced a small scroll from under its wing. After clearing its throat again, it began to read.

When long-legged little ones go chasing up the trees
Peel aloud the yellow bells and shake off all the leaves,

Then shall the hidden Silent Key be yours to take
Such a fitting tribute to the Lady of the Lake.

When at the summit of a string the key is flying free
The lake will dry its single eye, and paving you shall see.

The parrot folded up the scroll into a small paper plane and launched it in their direction. It made three impressive loops and landed neatly in Kip's hand.

He opened it up and the four of them read the riddle together.

'Paving? Could that mean the Crazy Paving?'

'That's why the Ark wouldn't shut up about it!' said Albert.

'Is peel spelt wrong?' asked Leela. 'Should it be p-e-a-l?'

'I think so,' Timmi replied.

'Eartha didn't make mistakes,' said Kip.

'I knew it!' said Timmi. 'I knew the Ark was going to be the eleventh riddle!'

‘Well, it’s about time,’ said Albert. ‘There have been nowhere near enough riddles for my liking recently. Team Glowflyer’s back!’

‘Hey parrot, give us a clue!’ shouted Leela.

But the parrot was hopping into the ditch at the side of the road where it landed in a little boat made of onion skins. Squawking merrily, it rowed away across the ditch water using two wooden spoons as oars, and disappeared into the distance.

‘So what do we do now?’ Kip asked. ‘How do we get out of the Ark’s dream?’

‘Oh, that’s easy,’ said Leela. ‘You just spin around really fast.’

Albert made a for-real face.

‘Honest,’ she said. ‘Like this.’

They watched Leela twirl around on the spot until she was just a blur, and then a cloud, and then … nothing.

‘Well, I suppose it’s no more spaceybrains than anything else around here,’ said Albert.

As Kip spun round and round himself in a dizzying whirl, the last thing he saw of the Ark’s dream was the cabbage rolling past again, smiling.

Danger Velcro

Once he’d left Eartha’s Dreamwave town and became aware of the bedroom again, Kip expected to find himself spinning on the spot. But he was standing perfectly still, his arms at his sides.

His thoughts were racing, as if he'd just come out of an action film. The Strange Energy of the Dreambomber had stirred up quixars from head to toe. This, in turn, had quickened the puzzle-solving powerhouse in his mind, and the memory of the parrot's cryptic poem was churning in the afterglow of the dream. He grabbed a pen and a sheet of paper from a notebook on the floor. Then, with everyone helping, they pieced together the three verses.

'We have *got* to tell Professor Steampunk,' Kip said.

'Let's go now,' said Leela, collecting up the Psychogenic Berets. 'We haven't got any plans. Unless you count giving the mowl a bath. And I can't find my body armour anyway.'

There was a hiss under the bottom bunk bed and one orange eye blinked in the shadows.

'Come on, cuddlemunch,' said Leela. 'Looks like you've had a lucky escape. No bath for you today.'

The mowl rolled out triumphantly from under the bed and whip-slurped Leela's ankle with his long, thin, orange tongue.

Kip picked up the Ark carefully and they piled out of the window on to the three waiting Skimmies. Timmi hopped on behind Leela again.

'I can't wait to see the professor's face,' she said.

'It'll probably do a backflip,' Leela said.

'*Just* a backflip?' said Albert. 'Unlikely. More like a triple-twizzle, half-pipe, crunch-tuck backflip.'

But the door to the laboratory was locked.

'Ballmoth, take us to Professor Steampunk,' said Kip.

The glowing white sphere materialised before him but didn't move. A voice came from nowhere and everywhere, as cool as an Arctic fox.

'Professor Steampunk is in a meeting,' said GENI.

'Thanks GENI, we'll leave him a message,' said Kip.

He double-tapped the Quicksmiths pin badge on his T-shirt – the red candle with a white flame at both ends, each containing a golden eye. The Carousel opened up and, a little hesitantly, he swiped through the Touchlight, sending the floating wall of icons flying until he reached the speech bubble symbol and left his message for Professor Steampunk.

'To Eartha's study?' said Albert, once they had left the labs and walked over to the Skimmies.

'To the Great Globe,' agreed Kip. 'We still need to take the Ark back.'

'Can I see the poem?' Leela asked. 'From the dream?'

Kip felt a little eddy of glee shake up his stomach as he remembered that Eartha had found a way to set them another quest. He took the paper out of his pocket and passed it over.

'It's funny that the Futurescope isn't mentioned,' said Timmi. 'But the dream-parrot said we have to find it.'

'Guess we solve the poem and that will lead us to it,' said Albert, with a shrug.

'What do you think the Silent Key might be?' Leela asked.

'All the buildings at Quicksmiths have rooms that lock, don't they?' said Kip.

'Yes,' Leela replied, 'but most of them lock with Thoughtwave readers, not keys.'

'But there *are* keys at Quicksmiths,' Timmi added. 'And some of them are bound to be really ancient.'

'Bagsworth has a big bunch of them,' said Albert, 'for the oldest buildings – I've seen it in the Porterhouse.'

'Great thinking,' said Kip. 'The Silent Key could be just sitting there on his key ring!'

'Good ol' Baggy,' said Timmi. 'Lucky for us he has a soft spot for Kip.'

'He has a soft spot for all of us really,' said Kip. 'I just cheered him up when he was down.'

'Forget about Bagsworth's keys,' said Leela. 'What about those chests and cabinets in Eartha's study? I'm sure at least one of them was locked when we were searching around for riddles. We're going there anyway…'

'SEAGULL!' Albert shouted, out of the blue.

Kip looked around and spotted the open-beaked bird looming overhead. His hand went protectively to the big side pouch of his cargo shorts – where

Pinky was asleep – to check the Velcro was done up properly.

'Am I missing something?' asked Timmi.

'We had a close call about a week ago,' Kip explained. 'You two were packing for your field trip and Albert and I were testing our Skimmies. This stray seagull flew out of the Garden of Giant Leapfrogs – must have come through a wormhole – and cornered Pinky, who was pinkying about in a flower bed.'

'Luckily we were right there,' added Albert. 'Kip did a kind of flying karate chop, and I barked at the gull and it scarpered.'

'So then we realised we needed a way to keep Pinky safe if there was danger around. Especially now she's waking up during the day more.'

'How does fastening that keep her in your pocket?' Leela asked. 'She could easily squeeze past the closed bit, or nibble her way out.'

'I trained her,' said Kip. 'She knows that when the Danger Velcro is done up, it's not safe to come out.'

'She's so well behaved,' said Leela. 'What other smarts does she have?'

'Mostly food-related stuff,' Kip replied. 'But also "stay", "run" and "jump". And "fly" of course.'

'What about "find riddles"?' asked Timmi.

'She's a natural, doesn't even need training.'

'Speaking of riddles,' said Albert, 'here we are! Our old riddle-hunting ground.'

Chapter Six

Invention House

Late morning sunshine trickled through the arched skylights of the Hall of Maps, turning the air hot and hazy. The Great Globe rested on its wooden deck like a beachball for giants. It had been at the heart of the hunt for the Ark, hiding in plain sight as one of the college's centrepiece inventions, when secretly it had contained not just Eartha's study but five of her ingenious riddles too.

Kip looked at the others and their faces were lit up in the sunny glow. Like them, he turned to the globe and soaked up this feeling. The adventure wasn't over.

The door disguised as the great continent of Africa was open, and someone was waiting at the bottom of the wooden stairs to greet visitors.

'Welcome all,' said the attendant, in a voice that Kip knew straight away.

'GENI?' he said, surprised.

'I didn't know Strange Supercomputers had bodies,' Albert said.

'The Strange Reality Drive is my eyes and ears. But sometimes it is helpful to take a physical form too.'

GENI was beautiful in her flowing robe. She had skin the colour of burnt sugar and eyes the colour of sunsets. And she was a graceful blend of opposites, a delicate balance of old and young, male and female, wise and innocent.

'What's your body made out of?' asked Albert. 'Bits and bytes?'

'Mostly energy,' said GENI. 'Touchlight. A mist of water. A sprinkle of Strange Elements. But it uses up a lot of power so I dwell in it sparingly. And I only take this form when I am not too occupied elsewhere.'

'Is the exhibition busy?' asked Timmi.

'No, you have arrived at an excellent time. May I advise you start at the model of Eartha's Invention House, where you can see many of her creations. It was made specially for the exhibition. The Memoria Technica is also highly recommended.'

'We're allowed to play it now?' said Leela.

She shot up the wooden stairs, calling back over her shoulder. 'I'll find you guys in a sec!'

'What's a Memoria Technica?' asked Kip, as they followed.

'A musical instrument, I think,' Timmi replied, with a shrug. 'But Leela's the music maniac – you should ask her.'

Not much had changed inside – the inner room of the globe was bursting with Eartha's reservoir of riches. Books, measuring instruments, curios, papers, charts, and tools were squashed into every available space, and stacked on every surface of the cabinets, trunks, shelves and tables set around the circumference of the study.

'It's definitely bigger on the inside, isn't it?' said Kip, looking across the large empty space in the centre of the circular room.

'Oh, lots of places at Quicksmiths have extra dimensions,' said Timmi.

'Sometimes it's hard to believe what happened in here,' said Albert, as they crossed the creaky wooden floor.

'I wonder if the puzzle box is still under there?' Kip thought aloud, staring at the floorboards where the giant cube containing the last of Eartha's riddles had risen up.

'No,' said Timmi firmly. 'I heard it was taken away to be studied.' She shuddered. 'Those red skulls.'

Albert caught the shudder, and looked down at the small bumpy scar next to his thumb, the same pale brown as his palm. 'And the Clockwork Soldiers.'

As Kip's memories chased each other down the

avenues of the recent past, he went cold inside, catching the shudder himself. He had found the enigmatic Grandfather Clock here, in Eartha's desk. Then came the struggle on the clifftop. And the terrible torrent of Timeyarn that had streamed out of the clock and almost consumed Gorvak entirely, leaving him half-decayed.

'I wonder where he went,' Kip mumbled.

Albert began to ask something but the look on Kip's face must have made him change his mind.

'Hopefully he fell off his stupid cloud ladder. And got eaten by passing vultures,' Albert said chirpily.

'Doubt it,' said Timmi. 'Vultures have better taste than that. And vultures *love* rotten things.'

'You're probably right,' replied Albert. 'Not even vultures would've taken a bite.'

It was easy to hate that backstabber, easy to be angry about what he did. But even though Gorvak had started the fight, and brought the consequences on himself, Kip wouldn't wish what had happened on anyone. He shook off the heavy guilt, looked at Albert and Timmi and made himself smile.

'Yeah,' he said, absent-mindedly. 'Not even vultures.'

But he was still thinking about who could have helped Gorvak escape.

Timmi bumped shoulders with Kip.

'Come on,' she said. 'Let's put the Ark back where it belongs.'

It was hard to miss: hanging on a silken cord, it swayed gently at about eye-level. The jewelled birdcage was empty and the door was ajar.

'Guess what? This cage has a keyhole!' Albert whispered. 'Silent Key!'

All three of them got as close as they could without bashing foreheads.

'There's no key in the lock,' whispered Kip.

'Looks like this would be more of a Squeaky Key, not a Silent Key anyway,' whispered Timmi. 'Look at that rust around the keyhole.'

Kip placed the black parrot on the floor of the cage, propping it up against the bars.

'Bye, Ark,' he said. 'Keep your dreams safe.'

He turned to Timmi and Albert.

'Come on, let's go and find the Invention House.'

A Touchlight sign of words like pearly bubbles floated above a large, open display case. As they got closer, they saw a pleasant model building, with a thatched roof and oat-coloured plaster walls inlaid with blue buttercups.

'It says here that they've reproduced the Invention House brick for brick,' said Timmi, 'based on Eartha's building plan and paintings from the time.'

'It's a bit small,' sniffed Albert. 'Not being funny, but a doll's house is not my idea of fun times.'

'Small is beautiful,' said Timmi mysteriously. 'Come on, we should take a look.'

Albert still looked unconvinced.

'Take a look at what? It's right there.'

'OK you can stay here,' said Timmi. 'Kip and I will go explore.'

She pushed on the door handle of the model house with her fingertip. An after-effect of light wavered in a Timmi-shaped space, and she wasn't standing next to them anymore. There was only one place to look. Kip bent down and saw a miniature Timmi waving from a window inside the doll's house.

'It's a bit like the first riddle,' said Kip. 'Remember? When we went inside the painting.'

'We never did ask about how that worked,' Albert replied. 'Did we go through a wormhole to an actual courtyard somewhere, or did we shrink and turn two-dimensional?'

'Maybe we'll find out inside.'

When Kip leant forward and copied Timmi, the study dissolved away and he found himself in a spacious warehouse. All around were Touchlight replicas of Eartha's fabulous contraptions, ranging from the size of a toaster to a double-decker bus.

Timmi was standing at an exhibit not too far away, in conversation with GENI at her side.

'So, you're outside, and also in here?' said Kip.

'Strange Supercomputers can be in several places at once,' GENI replied.

'I suppose I shouldn't be surprised,' Kip said, nodding.

Albert came trotting up to join the group. 'How come we know what the inventions look like if they were destroyed?' he asked.

'Some pieces of the original machines were gathered up and kept safe,' GENI replied. 'There is also much written about the devices by Eartha herself, by those who worked with her, and by those who witnessed her marvels. I have created impressions from these data. But we do not know for certain if they are correct.'

They strolled alongside the exhibits and came to one that looked like a huge blender with a large funnel on one side and a conveyor belt coming out of the other.

'The Homunculiser,' narrated GENI as they walked past, 'is referred to by many as the first shrinking device.'

'Why would anyone set fire to all these incredible things?' asked Albert.

'Someone was going to use Eartha's discoveries to do bad stuff,' said Kip.

'She wrote about dark forces, remember?' added Timmi. 'That's why she hid the Ark behind all the riddles, to try and keep it safe. And that's why she burned down her Invention House.'

'You are correct,' GENI continued. 'Eartha became

fearful that one of her devices would be transformed into a weapon, like many wonderful creations that have started out with great and good hopes. But we do not know which invention caused her so much consternation.'

'Oh look! There's the Futurescope,' said Timmi, pointing at a sign.

They all stopped and stared at a slowly revolving Touchlight question mark that stood nearly as high as Kip.

'Don't you know what it looks like?' he asked.

'We don't,' said GENI. 'Despite it being the most legendary of Eartha's inventions, she was very secretive about her Futurescope.'

'I know this might sound stupid,' said Albert, 'but what exactly did it do?'

'Scholars believe that it traced the rarely seen energy Aeon Light, enabling its user to glimpse the future.'

Kip saw a squirl surge up and coil itself around the question mark, but it quickly ebbed away.

'To broaden our understanding of Aeon Lightwaves, researchers at the college are examining drawings from Eartha's notebook along with sketches from the only other known Aeon Light observer, Kip Bramley...'

Me? thought Kip, squirming a little.

He looked around awkwardly. No one else seemed to have noticed except Albert and Timmi, who were beaming proudly. He screwed up his face in reply and they beamed more.

'You're famous,' said Timmi, when GENI had finished.

'Ermgh,' said Kip.

Albert clasped his hands together and batted his eyelids.

'Is your arm sore from signing so many autographs?' he asked. 'You're going to need a bodyguard to keep away all your screamy fans. I volunteer.'

'GENI only mentioned my name once,' Kip protested. 'And in case you hadn't noticed, no one seems to be paying much attention. Which is good.'

'Don't worry,' said Albert. 'We won't let all that fame go to your head. Although I bet I know someone who will...'

'Hey guys!' interrupted Timmi. 'The Crazy Paving!'

The Crazy Paving

The three friends exchanged excited glances as GENI guided them over to a Touchlight display that looked like a large, melted chessboard. Instead of rows of squares, its surface was made up of lots of different shapes that somehow all fitted together.

'Didn't Miss Twiss say it was still somewhere at Quicksmiths?' Timmi said.

'That is one theory,' said GENI. 'Despite the fact that Eartha's inventions were deliberately destroyed, legends remain. They say that the Crazy Paving is hidden somewhere in the college grounds.'

'What Strange Energy does it use?' Kip asked.

'It is one of only a few devices thought to tap into M-Waves – a form of unusual Thoughtwave that exists independently of human beings…'

Marvel-Waves, he thought. *Mystery-Waves … Monster-Waves*?

'Recent work by our Head of Thoughtwaves, Alexios Koriolis, has made great progress into M-Wave technology but we are still some way from reproducing Eartha's Myriad machines.'

Ah, thought Kip. *Myriad Waves.*

'Remind me what the Crazy Paving was all about,' said Albert.

'It allowed Eartha to travel to different worlds,' said GENI, 'or to be more precise, different realities called Myriads.'

'Like a multiverse?' Kip said.

'A bit like a multiverse, yes,' said GENI. 'But we try to avoid that word. It's used outside Quicksmiths to describe the Myriads, without understanding what they really are.'

Albert put his fingers up to the chessboard impression of the Crazy Paving.

'Does the pattern mean anything?'

'We believe that each of the shapes in the pattern corresponded to a new world. It's probable that every time the Crazy Paving was activated, the pattern would have changed to show a new random selection.'

'How many other worlds are there?' asked Timmi.

'It's likely there are many worlds, too many for one person to count. Even Eartha.'

'And how did Eartha actually operate it?' Kip asked.

'If my hypothesis is correct, then to reach a new Myriad she would have stepped on one of the shapes in the pattern of the pavement, or connected with it in some other way.'

'Can anyone use it?' asked Timmi. 'If they knew where it was.'

'Only if they have the activation device,' GENI replied.

The Silent Key? mouthed Kip, and Albert nodded.

'And it's hidden somewhere at Quicksmiths?' Timmi said.

'That is only a rumour,' said GENI. 'I was unable to find proof of this in any of the data I have examined so far.'

'Could it be under a lawn or something?' Timmi tried again.

'Nothing matching this description has shown up in any of my scans of the college campus.'

Kip took the scrap of paper out of his squirrel-free pocket and looked at Eartha's poem-riddle.

'Do you know anything about a Silent Key?' he asked.

'This is not something I have heard of,' said GENI. She paused and streaks of black and white flashed through her eyes. 'It is not mentioned anywhere in the Library archives.'

Albert leaned over Kip's shoulder.

'What about a lake? Is there a lake at Quicksmiths?'

'There is,' said GENI. 'The Old Boating Lake can be found north of the college.'

'That's a lake? I thought it was a big duck pond,' said Timmi.

'The original lake was bigger. But it was drained and resculpted many years ago.'

'Would it have been around in Eartha's time?' asked Kip.

'Yes, there are records that reference the boating lake before she was born.'

'OK thanks, GENI,' said Kip. 'That's been really helpful.'

The Strange Supercomputer smiled and followed them to the front door of the Invention House, where she stayed behind to wait for another guest.

'So how do we get out?' asked Albert, reaching over to the door handle, 'do we just...'

An Albert-shaped after-effect wobbled and evaporated away. Kip looked out of the window and waved up at giant Albert, who waved back enormously.

Kip and Timmi both stepped towards the door at the same time, both stepped back, laughed, and a few moments later were standing next to normal-sized Albert.

Chapter Seven

Memoria Technica

'Where have you lot been?' said Leela, galloping over. 'I've been looking for you for ages.'

'We went to the Invention House,' said Kip.

'Did you find anything out?'

'Lots more about the Crazy Paving.'

'Tell me later,' said Leela. 'I want to show you something.'

She skipped over to a squat glass box on the far side of the study. It had a single glass leg with a curved glass foot. There was something timeless about it, and no way of telling if it came from an orchestra of the distant future or a mystical minstrel from the ancient past.

'That's the smallest alien piano I've ever seen,' said Albert. 'Pinky could play it.'

'It's not actually a piano,' said Leela.

'Duh,' replied Albert. 'It's obviously the Memoria Thingia.'

Leela hummed happily around the side of the instrument.

'Memoria Technica,' she said, fitting her thumb into a sensor etched into the side. 'And I'd step back if I were you!'

Everyone retreated and watched in awe as the Memoria Technica came to life. Every square inch of its surface opened out and expanded, more than doubling the size of the instrument. Extra legs spiralled down at each corner and a stool spiralled up from a disc on the floor. And finally, the top swung out, allowing curly pipes to nose upwards like curious eels from a glass seabed.

Two long rows of thin metal spokes folded down from the instrument's front panel. The spokes had clasps at the ends, holding large oval buttons, also made of glass. One of the sockets was empty where a loose button must have fallen out.

'Plunk us a tune then,' said Timmi.

Leela sat down on the stool and rubbed her hands together gleefully. She looked for a second sensor on the body of the Memoria Technica and pressed again with her thumb. Long, bendy antennae grew out from each side of the instrument and, after Leela's adjustments, they almost touched her temples.

'Is it going to play our emotions like the Heartsichord?' asked Albert. 'I should warn you, I'm not feeling very feely today.'

'Not really,' said Leela. 'Yes, it's connected to Thoughtwaves, but in a different way.'

She rested her fingertips on the central buttons, before letting out an amused hoot.

'Watch this!' she sniggered, and played a single note with her left hand.

Pure and tinkly, it was exactly how Kip expected glass notes to sound. There was something quite cheerful, almost Christmassy, about it.

The air rippled around the mouths of the Memoria Technica's glass pipes.

'What's that?' said Timmi.

Something floated out of one of the pipes. Something small and furry and feathery. A miniature mowl. A mowl in a top hat, to be precise. Each new note produced a new mowl until there was a multitude of musical mowls parading up and down and around the Memoria Technica, and weaving among the four friends.

'That just might be the best thing I've ever seen,' said Albert, doubling up with laughter.

'That's unbelievable. Is it playing what you think?' asked Kip.

Leela nodded, concentrating on the music.

'The antennae pick up my thoughts.'

Timmi shriek-giggled and hunched her shoulders as a mowl note tried to skip into her ear. Lirriping uncontrollably, the real mowl appeared and dived into the visible music. Ruffling his head crest, he joined in the parade until all the mini-mowls fell into line to follow him like ducklings.

'Scratch that,' said Albert. '*This* is the best thing I've ever seen.'

Kip felt a shuffling in his pocket and remembered to undo the Danger Velcro. Pinky's face looked out immediately and her eyes widened with pure delight.

Picking up the pace, Leela began to play with her right hand too until she came to a broken button, which she tried pressing a few times.

'It's four hundred years old,' she mumbled with a shrug. 'One dead and one missing note isn't too bad.'

Her fingers carried on, and were soon flying furiously again. As the melody became more complex, the top-hat mowls formed a conga line and began to dance along the open lid of the instrument. Unable to resist, Pinky shimmied up a glass leg and tried to hug her way through the line-up, bursting the notes one by one.

'World's. Cutest. Broadway Show,' said Timmi.

Leela swivelled round on the stool, with a theatrical leer.

'Mwahahaa! You mere mortals have seen nothing yet. Not if it has a Memorabilia Panel…'

'What's that?' asked Timmi.

'It records the images from your mind as you compose. Then you can play them back together in a mix.'

She began to hunt around the Memoria Technica.

'Help me look for it everyone, it's probably a panel that flips down...'

'Like this maybe?' asked Kip.

He ran his finger over a dark line underneath one of the antennae.

'That might be it,' said Leela.

She plucked with one fingernail at the base of the antenna and, with a soft clunk, the flap fell down to reveal a console of metal switches.

'Let's hope Eartha made some recordings!'

Fingers wiggling, Leela's hands hovered over the console before trying a switch at random.

The Memoria Technica began to play a bold tune all by itself, just like a haunted piano in the saloon of a Wild West ghost town. Green dragons the size of mice sailed out from the pipe mouths and began to strike ballet poses across the surface of the open lid.

Eartha wrote this music, thought Kip in amazement. *All those years ago.*

He felt fleetingly close to her – the great Renaissance architect of ideas – and wondered at how a life lived so long ago could still touch their lives in the here and now so strongly, so enchantingly.

'Try another one,' Timmi said.

Leela turned off the dragons and flicked a second switch. The music changed to a shy melody and graceful spider-notes floated out of the pipes, dangling from silk parachutes. The mowl freeped and began to hop-waddle after them, flicking at them with his quick, orange tongue.

'More! More!' said Albert.

At the flip of a third switch, beautiful harmonies began to play and planets spun out from the Memoria Technica, settling into an orbit around each of their heads.

Leela muttered something and tried two switches together.

'Let's see if this mixes things up,' she said.

The dragon notes appeared again – only now each one began to chase its tail puppishly, moving faster and faster until each one had melted into a revolving hoop. Celestial harmonies began to weave in with the dragon's bold refrain, and the twinkling planets re-emerged from the pipes, gliding over to settle inside the spinning emerald rings.

'I can see why you were so excited,' said Kip. 'This thing is incredible, even if you don't know anything about music.'

'Does anyone else want a go?' Leela asked, stepping back.

They each took turns to choose the music at random. Cows jumped over moons, eggs hatched into birds-of-paradise, spiders turned into hot air balloons, and lemon trees fired fruit that exploded in golden fireworks.

Seeing all this mythical music, it wasn't long before

a group of Third Years began hanging around, waiting for their chance to play.

'Come on,' said Kip. 'We need to go and poke around the Old Boating Lake anyway.'

'What's that?' asked Leela.

'It's that big duck pond, said Timmi. 'You know, past Aristotle's Theatre. It used to be a lake…'

'Ah-hah!' said Leela. 'So maybe it's the lake in the poem?'

She tried to persuade the mowl to leave but he refused to budge and eventually she left him behind, frolicking after the notes with his almost-human hands held out, fat little fingers twitching. Pinky, on the other hand, had had more than enough excitement, and willingly crept back to Kip's pocket for one of her frequent daytime naps.

A Proposal

'Is that the time? It's snack o'clock,' said Albert, as they left the study. 'Anyone coming to the Buttery?'

'I might see if Chef Garibaldi has made me the bento cakes he promised,' said Leela.

'Ooooo, me, me!' joined in Timmi. 'He said there'd be snickerdoodles too. Just like Grandma Brown makes back home in Torrington.'

'All I can say is you'd better prepare your tastebuds to be blown away,' said Albert. 'Albert has requested fatcooks.'

'Bento cakes? Snickerdoodles? *Fatcooks*?' said Kip.

'You can judge which one is the best,' said Albert. 'I'll give you a clue: it's fatcooks.'

'Sounds like my kind of competition,' Kip said. 'I'll be waiting at the old oak.'

As he walked across the courtyard, Kip pictured his dad, Theo, in his chef's uniform, and wished he were here to join in the fun. Although everything at Quicksmiths felt perfect, it was hard not to miss his dad a lot. They only really had each other, and he hoped Theo wasn't too lonely on his own.

Maybe if we can borrow a wormhole everyone can come and visit me in the summer holidays, he thought. *Dad would like that.*

Sunlight shuffled sleepily through the gaps in the oak leaves. The sluggish heat crept over Kip and he yawned and leaned back against the trunk. He tried to run over the dream-poem but only remembered a few words and had to look at the scrap of paper.

When long-legged little ones go chasing up the trees
Peel aloud the yellow bells and shake off all the leaves,

Then shall the hidden Silent Key be yours to take
Such a fitting tribute to the Lady of the Lake.

When at the summit of a string the key is flying free
The lake will dry its single eye, and paving you shall see.

Long-legged little ones? he thought. *Yellow bells*?

At least it felt as if the meaning of the second verse was beginning to come together, though. There was surely a good chance that the Old Boating Lake was the lake in the poem. And that might help them understand the third verse. His eyes went to the last few words.

Paving you shall see.

'It has to be instructions to find the Crazy Paving,' he murmured.

Come on squirls, he thought. *How about a shortcut?*

He shut his eyes. The sunlight's slow dance with the leaves made patterns on his closed eyelids. Squiggly lines of electric-blue squirls – Aeon Light – flowed into and around these patterns. But they didn't give Kip some miraculous answer.

'What's that?' asked a breathy voice.

Kip yanked open his eyelids to find Iris standing next to him, staring at the paper. He crumpled it up hastily.

'Just a poem,' he mumbled.

Her searching gaze swept from the paper to his face. There was a hint of bluish shadow under dark, deep-set eyes.

'You're a poet?' she said. 'Can I see?'

'Er … no … I … it's a bit embarrassing,' Kip stuttered.

'Oh. It is about *someone*?' Iris persevered.

'No, no,' said Kip hurriedly. 'Nothing like that.'

'Where's your crew?' she asked, looking around. 'They're like super glue. Sheesh they just don't leave you alone for a second do they? I just love Leela and Timmi – they're so clever. And Albert's such a sweetheart.'

Kip had no idea where this was going and smiled nervously.

'But they're never serious for one second – how do you get anything done with all that constant twitter? I suppose it's great if you just want to kick back all the time, and they're really funny, especially Albert. But they kind of show off a bit too. You'd think they were the famous ones the way they go on.'

What's she getting at? Kip thought.

Iris looked him straight in the eyes.

'*I* would give you plenty of space. I'm loyal and brave, and I won't bother you with pointless jokes.'

Oh no, thought Kip..

'Listen, Iris,' he said. 'I really like my friends, even if they do show off a bit sometimes and make crummy jokes. And, well, I don't really know how to say this ... so I'll just say it ... I'm not really looking for a girlfriend.'

Iris's dark-rimmed eyes trembled for a moment...

Oh great, thought Kip.

...and creased into laughter.

'I don't want to be your *girl*friend,' she said. 'I want to be your business partner. With your Aeon Light and my marketing, we would dominate the Quicket Market.'

'Oh,' said Albert, back from the Buttery. 'Hello.'

'Think about it,' said Iris, making a cool retreat.

'Think about what?' asked Albert.

'She wants to be my … my … business partner,' said Kip, a little stunned.

'What? Iris?' asked Timmi, leaning on the old oak next to Kip.

'Kip's Number One Fan,' said Albert. 'Loopy O'Lala.'

'Aw sweet,' said Timmi. 'That's so hearts.'

'No, no, no,' said Albert. 'That's not sweet, or hearts.'

'For once,' said Leela, leaning on the other side of Kip. 'I agree with Albert. The way she acts around you is like a crayfish that's gone cray-cray.'

'With an extra splash of cray spray,' Albert added.

'She is very intense,' said Timmi gently. 'But what about Kip? Maybe Kip likes her. Like, *like* likes her.'

'I don't think "like" is the word,' said Kip, not wanting to say anything horrible. 'And definitely not "*like* like".'

'She doesn't seem to be making many friends, though,' said Timmi. 'Maybe we should invite her back for the tasting competition…?'

'Don't even think about it,' Leela interrupted. 'Team Glowflyer already has perfect symmetry. We don't need no crayfish.'

Chapter Eight

The Old Boathouse

For the Skimmi to detect his Thoughtwaves, all Kip needed to do was stare deliberately up past the old oak in its summer wig of green leaves. Then he was soaring smoothly skywards, following the others.

Spirited winds ruffled his shirt as his Skimmi scudded beneath the clouds. Below, a pathway snaked across the lawn like a chalk serpent. It meandered through a line of fir trees and out the other side and then veered to the right towards the Skimmidrome. Over to the left, beyond Aristotle's Theatre, the grass was overgrown and scattered with purple cornflowers and orange Marigolds.

'That's it!' said Timmi.

The lake looked up at them like an inviting blue mirror. Ducks disturbed the reflected clouds in its tranquil surface, as they slid among patches of algae. Along one side, the water's edge was fringed with thick bullrushes, and on the opposite side was a log-cabin boathouse built on a base of rough-hewn stone blocks. In this foundation, two majestic arches, half-submerged, captured the green aquatic light. Between the arches was an ornate doorway that connected the boathouse to a jetty made from slats of dark and pale wood. The scale of it seemed very lavish next to such a small lake.

'They used to sail here?' said Leela. 'It's only just about big enough for duck-boats.'

'GENI told us it was larger back in the day,' said Kip.

They landed next to a patch of marigolds. Leela folded up her Skimmi and left it in the scented wild grass.

'Aren't you going to leave yours?' she asked, as Albert slung his over one shoulder and adjusted its strap. 'It'll be safe.'

'No way,' he said. 'This goes everywhere with me. Even the bathroom.'

Kip slung his Skimmi over one shoulder too and began to cut across the knee-high stems. After a few steps he came to a faint, footworn path that took them to the land-side entrance of the building. A few mildewed steps led up to a black-wood door scrawled about with corkscrewed vines of ivy. He tried the handle.

'Locked.'

'Forget the Silent Key, we need to get our hands on a Skeleton Key,' said Albert.

'The door that leads on to the jetty is probably locked too,' Timmi said. 'But I'm sure I saw an open window. And we can easily get across.'

A ledge overhung the top of the stone foundation and went all the way around the side of the building to the front. It was just wide enough to shuffle across on tiptoe, if they hugged the wall.

'What's the worst that can happen?' said Leela.

Everyone knew Kip was a good climber, so they all hung back for him to go first. He pulled himself through the cracked frame of the open window and hopped down into the cool interior of the boathouse. It was hard to see anything except darkness after the bright afternoon light outside.

'Ew, it smells like a farm in here!' said Timmi, clambering in after him.

Kip swiped up along his Candle badge to turn on some Candlelight. The boathouse was spacious, and he could imagine it in Eartha's time, full of rich tapestries and sumptuous furniture. Now it looked more like a rarely swept barn, and ivy was growing down one wall from a long chink near the ceiling.

A yell detonated outside, and there was a loud splash followed by lots of smaller splashes. They rushed to the window to see Leela floundering about in the water, and a family of ducks flapping away with indignant quacks.

'Well, it happened,' she spluttered. 'The worst.'

She managed to find a few handholds in the stone but couldn't quite reach the ledge, so Kip climbed down to help her up. Her hair was plastered around her ears and festooned with bits of algae. Once inside she took off her trainers, pulled off her squelchy socks and poured out two trickles of lake water.

'Can someone tell me why we didn't just use our Skimmies to get in?' she complained.

'This was much more entertaining,' laughed Kip.

'So is our boathouse hiding anything?' asked Albert, last in at the window.

'More ivy,' said Kip. 'Cobwebs.' He ducked. 'And a bee.'

'And this?' said Timmi.

She focused her Candlelight on a splash of colour underneath the straggling vines. As they all pitched in to pull away the ivy, a few displeased spiders scuttled away from the light.

'I think it's part of a mural,' she said.

Although years of grime covered the wall, the plaster underneath still seemed in good condition.

'We need something to clean the crud away,' said Albert.

'You rang?' said Leela, twirling her wet socks around. 'Crud Removal International at your service.'

Being careful not to rub away the paint as well as the accumulated layers of dirt, Kip and Leela managed to gently sponge the mural clean with Leela's wet socks, while Albert and Timmi gathered up the broken ivy and threw it out the window. Bit by bit the images underneath began to show through.

'It's a scene of the lake,' said Leela, turning up her Candlelight too.

Kip stood back. The paint was faded but it was still possible to make the picture out.

Barges skimmed along the calm surface of the blue lake. But the boating didn't stop there – the air above the water was also full of punts. The gondoliers were using their poles to push off from the clouds overhead. Beneath the surface of the lake too, rowing boats with see-through domes weaved among the fish. Everyone was dressed in Shakespearean clothes with puffy sleeves, funny stockings and capes.

'I wonder if it was really like that,' murmured Albert.

A woman at the lakeside was chasing after diamond-shaped kites that soared over the lawn. She had already caught most of their strings and her feet were lifting off the ground.

Is that Eartha? Kip wondered.

'She must be the Lady of the Lake,' said Leela, her eyes sparkling with excitement.

'This poem is finally beginning to make a bit of

sense,' said Kip, uncrumpling the paper again. 'Now we've found the lake and the Lady of the Lake.'

'It's just the first line we need to crack,' Timmi said. 'If we could work that out, I think the rest would fall into place really quickly.'

'Say it out loud,' said Albert, closing his eyes.

'When long-legged little ones go chasing up a tree,' read Kip.

'There are a few trees around the boathouse … and there's the old oak of course,' said Leela.

'Would that have been around in Eartha's day?' said Kip.

'Oaks can live for a thousand years,' replied Leela. 'Anyway, does it matter? She had a Futurescope after all.'

'Long-legged little ones,' said Timmi. 'Baby giraffes? Flamingo chicks? They like lakes…'

'Read it again,' said Albert, with his eyes still closed.

Kip repeated the first line and had only got halfway when Albert opened his eyes wide.

'SPIDERS!' he shouted. 'Spiders. They could be the long-legged little ones.'

'Spiders?' said Leela softly. 'Weren't there spider-notes in the Memoria Technica?' Now I think of it, there were lemon trees too – and what do lemons have?'

'Peel!' said Kip.

An are-you-thinking-what-I'm-thinking look

bounced around the four friends. They climbed as fast as they could along the ledge and pelted back towards Leela's Skimmi.

One of Leela's wet trainers squeaked rhythmically, and she started squeaking along with it. In high spirits, Albert joined in, and then Kip and Timmi, until everyone had to stop to let the laughter out. One short Skimmi ride later, and they were sprinting and squeaking again – all the way to the Great Globe.

But just as they were about to scramble up the steps and into the study a voice echoed across the hall.

'You there! Second Year – yes you … er …' There was a whispered conference with GENI. 'Leela!'

Leela froze. 'Uh-oh,' she said.

'There's been an *incident* with your wild … creature … in my study. I need you to come with me right this instant and clean it up.'

Muttering something blood-thirsty at the floor, Leela turned to face the professor who had addressed her. He wore a drab brown jacket with fuzzy beige elbow patches, and had a thick head of hair, gelled into neat waves. On his chin was a very tiny beard; it looked like someone had stuck on a snippet of felt left over from the elbow patches.

'I'm *so* sorry, Professor Koriolis,' Leela said sweetly. 'The mowl is fully house-trained, but every now and then he does get excitable. My friends will come and help, and whatever he's done, I promise we'll fix it up as good as new.'

The professor turned on his heel and marched out of the double door that led from the Hall of Maps.

'We'll *what*?' said Albert, indignantly.

'Come on, you love the mowl and all his mowly antics. This is the price of love.'

'If we all help,' said Kip, 'we'll be back here quicker. We need Leela anyway – she's our Memoria Technica expert. The spiders and lemons will wait for us.'

'Well yes, OK,' said Albert good-naturedly. 'He is very lovable I suppose. But if it's mowl poop we're talking about, bagsy not me!'

Professor Koriolis

It was just a short walk to Professor Koriolis's study, and the whole of the college seemed to be out enjoying the good weather. Summertime heat rose up through the lawns with a heady, green scent. The weekend laziness was contagious, and the gardens were full of students lolling about on the grass, reading or playing music.

Up ahead, forming one side of the large courtyard that enclosed the Clock Tower, was the Singing Mill. Its stately white walls were framed in blackened wood, and clumps of honeysuckle grew out from overhanging balconies. Alongside the building, a huge golden wheel turned. As they approached, the air filled with faint whistles and groans, like distant whale song.

'What turns the wheel?' asked Albert.

'You do!' said Leela. 'Well, not just you. All of us. All that constant churning of thoughts in our heads makes an awful lot of Thoughtwaves.'

'Nuh-uh,' Albert said. 'I only ever have two thoughts: what's for dinner, and when's my next nap.'

'Are you sure you and the mowl aren't related?' said Timmi.

'Hey,' said Albert. 'I've just realised something. Do the buildings represent the Big Five Strange Energies? So if the Clock Tower is Timeyarn, Skycrackle Tower is obviously Skycrackle, the Singing Mill is Thoughtwaves … er … the Quantum Quarter is Wormholes and Atlas House is Slipstream?'

'Five out of five,' said Leela. 'You win a place in an elite mowl damage control unit.'

'So, who is that guy?' Kip asked. 'The mowl's latest victim.'

'Professor Koriolis, the Head of Thoughtwaves,' Timmi replied.

'What's he like?'

'He's OK, I guess. Not my favourite, but how could anyone's favourite not be Professor Mo?'

Timmi and Leela took them to a door on the

ground floor of the mill, and entered an anteroom lined with shoe racks.

'He doesn't like sneakers on the carpet,' Timmi said, pulling off her trainers and placing them in an empty space.

Professor Koriolis was already sat in a threadbare armchair lit up by a line of sharp sunlight that speared the open window. He was reading a book: *The Multifarious Interface Theory and Other Important 21st Century Advances, by A. K. Koriolis*. Above the armchair hung a large portrait of the professor. In it, he was posing in the same armchair. In the same clothes. Reading the same book.

Professor Koriolis looked across as his barefoot visitors entered the room.

'There!'

He pointed to a large plant pot that had been knocked over. There was no denying it – muddy mowl-shaped hand prints had been stamped all over an expensive-looking rug, and the unfortunate former plant was now lying in half-eaten shreds among the wreckage.

'You can find some cloths and special carpet cleaner in the kitchenette cupboard. Off you go!'

The professor's eyes flicked back to his book.

'Oh, no TV for you mowl, not for a week!' growled Leela.

'Rubber gloves anyone?' Timmi said, snapping on a pair.

When they had finished clearing up the mess, Leela approached the professor and began to speak, but he held up a palm.

'Just to the end of the page,' he said.

They waited in silence while Koriolis finished reading. Out of the corner of his eye, Kip saw Albert making a look-at-that face. He followed Albert's secretive finger-curl to the professor's feet, and swallowed a laugh. Clumps of luscious silky locks sprouted from all ten toes, as if their owner hadn't quite managed to change back from a werewolf escapade.

Kip made eye contact with Albert, who accidentally let go of a high-pressure snigger. He managed to turn it into a successful cough, but not before Professor Koriolis scowled at the two of them. He snapped the book shut and put it on a coffee table.

'Are you finished then?' he said, looking over at the restored rug. 'I won't find anything unpleasant underfoot later, will I?'

'Absolutely not,' said Leela. 'It's like brand new.'

'Good, well, thank you … uh … students. Goodbye.'

'Professor Koriolis,' said Timmi. 'GENI said you were doing some experiments on M-Waves. Can you tell us more about the Crazy Paving?'

'Hmmm,' said Koriolis. He looked at the line-up before him more closely. 'Is that so?'

He stood up and went to a bookcase, where he pulled a weighty book off a shelf.

'Enlighten me with what you know about M-Waves,' he said.

'They're a type of Thoughtwave which can't be measured in the usual ways,' Leela said.

'But we can predict they exist because of the effect they have on other types of Thoughtwaves,' Timmi added.

'Good, good,' said Koriolis. 'And what does the "M" in M-Waves stand for?'

'Myriad,' they all chorused.

'Myriad,' said Professor Koriolis, walking slowly across the plush rug towards the window and leafing through the book. 'Myriad Waves.'

He put the book on the windowsill, and looked out at the sky.

'Any thoughts on what the Myriads are?'

'Other worlds,' said Leela.

Professor Koriolis turned back and looked at the group.

'Indeed. Now here's what you probably don't know. There are some who believe Myriad Waves are very similar to the Thoughtwaves made when we dream. One popular theory about Myriad Waves is called the Strange Dream Theory and what it says is this…'

The sunlight caught the profile of his face, making one eye glitter magically.

'…the Myriads, the other worlds that exist outside of our reality, are actually the dreams of the Universe.'

Kip looked around at the contents of the room and then back down at his own palms.

Does that make us just a dream of the Universe too? he thought.

'Are we part of it?' he asked. 'Is our world a Myriad?'

'Perhaps,' said the professor.

'So we're … everything … is just a blip inside a giant brain?' asked Albert.

'Just like that. Only not like that at all.'

'What happens if the Universe has a nightmare?' asked Timmi.

'Well, what if it did?' said the professor. 'We have nightmares all the time, and they can't hurt us.'

That's a weak answer, thought Kip, but the conversation had moved on.

'Because Myriad Waves are so similar to human Thoughtwaves, we might be able to see, and interact with, these other worlds. But first we would need to find them.'

'Are the Myriads illusions then?' asked Leela.

'Who's to say what's real and what isn't?'

'I know what's real,' said Albert.

'Do you now?' replied the professor, looking a bit annoyed. 'Doesn't a dream feel real enough to you, when you're in it?'

'How about the Crazy Paving? That's real, isn't it?'

The professor looked down at Leela for a split second and then smiled back up at the sky.

'Ah yes. The Crazy Paving. Despite our most earnest scientific efforts, we have failed spectacularly so far to interact in a meaningful way with Myriad Waves. Except, of course, for Eartha.'

'Eartha Quicksmith,' said Leela. 'From little orphan girl to Queen of the Quixars.'

Professor Koriolis smoothed out a wave of his hair with one finger.

'She took it all with her though,' he said, with a bit of a snap.

'Do you have any idea where the Crazy Paving might be?' asked Timmi. 'We were in the exhibition in the Great Globe today. We thought you might know something GENI doesn't.'

The professor looked pleased to hear this, and sucked his cheeks in.

'All sorts of theories are roaming around out there – they're all quite preposterous of course … it's hidden in a dimensional twist in a corner of the Library. It's been shrunk to the size of a slice of bread and placed in a Timeyarn capsule under the Clock Tower … it's one of the windows somewhere in Celestial Hall…'

'Miss Twiss said once that the Crazy Paving was like a doorway to a labyrinth,' said Leela. 'So could it be an actual doorway, somewhere at the college?'

Alexios Koriolis smiled behind his hand.

'You must think about these things *metaphorically*. "Sideways", as Professor Mo would say. Miss Twiss wasn't talking about doorways like the ones we use every day. As for the labyrinth part … there are many types of mazes…'

'So if it's not a doorway, how does it get you into another Myriad?' Leela persisted. 'Does it pinch space together? Is it like a wormhole?'

'No, no, no,' said the Professor. 'No wormholes. It works like this, or so we think: the Crazy Paving would create an energy chute of M-Waves leading to an entrance point in each new world. Because of the nature of Myriad Waves, it's possible that the Crazy Paving would also create a different exit point, a bit like the arrivals and departures terminals of an airport. These exit points might look like the original Crazy Paving. Or, as every Myriad is unique, they might look entirely different.'

'But where would it *actually* take you?' asked Albert.

'How far apart are two dreams? Nobody knows. Where are the Myriads? Nobody knows. Just like your dreams. Where are they exactly? Inside your brain? If so, then where inside your brain? Inside the chemicals? The electrical impulses? Inside the cells? Inside your mind, your soul? You see, it's very hard to answer. There's a reason why scholars used to call them the Nowhere Lands.'

He stopped and looked askance at the four friends.

'Why so much interest in the Crazy Paving anyway? I don't think you'd want to go inside even if it were right here. It's flawed you know.'

'How?' asked Kip.

'In order to use the M-Waves in the way she did, Eartha's machine must be one-way. That is, unless she had some clever way of reversing the tunnel's direction, which I personally think is quite impossible. Once you went in, you might have to keep travelling forever.'

'Wouldn't travelling through an energy chute turn you inside-out or something horrible, anyway?' asked Timmi.

Professor Koriolis seemed to enjoy this and laughed all the air out of his lungs.

'Perhaps you should ask Eartha,' he said.

Long-legged Little Ones

'Did you notice how he couldn't remember our names?' Timmi grumbled as they left the mill. 'And this is our second year in his class.'

'Maybe we should forget *his* name next time,' Leela suggested. 'Or get it wrong.'

'People, people,' said Albert. 'Have you forgotten we are *this close* to solving Eartha's poem? The long-legged little ones are waiting for us.'

He broke into a run and the rest of the group sprang after him, sprinting the short distance back to Atlas House.

'It's amazing really,' panted Leela. 'What good shape it's in – the Memoria Technica – after four hundred years – only one of the buttons has fallen off and only one is dead...'

Leela and Kip stopped running. It was as if an invisible bridge opened up between their two minds, as the thought occurred to them both at the same time.

'We've been calling them buttons ... because they look like buttons,' said Kip.

'But what if Eartha didn't call them that at all?' Leela followed on. 'Musical instruments like pianos usually have...'

'...keys!'

'The Silent Key!'

The well-worn wooden steps of the Great Globe creaked in complaint as they clattered up.

'I hope it's still got all of Eartha's original recordings,' said Albert between gulps of air. 'What if someone played over them?'

'It's been safe in here all this time, hasn't it?' Kip said. 'No one would record over Eartha's stuff.'

'Except Gorvak,' said Leela. 'He snuck in alone when we were all looking for the Ark.'

Kip felt his smile collapse.

'You're probably right though,' said Leela. 'He was too busy being a massive, mouldy toerag. He didn't have time for anything like that.'

Timmi was looking eagerly through the scattered visitors.

'It's free!' she said. 'Quick!'

They raced over and Leela pulled gently at the button that hadn't worked earlier.

'Are you the Silent Key?' she whispered.

But the Memoria Technica wouldn't let it go.

'Can you find Eartha's recording of the spiders again?' asked Albert.

Leela stared at the Memorabilia Panel, hesitated, and flicked up one of the switches. Dangling from their silken parachutes, spider-notes floated out of the glass pipes that curled from the open lid.

'Yessss,' she said, beaming with satisfaction. 'Now the lemon trees.'

She flipped a switch, waiting for a short while to see what music it produced before moving on to the next.

'Lanterns. Nope. Knights. Nope.'

After a few more attempts, golden seeds began to waft out of the pipe mouths alongside the spider-notes and Leela hesitated. The seeds planted themselves in the air by putting down yellow roots. In double-quick time, an orchard of lemon trees had sprouted up all around them, swaying in time to the music. The other visitors around the exhibition began to take notice and a small but enthusiastic crowd gathered.

'First time in my life I don't want an audience,' Leela said, under her breath.

The spiders breezing across from the pipes began to land on the quivering trees. They scaled the trunks deftly and leapt from lemon to lemon, causing the fruit to swing back and forth. Soft chimes blended into the music like the sounds of a tiny glass church.

'The lemons are the yellow bells!' said Kip, in a low voice.

All around them, musical leaves fluttered away from their trees to form a swirling, tinkling cloud around the Memoria Technica.

Then shall the hidden Silent Key be yours to take.

'Now!' hissed Kip.

Veiled from the audience by the cloud of leaves, Leela pulled at the glass button. This time it lifted up easily from the metal clasp.

'Show's over,' she said, switching off the music. 'The Memoria Technica's all yours!'

They parted their way through the curtain of dwindling leaf fall, no one saying a thing until they were out of the Great Globe, out of Atlas House altogether, and had scouted out a quiet bench in one of the courtyards. Here, they passed their discovery around, turning it over and inspecting it like a rare jewel.

Now that it was detached from the Memoria Technica, they could see the flat, oval button more clearly. It was completely made of glass – opaque like chalky water – and its upper face was perhaps double the size of a fingertip.

Albert turned the Silent Key over. On its base there were four small metal wheels, just like the rollers of a combination lock. Each one displayed the letter A. He scrolled one of them a few times.

'B, D, F…'

'Must be a password,' he said, looking up at the others.

The Memoria Technica had given up its secret, and yet each new secret seemed to lead to another. Kip realised how much he'd missed the thrill of the chase.

'Can you get addicted to adventure?' he asked.

'Very,' said Leela.

'I think we need to look at that mural in the boathouse again,' said Albert. 'The Lady of the Lake is waiting.'

The sun was getting lower in a blazing sky as they approached the overgrown corner of Quicksmiths. This time around they skimmied up to the open window and soon stood before the painted wall.

'At the summit of a string,' Kip mulled over the next line of the poem. 'That must mean…'

He ran his fingers across the mural, slowing down at the kites. One of them had an oval design at its centre, which caught his attention and he swept over the surface a few times.

'The plaster is lower here,' he said. 'Sort of sunken. Who's got the key?'

Leela produced the glass button and handed it over to Kip. It fitted the indent perfectly and clicked into place with a promising thunk. They waited.

'Shouldn't something be happening?' said Timmi.

'Albert,' said Leela. 'You eat more than anyone else I know. So how is your stomach always gurgling?'

'It's not me,' insisted Albert.

'Well, if it's not you, who is it?' said Leela.

'It's coming from outside,' Timmi said.

They ran to the window and looked out to find the water in the boating pond was draining rapidly.

'There is a *really* thirsty fish down there,' said Albert.

'The lake is drying its eye,' said Leela excitedly. 'This is the end of the poem!'

Unsure what to do about the dropping water level, the ducks still floated on the surface, bobbing lower and lower with the ebbing lake. Taking advantage, a seagull divebombed a nest of eggs, but was chased away just in time by the angry mother duck. Thinking quickly, Kip checked the Danger Velcro, which was already done up.

Timmi leaned out of the window, clapping her hands and shouting to scare away the gull.

'Scram!' she said. 'Go on, scram!'

The four friends watched impatiently as the fingers of receding water clung to the muddy sides of the lake. When the water had fully drained and the entire hollow was revealed, Kip was surprised to see the lakebed was flat with very steep sides, not curved like a soup bowl as he'd imagined.

'So what happens now if I do this?' Kip said, going back to the mural to remove the Silent Key.

He half expected the lake water to start filling up again, but it didn't. Leela shrugged.

'What about the jetty?' she suggested. 'We'll get a better look from there.'

They followed a ramp down to a sun-warmed porch that smelled of damp wood, opened the latch of the door and emerged on the walkway. Light and dark planks formed a striped pattern along the jetty's length, showing where rotting wood had been replaced over the years. A few sun-whitened posts rose up at irregular intervals from the sides, like the chipped tusks of a deepwater beast.

'There are steps at the end,' said Timmi, leaning on one of the posts.

The jetty was just about wide enough for them to walk in single file. Kip reached the stairs first to discover they were eroded but intact, and covered with algae. The steps went all the way down to the flat bed of the lake.

‘Why do you need steps at the end of a jetty?’ asked Albert. ‘For submarines?’

‘We’re about to find out,’ replied Kip. ‘Be careful, they’re slippery.’

Tightening his Skimmi strap so it didn’t swing over his shoulder, he looked over the side of the jetty. Droplets swelled at the ends of nails sticking out from the wet support posts. In them a hundred slipping suns flashed and plopped down six metres or so to the lake floor. He went down one step, and then another.

‘The Silent Key,’ breathed Timmi, who was right behind Kip. ‘It’s lit up!’

Kip’s attention had been on the lakebed that seemed strangely dry despite the dripping water. Now he glanced at the glass button in his hand, and saw it was glowing softly.

‘Keep going,’ Leela said.

After a few more steps, thin streaks of light began to surge out across the lakebed, joining up to make a haphazard patchwork pattern of paving stones. For a few seconds, Kip’s eyes took in the shapes clustered together, and his brain tried to make them mean something: a cactus, a shark fin, an anchor.

And then, with a thrill, he remembered GENI’s words.

Each of the shapes in the pattern corresponded to a new world.

‘We’ve only gone and done it,’ he said. ‘We’ve only gone and found the Crazy Paving.’

'Eartha, you sneakysocks!' said Albert. 'It's been perfectly hidden under this lake for four hundred years.'

Kip looked at the Silent Key. With each step closer to the bottom of the lake, it glowed a little brighter.

'They're definitely connected,' he said.

'We should tell Miss Twiss,' Leela said.

'We should tell everyone!' said Albert. 'This is immense.'

'Definitely,' said Timmi. 'And GENI can help us work out that password on the key.'

The last few steps were almost completely covered in weeds, and Kip didn't want to go all the way to the lake bottom anyway. He turned about face, taking care not to slip on the slimy wood where he stood, and looked up. Timmi was right in front of him, then Leela and Albert. His friends looked down at him, a just-won-the-lottery expression on their faces.

'Team Glowflyer does it again,' he said proudly. 'Let's celebrate at the Buttery and decide what to do next?'

'Yeah,' said Leela, patting her still-damp clothes. 'The sun's gone behind that big cloud now.'

'Here,' said Timmi, beginning to unknot the shirt tied around her waist, 'have this.'

Albert turned to face the top of the narrow stairs so he could lead the way back up. But as he swivelled around, his Skimmi knocked Leela in the face. In one fluid motion, she twisted to avoid it and took a step back, knocking into Timmi. With a yell of surprise, Timmi teetered and fell off the slippery steps.

'Sorry,' gasped Albert. 'Sorry, sorry.'

For a stretched-out moment, Kip held his breath. A terrible fear gripped him, a fear that Strange Energy would crackle up around Timmi from the lakebed, that some unknown force would consume her. But she stood looking up at them, blinking, with a slightly dizzy expression.

'Phew,' she said nervously, sweeping the back of her hand over her brow.

'Are you OK?' asked Kip.

'Fine,' said Timmi, looking at the weeds on the bottom steps, 'just need a hand up.'

She stretched up her arm to Kip and he reached down. As his hand grasped hers, his whole body felt a tremor. Sparks flew in the corners of his eyes. Something was wrong.

And then the lake was gone, like a light bulb being switched off.

Chapter Nine

Into the Myriads

Kip was slipping downwards fast, at a hair-raisingly steep angle. He was surrounded by the blackest night in which an occasional spark flashed, blinding him. There was a pressure in his ears, the kind you feel at the bottom of a deep swimming pool.

How am I falling? he thought. *There wasn't a hole.*

It felt as if he might slam into something at any second, and every time that thought reared up he couldn't help flinching.

'Hey!' he managed to shout. 'Guys?'

No one answered. He realised that he was gripping the Silent Key tightly and his hand was beginning to ache.

'Are you there?' he yelled again.

There was a sudden shift, like the lurch of a rollercoaster, and Kip felt something invisible pressing down on his chest, so that it took all his effort to breathe. In the next moment he felt himself lifting, and then falling again, lifting and falling, up and down, faster and faster, until he was like a ragdoll being shaken. And just when he didn't think he could take any more, it all came to an abrupt stop, releasing him into drifting freefall.

Kip found himself suspended in a thick not-quite-liquid. He fought back the urge to run – of course he couldn't – where to, and how? But it was hard to shut out the fear that was closing in on him.

I'm breathing, he thought. *That's good. But how? What is this stuff?*

There didn't seem to be a source of light anywhere, yet Kip could see quite clearly. The not-quite-liquid surrounding him was vacant for a few metres in all directions. Beyond this empty zone, globules as big as balloons were rising slowly like air bubbles in syrup.

'Hello?'

This time a faraway voice replied, muted, as if underwater.

'…here … energy chute … where … you?'

'Timmi!' Kip shouted. 'I'm here! Where are you?'

Her voice was getting closer, although he still couldn't see her.

'Falling in every direction … like astronauts.'

It *did* feel like falling everywhere at once. If Kip looked up, it felt as if he were drifting slowly down into a bottomless sea. And if he looked down, there was a sense of drifting slowly upwards into an endless night sky.

'... boy am I ... I thought I was in here on my own.'

Timmi's voice was unexpectedly close behind him, and he jumped. The best way to move around in the soupy atmosphere turned out to be a kind of clumsy frog-swim. Kip waggled his arms and managed a slow about-turn. There she was, looking scared but there nonetheless, and he felt a little stronger for seeing her.

'Are we dead?' she asked.

'You don't look it,' he replied, sounding more confident than he felt. 'No wings or harps.'

'You neither,' said Timmi. 'But it's hard to say. How would we know?'

Those words seemed to hang around for much too long.

'We came through Eartha's machine, didn't we?' said Timmi eventually. 'So it must be safe.'

'Hey,' Kip said. 'What about Albert and Leela?'

'Leela?!' yelled Timmi.

Kip joined in.

'Albert?!' they both shouted.

There was no reply, no faint, faraway voices. Just an almost-silence that rustled in Kip's ears.

'Whatever just happened only happened when you grabbed my hand...' said Timmi.

'...and I have the Silent Key,' Kip added.

That made him realise he was still holding it. Being

extra careful, he put it away in his most secure pocket and double checked the zip was done up properly.

'The key and the paving must've connected up through the two of us,' he said.

'Guess we didn't need that password after all.'

While they thought about that, the colourful globules floated around them, bouncing sluggishly.

'We're inside a lava lamp,' said Timmi.

'A lava lamp?'

'It's like a decoration thing. The convection heat of the lamp makes the goo bubbles float up and change shape. Then they go down again.'

She swim-flapped her arms elegantly, and although Kip was sure she must be more scared than she looked, it was reassuring. And he felt better when he joined in.

'Lava-Lamp Limbo, that's where we are,' she said.

'Are we still travelling through the Crazy Paving then,' Kip asked, a little confused. 'Or is this a Myriad?'

Feeling more confident now, he waggled his way to the edge of the empty zone to take a closer look at one of the globules. Something was enclosed in its wobbling outline: a strange island – half in shadow and half in bright sunlight. Pterodactyls skittered out of the shadowy half and flapped about over soft lilac waves.

'They've got tiny worlds inside them!' he said, with a rush of understanding.

He began to peer inside the globules as they rose

up before him. In one, a writhing mass of serpents made of fire and smoke travelled over a frozen plain, leaving deep channels in the ice behind them. Another contained a fabulous origami city made entirely of folded paper.

'So, these are the Myriads?' murmured Timmi.

Kip found his eyes drawn to a globule enclosing a familiar sight.

'Hey! Is that the Clock Tower?'

He frog-swam towards it, but some invisible barrier made it impossible to go any further.

'Kip!'

There was urgency in Timmi's voice but Kip could only turn around slowly. A globule was advancing towards them, invading the empty zone, becoming bigger and brighter than all the others.

'It's like it knows we're here,' said Timmi.

Kip stared inside to see a seaside scene.

'If it's not Quicksmiths, try to stay away from it,' Timmi said, attempting to backstroke in the opposite direction.

But it was impossible.

The globule broke open at the sides and formed gelatinous limbs that reached out around them, like a giant somewhere-in-space amoeba.

'It's sucking us in!' Timmi squealed.

'We'll be OK,' said Kip because it seemed like the right thing to say.

‘Hold my hand,’ said Timmi, nervously. ‘You have the key. I don’t want to get left behind here on my own.’

Trying to keep calm, Kip took Timmi’s hand and counted his own breathing as the globule expanded completely around the two of them.

Seven … eight … nine…

And on the tenth breath, the globule burst spectacularly in a shower of warm crackles.

Sandcastle

Something sharp was sticking into Kip’s face. He was lying on his front and tried to turn over but the Skimmi slung across his back stopped him from getting very far. Very carefully, he pushed himself up off a hard surface and a few pebbles fell off his cheek. Just in front of him was a clump of thick, blue-berried sea grass sticking up through a cleft in the rock…

Pinky!

Not knowing what he would do if Pinky were hurt, Kip checked the Danger Velcro and felt Pinky’s huddled form in his pocket. She sighed and sleep-squeaked, and he sighed too with an unwinding rush of relief.

‘How could you sleep through all that, furball?’ he said softly. ‘You just stay in there, nice and safe, until we figure this out.’

Timmi was lying face down too. Fearing the worst, Kip scrambled over and shook her shoulder gently.

'Are you OK?' he whispered.

Timmi groaned, but it wasn't a groan of pain.

'You know how you have to catch your breath after running?' she said, still not rolling over.

'Mmm-hmmm,' Kip said.

'Well, it feels like I'm trying to catch my mind.'

She rolled around and sat up, gently flexing her arms and legs.

'Nothing broken,' she said, with a grateful smile. 'You?'

Kip sat back, reassured, and nodded.

'So that was the Crazy Paving?'

'Well, Eartha sure got the name right,' said Timmi. 'That's the craziest thing that ever happened to me.' She scrambled to her feet and looked around guardedly. 'Where are we?'

Kip stood up too, eager to get a better look around this new Myriad. They were standing on an elongated strip of rock next to a beach. The clear blue open expanse of the sea and sky seemed to fill the world.

Timmi was pressing her Candle. She double tapped and swiped. Kip did the same.

'Question GENI?'

There was no answer.

'Worth a try,' she said with a shrug.

'Are they broken?' Kip asked.

'Could be,' Timmi said. 'Or maybe they don't work here.'

They each fell silent, thinking. Softly, softly, the drawn-out whispers of waves washed in the background.

'So if we're in a Myriad,' said Kip slowly, 'then we're inside a dream of the Universe?'

The hugeness of it was almost too much to fit in ordinary words.

'That's what Professor Koriolis said,' Timmi replied.

'If this is a dream, are we not real?' Kip asked. 'Are we like phantoms?'

'Dunno. I feel pretty real.'

'Me too,' said Kip. 'You know, if I'd known we were coming to the beach I'd have packed my swimming trunks…'

But Timmi didn't reply. Her eyes were searching the landscape frantically.

'Where's the Crazy Paving? It's gone!'

Kip felt a prickling of fear that threatened to sweep him away until a memory jumped in and saved him.

'The entrance and exit points are in different places,' he said. 'Remember? Professor Koriolis told us.'

Timmi nodded, a bit calmer.

'Like arrivals and departures terminals. I remember.'

'If Albert were here,' Kip said, 'he'd say that every Myriad has a Crazy Pav*in* and a Crazy Pave*out*.'

Timmi smiled distractedly, but it was a smile nonetheless.

'You know, the Silent Key lit up before,' Kip said. 'When it was near the lakebed. Maybe it's like a sort of Myriad Wave detector and we can use it to find departures?'

He took it out of his pocket and made himself believe that this plain glass button had the power to get them back to Quicksmiths. He rolled the alphabet wheels on its base at random.

'And we need to work out the four letters of the password,' he murmured. 'I wonder what it does.'

'I'm totally down for that,' said Timmi. 'Let's find the Crazy Paveout first, though. Over there's a good place to start.'

Perhaps a hundred metres away was a rock formation made of hundreds of pillars of varying heights. At first, these pillars were short and stumpy, and formed a long, even stretch of unusual stepping stones that rose only a few feet above the beach. Further inland they grew taller, pointing up at the sky like giant bony fingers.

Kip tightened the shoulder strap of his Skimmi, checked Pinky was still sleeping, and followed Timmi towards the rocks. But before they got very far, the sea began to do something very strange.

'Look at the tide,' he said.

The water was trickling back unnaturally fast,

leaving an expanse of damp sand behind. Something about it put Kip on his guard; he'd read about this.

'It could be a tidal wave,' he said urgently. He looked over at the tallest rock pillars. 'We might have to climb them.'

'A tidal wave?' said Timmi. 'How do we know for sure?'

'We don't,' Kip replied.

He was just about to start running for the rocks, when something twinkling under the shallows caught his eye. A sharp point became visible as the sea retreated, and then another and another, until the ebbing tide revealed a surprising secret.

'It's beautiful,' murmured Timmi.

The sandcastle was no bigger than any that might be found on an ordinary beach in an ordinary coastal town. But this one was built to perfection: its walls were inlaid with seashells; its pristine turrets were decorated with shining sea stones; and weedy flags fluttered from their pinnacles. There was a proper wooden drawbridge and a moat full of foamy brine.

'How is that not dissolved away in the seawater?' Kip asked.

'I think we should take a really quick look, in the interest of science,' said Timmi. 'Then we'll head for the rocks.'

Kip listened, not sure exactly what he was listening

for – the rush of a faraway tsunami perhaps. It was quiet.

'Who do you think built it?' Timmi asked, walking towards the castle.

'Well, we can assume not the fish,' Kip replied.

They were about five metres away when a faint blast from a conch horn rose over the distant sound of the waves. Kip looked over his shoulder.

'Someone must be coming. We should hide.'

'Someone *is* coming,' said Timmi.

Kip followed her gaze back to the sandcastle. The drawbridge was lowering. His eyes forgot to blink, and the threat of a tidal wave faded from his mind, as he watched the castle's inhabitants swarming out along the little bridge. Timmi's delighted laugh skimmed out over the wide beach.

'I love them!'

A dozen or so creatures that looked like miniature gorillas, each about the same height as Pinky, were riding wheeled chariots onto the sand. Kip squinted. From what he could see, they weren't hairy, but instead were covered in shimmering blue and purple scales. They began to fan out over the beach and, although Timmi was still chuckling at their tiny fierceness, Kip felt less at ease.

'They're trying to surround us,' he said.

'Oh, but they're too cute,' Timmi said. 'Do you think they'll let me pick them up?'

She knelt down and put her arms out to welcome the nearest one, who was racing towards her – tremendously fast from his small sand-gorilla perspective, but really rather slowly from Timmi's.

'Hello,' she said. 'What's your name?'

The charioteer didn't show any sign of slowing down or wanting to make friends. It occurred to Kip that as far as the sand-gorillas were concerned, he and Timmi were terrifying, invading giants, with deafening voices and devastating feet.

'I think we should leave them in peace,' he said. 'Come on.'

Timmi stood up reluctantly, but as she did so, a yelp of pain escaped her lips.

'Something stung me!'

She twisted around and tried to grab at her back.

Kip stepped quickly behind Timmi to find a needle-sized dart lodged in her shoulder next to the thin vest strap. Hanging from the blunt end was a curious decoration: a single coral bead like a tiny pumpkin.

'Are you OK?' he asked.

Timmi nodded as he pulled at the bead to dislodge the dart. It came out easily and Kip threw it to the ground. They looked around to see the nearest gorilla warrior reloading a crossbow fixed to its chariot.

'How could they?' said Timmi, with a hurt tone.

'We can easily outrun them. Let's get out of here!'

Side by side, they flung themselves across the beach, away from the castle and its angry inhabitants. The faint sound of the conch horn followed them but Kip didn't bother looking back – the sand-gorillas would never catch them. As they got closer to the rock formation, the edges of the nearest stepping stones lit up in a familiar glow.

Not slowing down the pace, Kip glanced at the Silent Key. It was lit up too.

'That's it!' he said. 'The Crazy Paving is insidc the rock.'

It wasn't far, just a few more strides … but there was a crashing sound just behind him, and Kip turned to find Timmi collapsed to her knees.

'What's wrong?'

'I don't think I can walk,' she said. 'My legs feel numb. Everything's woozy.'

Her words sounded thick and woolly and she retched alarmingly, sending Kip's heart into a runaway gallop. Timmi's eyes looked dull as he helped to haul her up and she leaned into him heavily.

'Poison,' she mumbled.

He shot a backwards look in the direction of their pursuers. Although the advancing sand-gorillas were slow, now he and Timmi were even slower, and they were catching up. The squeak of the conch horn sounded again victoriously.

'Please try,' begged Kip. 'It's only four or five steps, I'll help you...'

Timmi nodded and wobbled upright, her neck drooping. They staggered forward together, Kip taking as much of her weight as he could.

Breathless and afraid, he kept a tight hold of Timmi's hand and stretched out, just managing to reach the edge of a heart-shaped stepping stone, hoping that the touch of his fingertips would be enough.

It was enough and he gave silent thanks as the Crazy Paving spirited them away. But the rollercoaster journey through the energy chute felt longer than before. Kip could do nothing except wait helplessly, trying not to think the worst, until he was freefalling in Lava-Lamp Limbo.

'Timmi?' he called out.

It seemed like an age before he caught sight of her, spinning gently in the strange not-liquid. Her eyes were closed and her mouth open.

'Are you OK?' he shouted.

She didn't answer and Kip swam-scrambled towards her.

'Timmi?' he said, taking her hand.

Her eyes flickered and she groaned and spoke without opening them.

'Did we make it?'

'Yes,' said Kip. 'We're safe.'

'How does it look?' Timmi asked weakly. 'My shoulder?'

Kip frog-swam around to look. The whole of her right shoulder was swollen and had turned plum-coloured, almost black, around the dart puncture wound. Under the skin, dark, searching tendrils were beginning to spread up her neck.

'It looks OK,' he said, unable to admit the truth to himself or to Timmi.

'What are we going to do?' she said, her breath raspy. Round tears rolled out of her eyes and bobbed away to join the colourful globules.

If I'd been poisoned, he thought. *Timmi would invent something incredible to save me.*

'We'll be fine. I'll find you somewhere to rest soon.'

Timmi sniffed and leant her head on Kip's shoulder.

'Remember when we were talking about the Dreambomber,' she said so quietly Kip could hardly hear her.

'Yeah,' said Kip.

'And Professor Koriolis said nightmares couldn't hurt us.'

'Yeah,' said Kip.

'He was wrong,' she whispered, and fell quiet.

Gallery

'If this is all made of Thoughtwave energy,' murmured

Kip, half to himself, 'then maybe we can just think our way back? Influence whatever's inside the Myriads.'

A globule was approaching. Its insides wobbled and were hard to make out, but they looked promisingly summery. Kip shut his eyes, held Timmi's hand tightly, and thought homely things until he felt the next Myriad exploding into being all around him.

A velvet curtain formed one wall of the empty room. Next to him, Timmi groaned again and rolled over. She sat up and brushed the top of her shoulder lightly with a fingertip, and then pressed harder. Overjoyed, but frowning in confusion, she looked at Kip.

'It feels fine!'

Kip shuffled over on his knees to look. Where before there had been swelling and the insidious purple of poison, now there was just normal, healthy skin.

'Could the Lava-Lamp Limbo have done something?' he said, prodding her shoulder. 'You heal when you sleep, don't you? And if the Universe is dreaming, maybe that has something to do with it...'

'Whatever did it,' said Timmi, 'we sure got lucky.'

'We did. Even if the Myriads *are* just dreams of the Universe ... we have to assume that if we get hurt here, we get hurt for real. Exactly the same as our world.'

'I think the first thing we should do here is find the

Crazy Paving,' Timmi said. 'After that we can explore if we like, or find a place to rest, or whatever, as long as we know where departures is.'

'Agreed,' Kip said softly. 'It was well camouflaged in those rocks.'

They poked their heads through the velvet curtain. Outside was a much larger space where people milled about, looking at pictures on the walls.

'I think it's an art gallery,' whispered Kip.

'The people seem normal enough,' Timmi whispered back, 'except for maybe their clothes. They all look like fairy godmothers. And godfathers.'

Everyone had powdered faces and blueberry-coloured lips. They wore elbow-length silk gloves and pencil dresses with a strange tutu in the middle, both men and women, and carried pointless little paper umbrellas. Kip looked down at his cargo shorts and faded manga T-shirt, and then at Timmi's shirt and vest, cut-off jeans and pink baseball cap.

'It's going to be hard to blend in,' he said, 'but we don't really have much choice.'

'If anyone asks, we'll say we're part of a radical art group,' replied Timmi.

They parted the curtain and stepped out into a long atrium. It was lucky for them that the gallery occupants all seemed much too absorbed in the pieces of art to notice them, and the two visitors walked by unobserved.

'We'll keep an eye on the Silent Key,' murmured Kip. 'It should light up again when we're close.'

'When I did a search-and-rescue course once, we moved out in circles from our starting point, making the circles bigger and bigger as we went. We can't quite do that here, but we could start by exploring this room, and then all the closest rooms, and gradually work our way outwards.'

'Good plan. Hopefully departures should be fairly close to arrivals,' Kip said, 'just like in the last Myriad.'

The quixars in the back of his neck prickled as they walked past a picture and Timmi must have felt it too.

'I think this is a Strange Energy gallery,' she said.

The peaceful atmosphere put Kip at ease, and he found himself gradually relaxing, even enjoying the wonderful novelty of the displays. The atrium turned out to be full of scratch-and-sniff artwork, and he zoned in first on a pine tree, then a jar of jam that had gone mouldy, and a brightly coloured sea slug (which smelled of watermelon).

A full circuit of the gallery revealed no evidence of Myriad Waves and so they moved to the next room. Here, the walls were hung with plentiful small paintings along with a single extra-large one that was nearly as big as all the others put together. There was a sign hanging by the door.

See the bigger picture

But that was easier said than done. Every time Kip tried to look at the extra-large painting, it rippled away along the wall like a turbocharged flatworm. Dizzy from chasing it around and trying to catch it out of the corner of his eye, he gave up and zigzagged back towards the entrance.

'The Crazy Paving isn't in here,' said Timmi glancing around, 'otherwise the Silent Key would be lit up.'

'All right,' Kip said. 'Let's go back and try a different direction.'

Retreating to the scratch-and-sniff gallery, they continued to the far end and came to an archway, on which another sign was hanging.

Cave paintings

They ducked under the sign and entered a roomy hall full of pitch-black pictures. Hanging on hooks by the door was a row of torches.

'Guess we take one of these?'

Timmi picked one up and walked over to the nearest painting. When she turned the torch beam on the total blackout inside the frame, a hidden scene was revealed. The space behind the canvas stretched back to a rockface where stalactites hung down from the ceiling. Water dripped rhythmically from their pointed ends.

'Hah! It's not a cave painting. It's a *cave painting*.'

'Try another one,' said Kip.

She shone the torch into the next canvas. Its beam bounced back off the red eyes of hundreds of white bats clinging to the ceiling.

'We're spelunking!'

'Spe-whatting?' asked Kip.

'Spelunking,' said Timmi. 'It means exploring caves. It's my dad's favourite word.'

'I don't know my dad's favourite word,' said Kip. 'It's probably something to do with cooking.'

He stared at the painting. The deep perspective pulled him in, and he felt himself longing to let go of everything else and enter the cavern, clamber between the stalagmites and feel the clamminess of the prehistoric rock…

'Wonder if you can go inside?' he said.

Timmi shook his arm.

'Come on, don't want to get more lost, got to keep looking for the way out.'

Enter the Mindfield

The only thing in the next room was a low table near the entrance, on which rested a VR headset – an expensive-looking one. Next to it was a sign with the title of the exhibition.

Enter the Mindfield

'Can I have a quick go while you look for departures?' said Kip. 'It's just VR.'

Timmi chewed her lip. 'Go on then.'

Kip put the headset on. Wavy lines before his eyes began to morph into shapes all around him and he found himself standing in a park with an obstacle course – nowhere he recognised. His older sister Suzanna was climbing a rope web, and Kip and his mum were walking slowly, looking up and shouting encouragement as she reached the top.

'Oh,' he said out loud. 'Not what I expected.'

What kind of VR knows about my family? he thought.

Now Suzanna was scrambling back down and took Kip's hand in hers. He felt her warm fingers squeeze his own – it all felt so real – and for a moment Kip lost track of where he was.

'I'm inside a virtual reality, inside a dream,' he laughed.

And then, in a heartbeat, everything changed.

'No,' he heard himself mumble.

'What can you see?' Timmi asked, but Kip couldn't answer.

The ground beside him was crumbling and slipping away in a violent landslide. Suzanna was falling, her face turned up at a strange angle, her mouth open in surprise. Kip tried to pull her back but she was too heavy. A deep, dark dread took him over entirely as he watched the heaving earth swallow her up. His mum was pulling at his other hand now and Kip turned to her, only to see the land falling away on the other side of him too. He summoned all his strength and his mum looked up gratefully as he held her fast, her legs dangling above sharp rocks far below. Kip saw a close up of himself smiling. He was strong, he had saved her, and then … and then his feet were sliding on the grass and her weight was pulling him over and Kip could only watch helplessly as he let go, seeing his own face turn ugly with horror and regret.

He ripped off the headset and everything went blank. Timmi was watching his face anxiously.

'I don't think you should look,' said Kip, shaking his head to try and flick the images away.

'Why not? What did you see?'

Kip shook his head again. 'I think it runs on Thoughtwaves.'

Timmi glanced at the headset and took off her baseball cap decisively.

'I want to look,' she said. 'If I don't, I'll always wonder what I would have seen.'

'What about departures?' Kip said, still trying to put her off.

'It'll just take a minute. I can be brave too.'

Kip stepped aside reluctantly, wishing they hadn't come into the room. With the headset on, Timmi paced about restlessly. It was hard to know how bad the virtual reality was – her eyes were covered and her expressions obscured. Eventually she ripped off the headset too. Her face was pinched into a thin, pale shadow of itself.

'Should've listened to you,' she said, wrapping her arms around her ribs. 'That thing is *nasty*.'

She was putting on a good act, but Kip could tell she was really shaken. He stepped closer to reassure her but just then a group of two men and a woman entered the room and glanced over in their direction. The woman tutted and the three of them whispered behind their silk-clad hands.

'We'll talk about it later,' said Kip. 'Time to move on. We're getting noticed.'

They ducked back into the room of cave paintings and, as they speed-walked past, Kip glanced at the pictures hung on the walls. Before, up close, he had been captivated by them, but now he was seeing them from a distance, and something became clear. Each frame was roughly the same squarish shape, but each had a subtle difference – here a notched edging, there a decorative spike or a cut-off corner. The variations in the pattern were enough to make him stop.

'What's the matter?' Timmi asked.

He looked down at the Silent Key. Was it illuminated, ever so faintly?

'This might be it,' said Kip. 'Look at the shapes of

the picture frames. If you matched them all up, I think they'd fit together.'

'But we already ruled out this room – the frames aren't glowing. And neither is the key.'

'I think it is, a tiny bit. What if the Strange Energy in here is blocking its light? Something to do with the black cave paint, and the special torches?'

Kip and Timmi looked around; there must have been a hundred or so frames on the walls.

'Well, OK,' Timmi said. 'If this is the Crazy Paving, and each of those pictures is a Myriad, then which one do we choose to go home?'

'We could try and follow the shapes we already stepped on, in reverse order?' said Kip.

'I saw the paving stone,' said Timmi, 'on the lakebed. It was kinda like an acorn. But no clue what the last one was – in the sand-gorilla Myriad.'

Kip thought hard.

'I'm fairly sure it was a heart.'

They both scoured the walls, but none of the frames fitted that description.

As they searched a second time to be completely sure, Kip remembered something so awful he didn't want to say it. But it had to be said.

'Didn't Professor Koriolis think that once you were inside the Crazy Paving it was one-way? And you had to keep travelling forever?'

Timmi looked at Kip in horror. At that exact

moment, plumes of electric-blue light began to curl together out of nowhere and snake across the hall, and Kip found himself following the path of a squirl.

'Perfect timing,' he murmured.

Timmi shot him a questioning look.

'Aeon Light,' he explained.

Staring intently at the paintings, he watched the squirls spread out and loop in a tight coil around a diamond-shaped frame with two knurled corners.

'It's telling me which one to choose.'

'Well, Aeon Light shows you important things, right?' said Timmi, the relief softening her face. 'And getting home is important. Maybe the Aeon Light is showing you the way.'

Chapter Ten

Rescue Plan

'And then Kip and Timmi were just … gone,' said Albert.

They sat staring at Miss Twiss resolutely, unable to cover up the glumness inside. Albert's hands were flat on the table, Leela's in tight fists.

'We jumped down after them,' added Leela. 'Onto the lakebed – I mean the Crazy Paving – but the lights around the outlines of the stones had gone – we waited but nothing happened – Albert thought they might come back…'

'But they didn't,' Albert interrupted, 'so we came straight here.'

They had run all the way to Miss Twiss's office after landing their Skimmies, and his T-shirt was sticking to his skin.

'It was an accident,' said Leela. 'We had no idea. We were just about to come back and tell everyone…' she stopped tearfully.

It was hard to know if Miss Twiss was angry, with her face frozen in that forever wistful expression left by a long-ago illness. The muscles of her mouth didn't move even a millimetre, but Leela and Albert heard her voice clearly – a calm force in their turbulent minds.

'Go easy on yourselves,' said the Professor-in-Charge. 'It wasn't your fault.'

'It was kind of my fault,' said Albert, biting his lip guiltily. 'I bumped into Leela…'

'It was nobody's fault,' Miss Twiss's voice said again firmly. 'You must put these thoughts behind you now. They are not serving you, or Kip and Timmi. Now we must decide on the best course of action to help them, and to do that, we need to think clearly.'

She rose from her desk and walked to a machine in the corner of the room. Its nozzle poured out two glasses of fresh orange juice, the kind that has delicious bursting fruit cells inside. While they sipped their drinks, the Professor-in-Charge said nothing more. Albert and Leela exchanged a glance which said 'we need to do something quick', but somehow they managed to wait in silence, until Albert couldn't wait any longer.

'Miss Twiss, can you talk to them telepathically, through your Thoughtwave Lens?'

'Unfortunately, no. I've just been attempting to reach them, but without success. I have, however, spoken to

GENI. All of her non-essential processing power is now focused on a way to access the Crazy Paving without the Silent Key. She and I will investigate the lakebed and try to piece together how it works.'

There was a knock at the door, a few moments' pause, and Professor Koriolis entered. Miss Twiss must have been talking to him all this time, because they seemed to be in the middle of a conversation, in which Albert and Leela now found themselves included.

'Of course, finding the right M-Wave signature will be a challenge,' said Koriolis.

'I agree. But operating the existing mechanism without the key will be our biggest problem, Alexios,' Twiss said. She turned to Albert and Leela. 'Professor Koriolis is going to help us to make sense of all this and get Kip and Timmi to safety.'

He looked at Albert and Leela sympathetically.

'Have we tried their Mothballs?' he asked, leaning on the back of a spare chair.

Leela and Albert shared another glance – Leela self-critical, Albert hopeful. In their haste to reach Miss Twiss, they'd entirely forgotten about the tiny tracking devices that GENI could activate to find the whereabouts of each student in an emergency.

'GENI has informed me that their Mothballs appear to be located at the Old Boating Lake. But, of course, we know that is not the case.'

'Has anyone ever gone into the Crazy Paving and

come back?' asked Leela, her fingernails digging into her folded-up Skimmi. 'Apart from Eartha?'

'Well, we can never prove that she went,' said Koriolis. 'All her records on the subject – if there ever were any – are gone.'

'Are they lost in there?' said Albert. 'In the other worlds?'

'Without knowing how the Myriads are connected, or how to use the key,' said Professor Koriolis, 'then yes, it's possible that they are lost.'

'Even if they are lost, there's nothing to suggest that they're in danger,' added Miss Twiss. 'Kip and Timmi are bright and resourceful. And they know we'll be looking for them.'

'How far away are they?' asked Albert, wondering if they were on the other side of the Universe.

'If, as GENI has reported, their Mothballs are still here,' said Miss Twiss, 'then they are far away in a sense other than distance. Somewhere where the Mothballs can't follow.'

'How far away is your bedroom when you're having a dream?' Professor Koriolis said, rocking on his heels. 'Perhaps the Myriads are all in exactly the same place, the same way your dreams are all in your head.'

'Surely Eartha must have left some way to find them?' Leela said.

'I doubt it,' Koriolis said, snippily. 'She merely discovered a way to navigate the Myriads. That doesn't necessarily mean she mapped them or understood their full complexity.'

He straightened up and pushed down on the chair back until it creaked.

'Adelaide, this is the perfect opportunity to focus on the Multifarious Interface Theory.'

'Opportunity is hardly the word, Alexios,' replied Miss Twiss. 'But you're right. It's all we have. I'll leave it to you.'

A Hecka Strange Hole

As Albert and Leela closed the door to the office, someone was tying their shoelace on the bench outside.

'Do you think they'll let us help?' said Albert, stopping suddenly. 'We didn't ask.'

He didn't like being out of the picture, not where his friends were concerned. Leela made an I-don't-know face.

'Miss Twiss would, but if Professor Koriolis is in charge – well – he sometimes has his head in the clouds, and by sometimes I mean always, and by always I mean you can forget him even remembering we exist.'

'What's wrong?' asked a voice.

Iris loitered outside the door to Miss Twiss's study, her hand on the handle.

'Are you guys OK?'

Leela attempted a smile, but it was a terrible effort.

'Thanks Iris,' Albert said. 'We're fine. It's just...'

Albert and Leela looked to each other, each hoping the other might know what to say. Miss Twiss hadn't asked them to keep quiet about the Crazy Paving but it felt as if they should. It had been tiring, answering Twiss's detailed questions, and they had been in her office for nearly an hour. The prospect of more questions was not appealing.

'...it's personal,' said Leela.

'Oh,' said Iris. 'Oh. Well. OK. Sorry.'

They left her behind and took the back exit from Celestial Hall, walking beside the Change Your World wall. Its black stone was covered in the silver writing of the college motto in countless languages.

'Kip and Timmi didn't just change their world,' Albert muttered. 'They swapped it for a whole new one.' He looked at Leela with a weak grin. 'Show-offs.'

'Miss Twiss is right,' said Leela. 'They'll know we're looking for them.'

'If they can just sit tight,' said Albert. 'GENI will find them.'

'She will. She has to.'

'Hey, it's getting late for dinner. C'mon, we need to eat.'

Leela put her thumb and forefinger in her mouth,

pressed against her curled-back tongue, and whistled for the mowl.

'Probably up to no good somewhere. He gets especially naughty when he's hungry – we better find him first.'

Albert followed Leela around the side of the building, where she checked in a clover-edged burrow – which was empty – before carrying on towards Confucius Courtyard.

'I hope they're having an awesomic adventure wherever they are. What do you think the other Myriads are like?'

'It depends,' said Leela. 'What does a Universe dream about? There might be infinite possibilities. So you could have a Myriad where Albert Masvingo has a red puppy jumper instead of a brown kitten jumper...'

'I like my brown kitten jumper,' protested Albert.

'Or,' continued Leela, 'you could have a Myriad that is so un-normal that you wouldn't even know what you were looking at.'

'Like a Myriad with no cause-and-effect, so everything is random?'

'Exactly,' said Leela. 'Or a Myriad where life exists as – oh I don't know – solid electricity, or intelligent water – in ways that just aren't possible in our world. Or a Myriad made entirely out of cupcakes.'

Albert made his thinking face.

'But if that's true then there must be Myriads that are underwater, or which have no oxygen to breathe, or where the temperature is really hot. Eartha must have built in some safety factor, a way to filter out worlds that would be dangerous to us.'

'That makes sense,' said Leela. 'So at least we can be fairly sure that the Crazy Paving has sent Kip and Timmi somewhere safe. They just need to find a quiet place to hole up until GENI and Professor Koriolis can find them.'

'They're probably in a bouncy-castle Myriad,' said Albert.

'Or a mowl Myriad.'

That was a cheery thought and they were both feeling a little bit better as they spotted Bagsworth fretting around the trunk of the old oak.

'...the funniest thing,' Bagsworth's words mumbled out through the leaves.

'Hello,' said Albert.

'Do you need a hand, Mister Bagsworth?' asked Leela.

One hand on the base of his back, the porter straightened up with a grunt and turned around. A leaf was caught in the rim of his white Bowler hat.

'Hello Leela, hello Albert. It's all rather perplexing. I think it's another one of those strange holes!'

'What strange holes?' said Leela.

'The ones Professor Steampunk was looking into?' asked Albert.

'I believe so, yes,' said Bagsworth, smoothing down his huge moustache with a thumb and forefinger. 'The first ones were found by Chef Garibaldi in some apples. Now there's one in the old oak.'

'Can we have a look?' Albert asked, stooping under the fringe of leaves.

'Of course,' said Bagsworth. 'Be my guests.'

They all leaned in, faces just inches from the bark. A weevil weeviled around an irregular hole in the trunk, just underneath the tree's lowest branch. It was easy to see why Bagsworth had been inspecting it so closely. To begin with, the edges of this hole looked slightly charred. Looking deeper inside, they didn't see the usual darkness with a few spikes of splintered wood that you might expect from an average hollow-in-a-tree. Instead, it was filled with speckled static – the kind that appears on an old television screen when the antenna isn't working.

Then, before their eyes, a flurry of snowflakes breezed through the hole and wafted away, melting into nothing.

'That's a hecka strange hole,' said Albert.

'It just gets odder and odder,' said Bagsworth, pulling on one end of his moustache. 'I'll have a word with Professor Steampunk.'

He straightened up again and took a few steps, but then looked back at Leela and Albert.

'No Kip?' he asked. 'And where's Timmi?'

Albert toed a leaf on the ground with the end of his shoe and Leela sighed.

'We lost them,' she said.

'You *lost* them?'

'It was like this…'

Taking turns, Albert and Leela poured out the events of the last few days until the whole story had been told.

'It's not the first time there's been a worrying incident at Quicksmiths, and it won't be the last,' said Bagsworth, and his level-headedness made them both feel better. 'I'd trust Miss Twiss with my life. And GENI too. We'll get them back, just you see.'

If the Universe is Sleeping…

It was after eight in the evening by the time Leela and Albert found the mowl and got to the Buttery, and the crowds were thinning.

'I know there's only one Gravity Bracelet,' said Albert, 'but it does feel a bit like everyone's wearing one when you come in here.'

He put his left foot on the bare wall, and then his right, and began to walk up it, with Leela close behind him. In the blink of an eye, the wall became a floor.

'I keep asking myself "what would Kip do?"' said Albert, claiming an empty wall-table. 'But I can't ask him.'

'Same,' said Leela. 'And Timmi too.'

There was a pause.

'So, what *would* Kip do?' she asked.

Albert crunched on a mouthful of salad.

'Well, first of all, he'd wait for everyone to say what they thought and then he'd kind of just sum things up and casually drop in a plan of action.'

'That's what we need,' said Leela. 'A plan of action.'

'Don't we have one?'

'Miss Twiss has one,' said Leela. 'That's not the same as us having one. There must be something we can do.'

While they were talking, the mowl was crawling commando-style on his belly towards Albert's plate. Victoriously, he snatched a tomato and rolled it over to the middle of the table. Before either of them could stop him, he had jumped right on top of it, giving it an almighty squashing and sending tomato seeds flying everywhere.

'Argh!' said Albert. 'One went in my eye!'

'Lucky it wasn't a chilli,' said Leela. 'Mowl! Naughty! Go and get a tissue for all that mess!'

The mowl stamped happily up and down on the unlucky tomato, saw Leela's expression, thought better about defying her, and slunk away, leaving a trail of tomato gobbets behind him.

'What would Timmi do?' asked Albert, picking a pip off his cheek.

'Oh, she'd notice some minor detail that no one else had seen and make us all realise it was really important. Or she'd have some amazing invention under her hat that would just somehow fix everything.'

Leela started sticking the green runner beans on her plate into a hill of mashed potato, so they looked like green telescopes.

'Albert,' she said, pensively. 'If the Myriads are the dreams of the Universe like Professor Koriolis says, then the Universe has a mind – sort of...'

'Must have,' said Albert.

'And if they *are* dreams, then that means the Universe must be sleeping,' she said. 'Sort of.'

'Uh, sure,' said Albert. 'Maybe it has an eye mask and ear plugs and a big pink nightie.'

Leela couldn't help laughing even though she was trying to be serious and follow her thought to its conclusion.

'What I mean is ... if Kip and Timmi have gone inside a dream of the Universe...'

'Go on,' said Albert, 'I'm liking this.'

'... then maybe the Crazy Paving is like a Dreambomber for Universes?'

With a clatter, Albert's cutlery fell to his plate.

'Do you think we could use the Dreambomber to take us there, to wherever Kip and Timmi are?'

'Not quite,' said Leela, her eyes shining. 'The Dreambomber works using different Thoughtwaves – you know Dreamwaves not Myriad Waves – buuuuuut…'

Albert looked at her blankly.

'Buuuuuut…' she said encouragingly.

The blankness got blanker, until Albert clicked his fingers.

'We could use the Dreambomber to talk to Kip and Timmi when they're asleep!'

'Bingo! Come on, Miss Twiss might still be in her office.'

She was, and so was Professor Koriolis.

'It doesn't matter where Kip and Timmi are physically,' explained Leela eagerly. 'The Dreambomber can still be used to communicate with them when they dream.'

'Has your invention been tested?' asked Miss Twiss, directing the Thoughtwaves of her question so everyone could hear.

'Yes,' said Leela. 'We can make it work on the mowl and Pinky. And we managed – Timmi and I – we managed to get into each other's dreams a few times. We just couldn't make it stick. All the readouts confirmed it.'

She looked at Albert.

'All we need is practice. I *know* I can get it to work on them.'

'Have you considered that your connection to the dream might be stronger if both you and your subject are asleep?' said Twiss.

'I hadn't,' said Leela. 'But now you say it, that seems like it might work. We can give it a try.'

'Then it's decided. From now on, you will not go to any lessons: your work is to perfect your Dreambomber. And Professor Koriolis will help you.'

'We'd be far better using my Myriad Interface...' said Professor Koriolis.

Miss Twiss cut him off with the stop-sign of her hand.

'Do you have proof of concept, Alexios?'

'Well no, not yet, but...'

'Leela's Dreambomber has proof of concept. It's our best shot for communicating with Kip and Timmi and this is our immediate goal. Let's get Leela set up with some space in the Singing Mill. Do as you will with the Myriad Interface but make yourself available to help her. And make this your priority.'

Professor Koriolis looked like he was going to say something else, but he wisely swallowed his objection and turned to Leela.

'Come on then,' he said. 'Let's sort you out.'

'And Albert too, Miss Twiss,' said Leela. 'I'm going to need an assistant.'

By the middle of the next morning, Leela and Albert were settled into their new workspace on the second floor of the Singing Mill. A couple of Oddjob Drones were dragging an extra bean bag into place. Two hammocks were strung across the room and swung lazily from their wall hooks. Softening the background were the lullaby whistles and sighs of the Singing Mill.

'Unreal,' said Albert, looking around. 'When I think about all the times I got told off for falling asleep in class. And now they actually want me to?'

Leela set a toolbox on the table next to the Dreambomber and shook an empty mug.

'Oh, assistant! I think we need some more morning hot chocolate.'

Albert groaned.

'Make sure you put plenty of malt in it this time,' called out Leela, as he tramped over to the microwave in the corner. 'We need to stay extra sleepy, remember!'

The door squeaked open and Professor Koriolis poked his head in.

'Hello Leela, Albert. How's the room?' he said, looking around.

'It's perfect, thank you,' she said, rolling down the blinds. 'We had some really good results last night and I've taken some more readings. We just went for a quick run around the garden to tire ourselves out. Now I'm going to practise on Albert.'

'Turns out I'm even better at sleeping than the mowl,' Albert said, pouring milk into two mugs.

'We've got a pile of the world's most boring books from Big Obi,' said Leela. 'It's impossible to stay awake when you read them.'

When the Head Librarian had found out why Leela and Albert were looking for boring books, he had personally taken them into the oldest, dustiest corners of the Library, and plucked out the thickest, wordiest tomes.

'This one's called *A Compendium of Early Mediaeval Spoons*,' said Leela. 'And this one's a three-hundred pager on global facial hair trends from 1969 to 1972. Would you like to stay for the experiment?'

Professor Koriolis tapped his watch.

'I really shouldn't,' he said. 'There are some readings I need to take myself.'

He looked over at the table.

'Is that it?' he asked. 'The Dreambomber?'

Leela nodded proudly and patted the side of the machine. Koriolis looked at his watch again.

'There's just enough time for a quick show-and-tell,' he said, stepping into the room.

Leela turned the wheels that summoned the green cylinder, and then the yellow cylinder. The leafy rustling of the Dreambomber combined with the lullabies of the Singing Mill and even Professor Koriolis's eyes started to look a bit droopy. He must have been impressed as he decided to stay for a demonstration on the mowl, who was already sleep-wurbling happily in a shoebox full of cotton wool.

Cowardly Peacock

'It looks like he might just leave us alone to get on with things,' said Albert, after the professor had gone.

'You could be right,' said Leela. 'He seems busy with his own stuff. Although we can't bank on it. Now Miss Twiss is on his back, he's surprisingly aware that we exist. He actually even remembered our names.'

She held out an eye mask and some ear plugs.

'Oh wait! I have this for you too.' With a flourish, Leela proudly produced a beret big enough for Albert's afro.

'Mmm comfy,' he said, after pulling it on. 'My hair thanks you.'

'Your hair is welcome. All set? Ready for the world's shortest bedtime story?'

Albert took the eye mask and struggled clumsily into a hammock.

'Sure you're ready? World's shortest bedtime story. Here we go. Once upon … the end.'

Albert was still smiling to himself as his face started to relax and sleep crept over him. Referring back to some scribbled notes on the Touchlight scratchpad of her Carousel, Leela checked the Dreamwave Gauge. When she was satisfied Albert was out cold, she placed the Psychogenic Beret on her head, and stepped through the milky-white doorway of the Thoughtwave Lens in her mind's eye…

She was inside an empty circus tent. A smaller tent was pitched at the centre of the circus ring. Albert was in here, huddled over an iron safe with a red timer that was ticking down.

'Albert?' said Leela.

Albert was staring at the numbers changing on the timer. Except they weren't numbers. The counters showed a series of lions in different poses.

'Albert, it's me, Leela.'

'Shhhhh,' said Albert, opening the safe door. 'The clowns will hear you!'

He extracted gift boxes from a compartment in the safe and started opening them, only to find more gift boxes inside. Leela tried again and again to talk to him. The plan was that she'd give him a simple message which he had to bring back from his dream. She even helped him open some of the boxes, but Albert didn't realise it was her. In the end she waited so long that the dream started to weaken and fade by itself, and she found herself back in their workshop.

Albert felt a flick on his nose and pulled off the eye mask groggily.

'Where were you?' he said.

'Oh, I was there,' said Leela. 'You were in a circus tent with a safe. You said something about clowns.'

'But I didn't see you,' groaned Albert. 'There was this whiney lion that kept interrupting me, I think it was the cowardly lion actually, except it was covered in peacock…'

Leela smirked.

'That was you?' Albert facepalmed and groaned again through his fingers. 'Why didn't you look like you?'

'Dreams are dreams,' said Leela with a shrug. 'Nothing's what it seems.'

'I should have guessed,' said Albert, banging the side of his head with his hand. 'Stupid pebblehead.'

Leela patted his shoulder.

'S'OK,' she said. 'We'll keep trying. We're close.'

'You'd think dreaming would be much easier than classwork,' said Albert, swinging his legs out of the hammock.

'My turn,' said Leela, taking the eye mask from Albert's hand. 'Don't worry, I'll do my own bedtime story!'

But just as Leela was debating which beanbag looked the comfiest, there was a knock at the door. She was expecting Professor Koriolis as she turned the handle, but instead Iris was standing there.

'I heard about Kip,' Iris said.

Leela's mouth pressed itself into a tight line. It was irritating how fast gossip spread.

'Yeah,' Leela replied. 'And Timmi.'

'Who is it?' asked Albert, over Leela's shoulder. 'Oh. Hi.'

'Listen,' said Iris. 'I just wanted to let you know that … I know I haven't known Kip for very long. Or Timmi. But I want to help. The others do too, Maya and everyone. So I thought I'd come up and offer. To help.'

When she spoke, flashes of small, rounded teeth showed the promise of an intense smile.

'That's really kind of you,' said Leela, 'but…'

'I'm especially good at maths if you needed calculations while GENI's busy. Everyone's talking about it by the way. Your Dreambomber.'

With one foot she nudged a large canvas bag on the floor.

'And I've brought you some lunch from the Buttery, thought you might be hungry.'

'Actually,' said Albert, 'now you come to mention it…'

He picked up the bag and looked inside. It was full of takeaway boxes, cartons, fruit and pastries.

'Thanks,' he said, trying not to drool all over a pyramid of crispy, plump samosas. 'Really. That's hugely nice of you.'

'So, can I? Help?' said Iris.

'Sure, why not?' said Leela. 'But we're just in the middle of something. We'll give you a call later?'

Iris started off down the corridor but remembered something and turned back.

'The others had a suggestion,' she said. 'I don't

know if it will be any use, but maybe Kip can use Aeon Light to get home. Or maybe we can use his squirl drawings to figure out where he's gone somehow.'

Leela picked at the wood of the door for a second.

'Great,' she said. 'Say thanks to everyone. It doesn't really relate to what we're doing, but we'll tell Miss Twiss. She and Professor Mo are the ones who've been studying Kip's book.'

Iris's whole-tooth smile lit up the corridor.

'OK. See you soon.'

Leela closed the door and looked at Albert, who was already biting down on a burger.

'Here's a proverb for you,' he said, spraying a few unintentional crumbs. 'If you want to go fast, go alone. If you want to go far, go together. If you want to go with Albert, bring a snack.'

Chapter Eleven

A Face at the Window

Pale, knee-high grass whispered back and forth in a gentle tide. The early-morning meadowland stretched out towards a distant undulation of hills and was interrupted only by several copses of tall trees.

'This isn't Quicksmiths,' said Timmi.

There was a sharp edge of tension in her voice, and it plucked at hidden fears. Just a few minutes ago, awaiting transfer in the Lava-Lamp Limbo, everything had seemed perfect. They had discovered the Crazy Paving, glimpsed the other worlds, and the squirl was going to take them home, where Albert and Leela and everyone would be waiting to hear their stories.

We're getting lost, Kip thought, trying to keep the panic out of his own mind.

An unseen bird called from the trees, and he was grateful to be reminded momentarily of Eartha's parrot.

'We're supposed to find the Futurescope, aren't we?' he said. 'Maybe that's why the squirl brought us here.'

Timmi tried her Candle badge again. When it didn't work, she half-turned to Kip.

'Is the Silent Key OK?'

That's a strange question, thought Kip.

'Hope so,' he said.

He dug the thick glass button out of his pocket.

'It's fine, see.'

'Promise you won't let it out of your sight?'

'Of course I won't. It's our ticket out of here.'

Kip turned the button over to examine the four alphabet wheels on its base.

'What if the password is a like a homing device?' he said suddenly.

He turned the wheels one by one to bring around the letters H-O-M-E. But there was no immediate sign to tell him if he had guessed right.

'Do you want a go?' he asked, passing the key to Timmi.

She flinched and didn't take it.

'What's the matter?'

She didn't answer.

'Timmi?'

'It's nothing.'

Kip waited for her to say more but she just pulled down her cap – it was at least one size too big for her and covered her ears completely.

'We should look for the Crazy Paveout,' she said.

Small paws scrabbled in the flying squirrel pocket of Kip's cargo shorts. He undid the Velcro and lifted up Pinky so she could look around.

'Finally, she's awake. And the Mighty Furball demands to know why we disturb her slumber!'

'How have you been asleep this whole time?' said Timmi, trying to be chirpy. 'Wish I had a friendly giant to carry me around.'

Delighted by this new world, Pinky jumped from Kip's hand and landed in the tall grass where there were meadow moths to chase.

'I hope Leela and Albert are managing without us,' Timmi sighed, after watching her for a while. 'Bathtime for the mowl is really difficult. Albert won't know what's hit him if Leela ropes him in.'

'I expect bathtime for the mowl is difficult even if you have a dedicated special ops team.'

Timmi rolled her eyes and nodded.

'I keep thinking, what would Albert say,' Kip said. 'He'd have loads of good ideas right now, about what to do.'

Kneeling down, Timmi turned her hand into a finger-spider to amuse Pinky.

'I miss them. Can you do an Albert impression for me?'

Kip sucked in his cheeks which forced his lips together into a kind of beak – the face Albert made when he was thinking. He kissed at the air comically and squeaky quacks escaped from the sides of his mouth.. Timmi giggled uncontrollably.

'Your turn. Do me a Leela impression.'

'Sure … OK…' She put on a wise face. 'You know what they say … er … a hamster in a wingsuit does not a flying squirrel make.'

Kip sniggered and Pinky shimmied up onto his shoulder, hugging his neck before delicately gnawing at his earlobe, her fine whiskers tickling his cheek.

'That means she's hungry,' he explained.

Pinky squeaked.

'I don't have any food just now,' Kip said.

She squeaked again and tried the other earlobe.

'Or water. Sorry, Pinky.'

At the mention of the word Kip realised how dry his own mouth was. And emptiness sank its fangs into his own neglected stomach. How long had they been in the grip of the Crazy Paving? It felt like days.

'We'll find something soon.'

Pinky didn't believe Kip and searched inside his T-shirt, making him writhe and yelp. Then she launched over to Timmi to look for Timmi-food. Unable to offer anything edible, Timmi tried her baseball cap as a distraction. Pinky fussed around inside for a bit, looking for raisins.

'How are we going to get you home?' Timmi asked her.

Deciding to make the best of the situation, Pinky scampered up to Timmi's shoulder and dived off, into the bowl of the upturned cap.

'Listen, I think we need to keep a record of everything,' Timmi said decisively. 'It's just ... scientific. How about you and Pinky write down what we've found out, and I'll look for departures? Won't go far.'

'Where's that bit of paper with Eartha's dream-poem?' Kip muttered, searching through the numerous pockets of his cargo shorts. 'Oh, but we don't have anything to write with.'

Timmi unpopped a press stud on the side of her hat and produced a pencil stub a few inches long.

'Meet Stumpy,' she said. 'I never leave home without her.'

After fighting Pinky over Stumpy for a bit, Kip eventually won and the flying squirrel crawled defeated into a pocket to sulk. Kip sat down in the grass and tried to straighten out the sheet of paper against his knee as best he could. Then, starting in the left-hand corner of the page he sketched an acorn, a heart, and a diamond – the shapes of the Crazy Paving that had brought them this far. He added some arrows and notes to explain what they'd seen in each Myriad. When it was finished, he lay back in the long grass and closed his eyes just for a second...

'Kip Braaaam-leeeeeey,' said a high-pitched voice. 'Can you seeee meeeeee?'

Something kicked at his shoe and Kip leapt up.

'Who? What?'

'I said, "come on lazybones". Grab the Skimmi. I found something!'

Timmi led the way to the nearest copse and wove through the trees, stepping aside proudly where the small wood came to an end so Kip could share in her discovery. In a large clearing where the wild grass had been cut away, stood a stately four-storey house with neat peaks of red-wood turrets.

'It looks pretty ordinary,' Timmi said. 'Which makes it by far the sketchiest thing I've seen in a Myriad yet!'

Kip looked over at Timmi – a few dandelion seeds were riding on the saddle of her baseball cap. She smiled brilliantly and he smiled back.

'I'm so glad I'm stuck here with you,' he said. 'And not on my own,' he added hurriedly in case she thought he was trying to be romantic.

Timmi bent down and pinched off a tall stem of grass near the root. She waved this long-stalked wand at the house's ornate gate.

'I was thinking ... the Aeon Light must have led us here for a reason. Maybe the Futurescope's inside. And whoever lives there might have food and water too.'

An embarrassingly long whine forced its way out of Kip's stomach.

'All right. We knock and get ready to run if we have

to. If we're going to survive, we have to stay alert. You too, Pinky. Danger!'

Pinky stuck her head out of the pocket, wiggled her ears to show she understood, and disappeared back inside.

As they approached, Kip's gaze swept the outer walls of the house. He thought he saw a movement under the eyelid of a second-floor window. Was that a shadowy face behind the warp of the glass?

The vertical bars of the gate were twisted into occasional metal knuckles that caught the golds and oranges of the steadily climbing sun. As they both reached out, it creaked open by itself. Pinky shivered against Kip's leg.

'Hope the house isn't as hungry as I am,' whispered Timmi.

Unlike the gate, the front door opened silently when they pushed, letting them tiptoe into a grand entrance hall. It had a polished marble floor that made their footsteps sound bigger than they were.

'Reminds me of the Hall of Maps,' Kip whispered.

On the walls hung charts as big as sails, of lands he didn't recognise. Light blossomed from behind grilles set at intervals between the hangings. At the other end of the hall was a high-arched door, panelled in silver.

Before they had walked too far, the door opened. As someone stepped forward into the hall, Kip blinked away a powerful surge of spectral ice-blue squirls.

A Stranger and a Friend

The girl looked a few years older than Timmi and wore an olive-green tunic with a belt the same colour. Her leggings were the colour of a spring sky, and wide-brimmed grey boots came up to her knees.

'I have been waiting for you,' she said.

It was absolutely the last thing Kip might have expected her to say.

'But we just came through the Crazy Paving,' he replied. 'And we're lost.'

'You must be thinking of someone else,' added Timmi politely.

The girl stared at them for a moment. The overgrown tangle of honey-brown hair that fell past her collar looked like it hadn't seen a pair of scissors in a long time. Her face melted into an irresistible smile and she let go of the door and walked towards them.

'I spoke the truth,' she said. 'It is you.'

She was speaking English, but her accent was hard to place. Kip wasn't sure if it was American or Irish or Australian. As she came closer, he couldn't help being drawn to her eyes. They were turquoise as ocean sinkholes, scattered with silver threads of sea sparkle. And so familiar to him.

'Do you not know me?' she said finally, the smile now turned into a teasing curl under a half-winked eye.

Kip frowned.

'I kind of do,' he said. 'And I don't.'

'Same here,' said Timmi.

'Listen to the light,' said the girl.

It can't be!

Those words were with Kip always. He could never forget that mysterious line in the letter he'd found in the secret study during their hunt for the ten riddles. The letter from Eartha that explained about Aeon Light. Words failed him, while his brain went into high speed, calculating all the possibilities.

'But you're dead,' he managed to say eventually.

'Who's dead?' said Timmi.

'It's her,' said Kip, turning to Timmi and back to the girl. 'It's Eartha!'

Timmi's face was a mirror of Kip's sheer surprise.

'What?' she said. 'How can that be possible?'

Young-Eartha smiled again, warmly and welcomingly.

'Time is not our friend for long. Come.'

She moved quickly after that, giving them no chance to talk as she strode ahead into a side room where rough-cut roots crackled merrily in a deep stone hearth. As soon as they entered, Eartha flipped a sand timer the length of her arm, which was set against the wall.

'All these years I've waited,' she said. 'So much to tell you, and only a few precious moments caught in Time's net.'

Kip remembered the day he first went to Quicksmiths and his questions had all collided into each other, spilling out more and more. It felt like that now.

'What's going on? Are we still in the Crazy Paving? Have we gone back in time? Did the squirl know you were here?'

Standing on the other side of Eartha, Timmi had become a question catapult too.

'How did you pin the Dreamwaves inside the Ark? What else did the Futurescope show you? How do we get home?'

'You are hungry,' said Eartha. 'Eat while I answer your questions. A long and hard journey lies ahead, if you choose it.'

She gestured to a table set with enough food for ten people: loaves of crusty granary bread, piles of unfamiliar fruit, bowls of mixed nuts and seeds, and a tureen of steaming stew. Timmi was already ladling big spoonfuls of it into wooden dishes.

As Kip sat at the notched table, he undid the Danger Velcro. Pinky burst out to run up his torso and along the underside of his arm, and dived into one of the nut bowls. While the stew cooled, he poured some water and gulped it down.

'In the lively halls of Quicksmiths,' said Eartha, 'four hundred years ago, I looked in the Futurescope and saw us here in this moment. I did not know I was looking upon myself; I thought the young girl I saw was a stranger. Many more glimpses the Futurescope gave me – each a wondrous and terrible gift. When I gazed on one of my own creations at the centre of an abyss of evil, I knew I must act.'

A red fruit burst in a firm crunch as Kip sank his teeth in. It tasted like a raspberry grape. In four bites it was gone and he started on the stew.

'With the help of the Futurescope I made elaborate plans. I set fire to my warehouse, so that all the world would know. No one suspected that my treasured inventions were not inside…'

'Sorry?' asked Kip, unable to stop himself from interrupting. 'So you didn't actually burn all your inventions?'

'That is indeed my meaning.'

'But why?' Timmi asked.

'The Futurescope showed me what to do. Once I had convinced everyone that they were destroyed, then in secret spaces, whispered to no one, I diminished every one of them until they were no bigger than that spoon you hold, disguising them artfully as everyday objects – a pendulum, a pin cushion, a thimble, a locket, a wax seal…'

Kip froze in amazement, the spoonful of stew just centimetres from his mouth. He looked around the room, wondering if the things he saw – the handle on the door, or perhaps the clasp on Eartha's belt – might be world-shaking inventions in disguise.

'The Crazy Paving gave me a way to spread the power I had created, to hide my machines deep inside the Myriads. And the Ark – my beautiful black bird – was the map to their many whereabouts.'

Gorvak, Kip thought, as his insides turned to lead. *He got to the Ark first.*

'Once I had set out the ten riddles, I made ready this safe house, for I knew the Aeon Light would lead you to me, Kip. The plan laid, I wrote my letters, said goodbye to my friends and left my home forever to travel to this far-off, time-twisted land.'

Eartha's blue eyes blazed heroically in the firelight and Kip had the feeling that there was nothing she couldn't do. It was contagious.

'But even if you disappeared from our Myriad and came here, you're, like, centuries old,' Timmi was saying. 'I'm no Albert, but even I know people can't live for 400 years.'

'In our world, time races forwards, or at least so it seems to us. Here, time rolls backwards. You are right to say I have lived four hundred years. But as the thousands of hours passed, I lost my age wrinkle by wrinkle.' Eartha glanced at the sand timer. 'Younger I grew, grain by grain, and shrank in size, casting off my older self.'

Kip put down his spoon and stared at Eartha, blinking as he took that in.

'Even if it's going backwards, wouldn't you have been … unborn by now?'

'Some Myriads move slowly in the leisure of a soft meander. This is one of those Myriads.'

'So four hundred years in our Myriad,' said Timmi slowly, 'isn't four hundred years here?'

'What is Time to a Dream?' Eartha replied.

'But how come we can understand you if you're going backwards in time?' asked Kip. 'Wouldn't you be speaking backwards gibberish?'

'It's not like that at all,' said Eartha, laughing generously. 'Here, the Universe is dreaming us backwards. You as well.'

Kip spun a fruit core on its stalk while he thought about that for a while, and then spun it the other way.

Everything sounds so simple when she says it. Somehow it makes perfect sense.

'It's the greatest riddle,' Eartha broke the silence. 'A tangle of Timeyarn I shall chase into the grave.'

She didn't seem sad to think about that, only excited.

'Our friend Albert is a bit of a Timeyarn fanatic,' said Timmi.

Eartha nodded as if to say she knew.

'He's going to freak the freak out when he finds out about this,' Timmi continued.

A fleeting friendsickness unsettled Kip's heart.

What's Albert doing now? he thought. *And Leela? Have they told Miss Twiss? Are they looking for us? I wish I could tell them we're OK.*

He contemplated the rosy reflections of the fire in the glass of the sand timer. The grains kept on falling, as sure as breath itself.

'Dreams are really short, aren't they,' he said. 'When we have them. Like a few seconds, but it can seem like years and years. Is that why time is different in the Myriads? Because we're inside the Universe's dreams. Four hundred years, or four hundred thousand years, is like four seconds to the Universe?'

'I hope there isn't a big time difference,' said Timmi. 'We're already in our third Myriad. What if we get back and everyone else is old?'

'A moment can be a lifetime, and a lifetime but a moment,' Eartha said, in answer to both their questions. 'Our path is more important than either.'

Everyone fell silent to think about that while the fire crackled away. Pinky gnawed furiously on a nut, and then swapped the half-gnawn nubbin for a bigger one.

'I saw an illusion once,' said Timmi. 'It's an image of a ballerina – she's dancing, spinning in one direction. And if you concentrate REALLY hard and block everything else out, you can make her dance in the opposite direction. It's like Thinking Sideways … only Seeing Sideways. Or maybe Feeling Sideways.'

Eartha gave Timmi a reflective look and nodded. Kip looked at Timmi in admiration – she'd given the great Eartha Quicksmith food for thought. Timmi muttered shyly and picked up a handful of dried fruit.

'But you've been here four hundred years! Weren't you lonely?' she asked, arranging the fruit into two piles of cubes and slices.

'The time has been well spent. And I have friends to keep me company.'

'Friends?'

Eartha pressed a button on the wall and Kip heard the distant tinkling of a bell.

Incognita

'So, let's go and find all your inventions and go home then,' said Timmi and then she put her hand to her mouth. 'Oh no! Will you crumble to dust if you leave?'

'If I left this place, the Universe would dream me forwards and I would only begin to age again,' said Eartha. 'I would not crumble…' she shook her head fiercely '…but I cannot go with you.'

'But why?' said Kip. 'We have the Silent Key. Everyone would fall over themselves to meet you.'

'The plan is not complete,' said Eartha. 'To travel with you now would mean the destruction of our Myriad. There is only one moment when I can and must return. Yet it all hangs on a fragile thread.'

She stopped and clapped her hands together.

'But here you are! The most important thing is that you found my dream inside the Ark and it led you here. And besides, there is still plenty to tell you. When you have heard it all, you may decide it is too early to go home.'

There was a clang over on Kip's right and, as he turned, he saw a square hatch begin to open halfway up the wall. A face peered through. This face was made up of very fine silvery chainmail. On the crown of its head where its hair might be, the chainmail grew thicker and turned to deep bronze, and a rosy gold blushed the metal of its lips. Its eyes were like old watch faces.

'Incognita, my dear. Our long-awaited guests have arrived.'

The chainmail rippled into an expression of surprise and the lace-metal eyebrows of the android shot up high. With a scraping sound, the hatch closed, there were sounds of light footsteps, and Incognita appeared at the main door.

Her body and limbs were made of the same finespun and flexible metal links. In her chest was a glass pane through which Kip could see a toothed sphere turning this way and that, its blunt spikes rising and falling. An arc of tiny wheels whirred and rolled responsively above the sphere.

As Incognita bowed elegantly, the edge of the glass pane glinted in a long blue crescent.

'Honoured to meet you. I am gladdened that your journey brought you safe to us.'

Her voice sounded a bit like Eartha's, only deeper, and each word was clipped neatly. Incognita looked at the final grains falling into the bottom half of the sand timer.

'This room is complete,' she said to Eartha, who followed her gaze and nodded.

'We must continue.'

Pinky watched as Kip shoved handfuls of nuts into a couple of his pockets and then launched herself from the tabletop to scrabble up onto Eartha's shoulder. Eartha reached up and stroked her cheek, and in reply Pinky hugged her finger.

'We are doing well,' she said over her shoulder as they all followed Incognita out of the firelit parlour. 'There's time for more questions.'

There was still much unanswered; yet Kip felt that if he could spend another four hundred years here with Eartha he wouldn't be able to understand it all.

'Does the password on the Silent Key take us home?' he asked.

'Yes. That will reverse the Myriad Waves, and return you to Quicksmiths.'

'What is it? The password?' asked Timmi.

'You will know what it is when you need it.'

Eartha hesitated at a door in the corridor and pulled it open a few inches. Spurts of energy burst out through the thin crevice and flickered around the ceiling like shoals of juvenile fish.

'The sun is setting on my memory,' she said, with a laugh. 'Wrong door.'

'What's inside there?' asked Timmi.

'That is where we work on my final invention,' replied Eartha, almost fondly. 'It's perhaps the most important thing I will ever do.'

Incognita tapped at a panel on her wrist. Amazed, Kip watched as her hand hinged back, away from the arm. From out of the socket extended a long pole, at the end of which dangled something like a butterfly net. She held the net high and chased after the energy-bursts, as Eartha paced ahead down the corridor.

'So, if you've been waiting for us,' said Kip, matching Eartha's stride, 'why are we here?'

'I need your help,' said Eartha.

Kip felt his footsteps lighten and his shoulders lift with pride. The great Eartha Quicksmith needed them.

'What can we do?' he asked. 'Is it about the Futurescope?'

'Yes. The two of you,' Eartha stopped and bent her head to Pinky, 'three of you, must find my Futurescope. But the journey will be harder than anything you have ever done. Do you accept it?'

Eartha wiped the unkempt hair from her face, and briefly looked so childlike, so tired, that Kip wanted to put his arm around her. He looked over at Timmi, who appeared to be thinking the same thing.

'Of course we do,' said Timmi.

'It must be kept safe from the Myriad Pirates at all costs. Nothing else matters.'

'Who are the Myriad Pirates?' asked Kip.

'They sail from world to world – slipping through the cracks between Myriads – pillaging, burning, trampling all they find. They are the worst of all life beneath the many skies. Your paths cross, and more than once.'

Eartha's hands came together and her fingers unlocked and locked again as if she were trying to mend something unseen.

'I let them into the Myriads. But I had to. If I had not they would have still found a way, and everything would have been out of time. We wouldn't have had a chance to stop them.'

'You once wrote "the shadows are gathering",' said Timmi abruptly. 'Did you mean the Prowlers?'

Eartha looked blank.

'In your letter to Quicksmiths,' Timmi tried again, 'you talked about them. It sounded like they were chasing you.'

Eartha pursed up her face and closed her eyes.

'I don't remember,' she said, with a single shake of her tangled hair.

She hurried into a second room and set off another sand timer on the wall. Next to it was a wooden rack which held transparent bottles of liquids that were churning and sloshing all by themselves. Above that were jars of gleaming orbs that looked a bit like Ballmoths. Further along, a cabinet held manuscripts covered in strange symbols and a collection of striped shells the shape and size of turbans.

'It looks like your study at Quicksmiths,' said Timmi, looking around approvingly.

Sketches of squirls spilled out from a binder, and Kip picked up a leaf of paper. It looked just like the ones he used to draw when he was younger.

'Can you tell us about Aeon Light?' he said.

Lately, Kip had been seeing squirls less and less with his eyes closed, and more in the world around him. Now that one had brought him through the Myriads to Eartha, it felt like they were becoming more purposeful.

Eartha gave Kip a knowing look.

'Aeon Light sails from the last uncertain breath of the Universe towards its birth. In its raw form, as you and I see it, it reflects off those things that can change many paths, many worlds. It flickers and dances like a map to the future that keeps redrawing itself.'

'Do you see it all the time then?' asked Timmi. 'I mean lots of things, and people, must have the potential to change worlds.'

'Yes, Timmi. The light is in many places and in many faces where I look. At times it is so blinding it is a hindrance. You are both bright to me, and so are the pirates. That is why I built the Futurescope – to enable me to focus my attention in those places where I need to know more.'

'I don't see squirls everywhere,' said Kip. 'Only now and then. And they've been quite helpful.'

'Aeon Light has no intention and no moral; it simply is. I think you are still learning and growing, Kip. Your ability has yet to find itself.'

'But why can only you and I see it?'

'There may be others, I do not know. As for you and I, we share an experience, which makes us who we are.'

'What experience?'

'We change the world together, Kip,' Eartha replied. 'Our story has hardly begun.'

She moved aside a winged pyramid and a horned skeleton the size of a cat, so that Kip and Timmi could sit down next to a glass harmonica. Ever inquisitive, Pinky glided down from her perching post on Eartha and began to explore.

'Here I am always at home,' said Eartha, brightly. 'Always myself, however my memory may fail me.'

She looked at her hands and turned them around in fascination for a few moments before looking up at Kip and Timmi again.

'I should explain. As I become more youthful, I am forgetting, losing everything I've learned. So, I began to write down my thoughts and memories. Much of what I'm telling you I know only because I captured it in ink years ago.'

They followed Eartha's gaze over to a corner of the room stacked high with thick books, some old and covered in dust.

'I wish I could say there was time for you to look through them, in case there is something that will be of use to you. Instead, we must trust in my summary.'

'Eartha,' said Kip, and he felt a tremor catch in his voice. 'Is something there – in those books – to help my mum?'

Eartha's eyes welled up with kindness, and her smile was bittersweet.

'You already have what you need,' she said. 'But you do not know what it is yet. There is no single cure, Kip. Only a series of steps, each of which will bring you closer to her. You might think each step is the end, but you will need to find more strength within so that you may carry on.'

Kip nodded. He had hoped Eartha would have an instant solution, a magic wand. But he was learning that life didn't just hand out magic wands.

'Whatever it takes,' he said. 'So, what now?'

'I've just thought of something,' said Timmi, before Eartha could continue. 'How will you leave when you're ready? Won't you need our key to use the Crazy Paving?'

'There are three keys,' said Eartha.

Kip and Timmi exchanged a glance.

'Three?'

'Yes, I have one with me here and there are two hidden in the Memoria Technica.'

'Didn't Leela say there was a missing button when she played it?' said Timmi, aghast.

Kip groaned.

'Gorvak was in the study,' he said, reluctantly. 'He got to your Ark first and listened to everything before he broke it.'

Eartha raised her eyebrows in an unspoken question.

'Gorvak G. Gorvak,' said Timmi.

Eartha looked uncertain and Kip remembered that the Futurescope gave her only glimpses – perhaps she hadn't caught his name. Or she'd forgotten.

'Reddy-blonde hair,' he said.

'Your fifteenth great-grandson,' Timmi added.

'I have children?' Eartha frowned. 'I do not remember.'

She looked from Timmi to Kip and her eyes seemed to sigh a faraway sigh. Kip felt a deep-down flicker – an old sharp-toothed sadness sleeping close to his heart.

Like mum, he thought.

'Is he a good man, this Gorvak?'

Eartha saw the expressions on Kip and Timmi's faces and her own face fell.

‘It cannot be helped,’ she said. ‘You have all the goodness we require.’

The glass of the sand timer reflected Eartha’s calculating eyes.

‘Very soon you must leave. They are coming and I must face them alone. Your time to face them will come.’

‘How do you know?’

‘It’s in my notes. Now we must hurry: the book.’

The Book of Poems

Eartha walked over to the volumes of writing and selected one that was set apart from the rest. She handed it to Kip. It was bound in a moss-green cloth with tarnished metal corners.

‘Hidden within the pages of this book are two sets of instructions. Each is written in verse to conceal it from the pirates. Look to the eleventh and twelfth poems.’

Incognita entered the room and handed Kip a drawstring bag made of coarse sackcloth, with a single thick strap. It was heavy and when he looked inside, Kip saw it was stuffed with food, a large water flask, and a couple of blankets. As he wedged the book of poetry between two loaves of bread, the blast of a bugle sounded somewhere within the walls of the great house. Incognita held her ear to a round device on the wall next to the books and listened.

'Pirates,' she said.

Eartha nodded. More bugles sounded in reply to the first, closer and more urgent.

'We can't leave you,' said Kip obstinately.

'You must,' said Eartha. 'And you will. Otherwise we shall all perish. And then which one of us will change the world? Incognita will take you to the Crazy Paving.'

Kip found himself hugging Eartha. Her hair smelled of firewood and fruit. She squeezed Kip tight and kissed his forehead. The walls of the house shook and Eartha turned to Timmi, taking her hand. Those remarkable four-hundred-and-forty-year-old eyes flashed with anger and sadness.

'You are stronger than you think,' she said. 'It's only your mind playing tricks.'

Timmi looked bashful, shook her head, and looked away. Eartha touched a charm on the Gravity Bracelet with the tip of her forefinger.

'This is a truly special thing you have created,' she said. 'It will save you more than once.'

While Timmi stuttered out her thanks, Eartha took Kip's hand too, joining the three of them in a momentous circle.

'When you see the world through each other's eyes,' she said, 'only then can you really trust each other.'

With a last squeeze, she let go of their hands and

ran to a cupboard where she began pulling out equipment. Looking back at them one last time, she gestured towards the door.

'Now go! Be safe.'

As soon as Kip called, Pinky dashed over and pocketed herself away in a scurry of whiskers.

'Give me the Skimmi,' said Timmi, 'you can't carry everything.'

Then they were following Incognita's rattling lope through the corridor. More metalwork androids streamed out of doors everywhere, heading back towards Eartha. Kip and Timmi ran against this current, keeping up as best as they could with their guide. Down some stairs two at a time they sped, and down more stairs, until Incognita stopped in a cold, dimly lit cellar. Her chainmail arms strained as she heaved aside a giant barrel and pulled at a metal ring in a flagstone in the floor.

'Down here,' she said, taking a key off a hook and handing it to Timmi. 'Follow the tunnel all the way to the end and open the door. The Crazy Paving is twenty paces from the doorway. Step on the arrow.'

'What do we do after that?' asked Timmi.

'You will find your way,' said Incognita. 'Eartha has left you signposts in the book of poems – shapes that will lead you through the Myriads.'

Kip hesitated as he faced Eartha's companion.

'Aren't you coming?'

Incognita's eyes glistened in the dark like bewitching moons.

'You must hurry,' she said, pushing him towards the trapdoor. 'We are down to the last seconds. If you stay longer, you will never return home.'

The flagstone closed above their heads and the roof scraped as Incognita heaved the barrel back into place. Timmi was already running, stooping slightly, and Kip sprinted to catch up, his footsteps dull on the hard dirt. Grilles glowing with an alarming red light flashed by and died behind them as they passed.

Gasping for breath, they reached a round wooden door framed by tree roots and cobwebs. As Timmi put the key in the lock Kip listened down the tunnel, just in case footsteps were following. But there was only silence. The lock was stiff and they both tried the key several times before it finally turned, and it needed the two of them, shoving hard, to get the door open wide enough to squeeze through.

Spangles of daylight fell on Kip's arms and the scent of mown grass flooded the air. They rushed up some rough steps that emerged near a copse of trees behind Eartha's house. The muffled booms of explosions shook the meadowlands and when Kip looked back, he saw spirals of white light rocketing up from the roof.

'What did she say? Twenty paces?' whispered Timmi.

They paced forward, whisper-counting together.

'… eighteen … nineteen … twenty!'

The final step brought them to the edge of a short slope, at the bottom of which was a lovingly tended lawn. Against a light-green background, patches of darker grass stood out – the shapes of the Crazy Paving. The arrow was easy to find and they made their way across the lawn to stand at its edge.

'On three,' Timmi said. 'One…'

'Wait,' said Kip.

He looked back at the house again. A cloud of billowing smoke and brick dust obscured the gate. But there, on one of the turrets, was an unmistakable figure. Timmi saw it too.

'What is that?' she gasped.

It was like some remnant of a petrified forest had been brought to life, and given the dexterity of a snake. The sunlight flowed over its slinking black-and-silver limbs. A crust of a face turned their way, and Kip saw a glinting white eye.

'Prowler!' he mumbled, hardly hearing himself.

'*That's* a Prowler?' she whispered. 'It's…'

She didn't need to finish.

'We have to go back and help her,' said Kip. 'Prowlers only ever turn up when something bad is going to happen!'

'We can't. You remember what Eartha said – if we stay, we all die. The best way to help her is by doing what she asked.'

Something hooked Kip's attention – a swishing in the longer grass near the treeline – and he grabbed Timmi's hand.

'On three,' he said. 'One…'

'Two,' said Timmi.

'Three!'

Chapter Twelve

Sleepover

The sounds of lunchbreak livened up the courtyard outside, as Leela and Albert sat hopefully in the Professor-in-Charge's study. It was like watching someone mark their papers for a very important exam.

Miss Twiss tapped one finger against the arm of her Airchair as she scrolled through the report.

Saturday 21:39
Subject: Mowl
Dream 03
…the subject was looking after a tiny bird the size of an apple seed. It jumped inside a tomato and hid behind the pips…

Saturday 22:37
Subject: Mowl
Dream 04
…Leela Lee and Albert Masvingo successfully

introduced a giant Swiss cheese to get the subject's attention. They helped him to build a burrow inside the cheese after which he recognised Leela and responded to instructions…

Sunday 11:45
Subject: Albert Masvingo
Dream 09
…dream quality was strong but the subject was unable to recognise Leela, instead seeing the cowardly lion with peacock-patterned fur…

Sunday 14:02
Subject: Leela Lee
Dream 12
…a poker game; the deck of cards was hourglass-shaped, and each of the cards in her hand was an Ace of Jesters … but the subject failed to see Albert place the highest bet…

Monday 10:10
Subject: Albert Masvingo
Dream 21b
…Leela attempted to deliver the simple message "the sky is red". Although the subject didn't bring back the message from the dream, he did remember picking up a meteor and throwing it over the mountain, which caused a red explosion. This shows progress. We will try adjusting the Dreamwave tuner…

'As you can see, we're very close to getting a message through,' said Leela. 'We should be ready to try communicating with Kip and Timmi any time now.'

'This is excellent work,' said Miss Twiss, closing the report. 'GENI has made little headway with accessing the Crazy Paving without a key, so this is still our most promising route of action.'

'We'll get back to it then,' said Leela, looking at the clock on the office wall.

'Time for a lunchtime nap,' agreed Albert.

Miss Twiss looked at Albert and then Leela.

'You look exhausted,' she said.

'Impossible,' said Albert, 'we've been asleep most of the time!'

'Nonetheless,' insisted the Professor-in-Charge, 'this is hard work. Go and get something to eat, and we'll find someone to help you this afternoon, so you can take a breather.'

Reluctant to disobey the Professor-in-Charge, and knowing how wise she always turned out to be, Leela and Albert headed for the Buttery, which wasn't far from Miss Twiss's office. Not wanting to waste any time, they bypassed the hot meals and went straight to the sandwich station.

'Hey Albert!' shouted a voice.

Albert looked up towards the high, glass-paned ceiling. The Buttery looked like someone had upended a long, thin room, and turned it into a tall, thin room. Diners sat at picnic tables clinging to the walls, as if there were nothing out of the ordinary.

'There's Badger and the others,' he said, waving back.

With Leela close behind, he stepped onto the nearest wall and began to walk up it towards the table. The circle of friends from his class cleared their plates to make room.

'Hi guys,' said Albert. 'Don't tell me. The new girl has been looking for us?'

'Which new girl?' asked Maya.

'Iris. Short black hair. Starcy. Looks like a mini terminator?'

'No idea,' said Badger with a shrug.

'We heard about your Dreambomber, Leela,' said Em, a little shyly. 'Professor Mo told us.'

'Have you got in touch with Kip yet?' asked Badger.

'We've been really worried,' Penny said.

'It's taken a bit of time to get things ready,' said Leela. 'But we're close to reaching them now.'

'When you look for Kip and Timmi with the Dreambomber,' said Badger, 'they have to be asleep right? So how do you know they're not awake, whenever you try? It's just pot luck really, isn't it?'

'We might be out of sync,' agreed Leela. 'And we don't really know if there are any time differences between the Myriads. The best thing we can do is make sure the Dreambomber's broadcasting as close to 24/7 as we can get.'

'That sounds like a lot of work,' said Em.

'Can we help?' said Penny.

Leela looked at Albert.

'Actually, that might not be a bad idea,' she said. 'We could do with a few volunteers, at least for this afternoon. Miss Twiss told us we have to take a break. Now I think about it, it might help me tune the machine better if I have some inputs from different people.'

Vigorous nods and pleased mutters chased each other around the table as everyone imagined rescue plans on a big scale. Em's henna art began to whirl around on her skin, like animated helicopter blades.

'We can take our sandwiches with us,' said Leela. 'Come on, let's ask Miss Twiss if you can skip lessons this afternoon.'

'It's time to buckle in your brains,' Albert said. 'We are going to turn those shower caps up to ten.'

'Shower caps?' said Maya.

'Ignore him,' said Leela. 'I'll explain everything.'

Night at the Lake

The four new recruits took to the Dreambomber like dream ducks to moonlit water. While they stepped through Thoughtwave Lens doorways to explore the worlds of each other's imaginations, Albert wrote down their feedback and Leela made adjustments to the machine's settings. In the end it was Badger who managed to get a message to Maya about penguins liking sushi. After that, there had been some dancing – a lot of dancing – around the workshop, and quite a bit of yelling. It was time to tell Miss Twiss the good news.

As the reinforcements left to get dinner, Penny made Leela promise to call them as soon as there was any update.

'And we're here whenever you need us,' Em said.

'Random suggestion,' said Albert, looking around the messy workshop when they'd gone. 'Once we've told Miss Twiss, let's get a takeaway dinner and spend the night down at the lake? Maybe being closer to the Crazy Paving will give the Dreambomber a sort of natural booster? And fresh air is supposed to send you into a really deep sleep.'

Leela looked out of the window past the ever-churning wheel of the Singing Mill. It was midnight-picnic-perfect weather.

As they reached the lake, the darkening summer sky was still smudged with pigeon pinks and soft blue-greys. An owl hooted somewhere close by and the mowl ruffled his head crest and went to investigate. A warm breeze tugged at Leela's hair, and she sighed.

'Hope they're having nice weather too, wherever they are.'

Albert was staring at the empty lake.

'Why?' he said.

Leela finished putting down the Dreambomber and straightened up.

'Why do I hope they're having nice weather?'

'Why are the rushes like that?'

Lining the lakeside was a thick fringe of very ordinary reeds.

'I don't get you,' said Leela.

'Well, there's a breeze isn't there?' said Albert. 'But the rushes aren't moving, not even a whisper.'

'It might be something to do with the Myriad Waves?'

'Question GENI…' said Albert.

But GENI didn't answer. Instead a recorded message played, saying that she was unavailable except in the event of an emergency.

Leela shrugged.

'We'll ask Professor Koriolis tomorrow. Come on, let's get set up. I have a good feeling about this.'

'Oh dear,' said Albert, as they were getting everything ready, 'there's one very important thing missing.'

He waited just long enough for Leela to start double-checking the equipment.

'We forgot dessert.'

'No problem,' she said, not batting an eyelid. 'We have plenty of ice-dream cake.'

It must have been around midnight when Albert drifted slowly out of sleep again. He blinked awake and looked up at the stars.

That's strange too, he thought. *The moon hasn't moved all night.*

He shifted over on to his side and froze. A cyclops was leaning on its crooked arm, staring at him with its single eye. Beside it, a strange barrel turned, sending out an alien Morse code of blue shapes. The creature rustled like dry leaves trying to talk and the frills of its head waved gently as it reached out another arm…

'Yeeek!' shrieked Albert, and his heart leapt up and hit the ceiling of the night sky.

'Yeeek!' shrieked Leela back. 'Why are we screaming?'

'Oh, it's you,' gasped Albert, with an embarrassed laugh. His heart climbed bashfully back down towards the middle of his body. 'I forgot we were here, doing this. Did you get anything?'

'Nothing much,' said Leela. 'You?'

'I went to the Lost City of the Mowls actually,' said Albert. 'There were mowls *everywhere.*'

'We'll get through eventually,' said Leela, rolling over onto her back.

'Wait, I haven't finished,' Albert carried on. 'I think I saw Kip too. I *think* so. Something about a lobster. But everything just dissolved too quickly. It's like I can't tell the dream's started. My brain gets diverted thinking about other stuff and it goes off to the wrong place.'

'Some dreams don't really have an exact beginning and an end,' said Leela. 'They just are and then they aren't. You have to sort of wander in. It gets easier when you use Deep Thinking.'

'Gah!'

For a long moment, Albert felt like it was all too much and covered his face with his hands. He was just a First Year. And the Dreambomber was Leela's. She was the Thoughtwaves girl, she had an A+ in dreams, not him. Badger had got the first dream-message across to Maya. But he, Albert Masvingo, was useless at Deep Thinking. Worse than useless. If you added up all the useless in the world, it didn't nearly make up how bad he was at it. But then he remembered Kip and Timmi, lost in the Myriads and facing who-knew-what, and he pulled himself together.

'Teach me,' he said.

Footprints

Albert was sitting at the edge of the lake, his feet dangling over the side into the dry space below. Brushing away a mowl feather that had decided to visit her chin, Leela sat up and shivered.

'We forgot the morning dew,' she said, feeling how damp her clothes were.

Albert turned around. He was holding the mowl, who lirriped when he saw Leela was awake and bounded over to her.

'Wasn't expecting you to have a lie-in,' Albert said cheerfully, unrolling his Skimmi. 'It's been breakfast time for the last half-an-hour. The mowl's been eating daisies and duckweed. I was *very* tempted.'

The thought of a hot breakfast and fresh clothes was irresistible. Taking a mostly dry tissue from her pocket, Leela swiftly brushed away the moisture that had collected on the Dreambomber's cylinders. While she turned the wheels to close the box, Albert folded up the berets. Before long they were boarding their Skimmies and rising up above the shadowy arches of the boathouse and the empty lake. The sun was waxy behind the low-lying dawn clouds, but it was light enough to see a trail of dark footprints on the dew-covered jetty.

'Did you see anything?' she called over to Albert.

Albert looked back at her quizzically.

'On the jetty?' she continued. 'Anything new, something we missed before?'

'I didn't go on the jetty,' he said.

They stared at each other, and then down towards the wooden walkway.

'It might be them!' Leela yelled. 'What if they came back last night and didn't see us?'

They swung their Skimmies back around and down until they were within touching distance of the planks. The footprints stretched all the way along and down the steps to the lakebed.

'There's only one set of footprints,' said Leela, horrified. 'Not two.'

'They're going the wrong way though,' said Albert, slowly.

His eyes turned up to Leela's.

'It can't be Kip or Timmi. Someone else must have a key to the Crazy Paving!'

It was the only possible explanation.

'There was a button, a key missing,' Leela gabbled, tripping over the words. 'On the Memoria Technica. That could've been it?'

'So who has it then?' asked Albert.

'It could be anyone.'

Albert looked down at the footprints, made his thinking face, then looked back at the boathouse.

'What about a camera feed?'

'Albert, you're as clever as a whole country!'

He bowed comically. 'Well, perhaps just a little one.'

'We can easily set up a Carousel camera to record the lake from now on. If someone uses the Crazy Paving again, we'll know who it is.'

'Awesomic!' said Albert. 'While you do that, I'm just going to take a closer look at one of those paving stones.'

While she worked quickly in her Carousel, Leela watched Albert out of the corner of her eye, wondering what he'd seen. The Crazy Paving couldn't possibly swallow them up like it had Timmi and Kip, as neither she nor Albert had the Silent Key. But they still had to be careful. If they got Crazy-Pavinged too, who would save the others?

'I was right!' said Albert.

He was staring down at the flat, patchwork stones on the lakebed.

'Check out this one that looks like a piggy bank.'

Leela skimmied swiftly to his side.

'There! Another one of those holes Bagsworth showed us.'

Albert was already getting down on his hands and knees and putting his eye up to the hole.

'Don't touch it!' squeaked Leela.

'I won't. Come and take a look.'

Leela disembarked and knelt next to Albert, getting as close as she could risk. The hole was very similar to the one they'd seen in the oak tree – charred around the outer edge and speckly inside. As they watched, there was a slight pressure change, enough to feel on the skin of their cheeks. Seconds later, an off-white, gummy feeler unrolled out of it and began to search around with its snail-like eye. Leela and Albert pushed themselves back in amazement.

The wind flew past their ears as they raced to the

Singing Mill. Below them, the mill wheel dipped and rose endlessly, churning invisible thoughts, putting to good use all the fleeting energy of human minds.

Abandoning their Skimmies on the lawn, they ran flat out to Professor Koriolis's study. Leela didn't even wait for Professor Koriolis to speak first, and he looked displeased; but his frown stood no chance beneath the deluge of words.

'We spent the night at the lake – and we sort of got into Kip's dream, even if he didn't recognise us – then we saw one of those holes in the Crazy Paving – like the ones Chef Garibaldi and Bagsworth saw – something came through – a creepy little eyestalk – and we saw footprints too, going down the jetty – at first we thought they were coming up, that Timmi and Kip had come back, but Albert saw that the footprints were going the wrong way…'

By this time, Professor Koriolis had put down his book and made his way over to where Leela and Albert were standing on the thick rug by the window.

'Slow down,' he said. 'Did you take the Dream-bomber to the Crazy Paving?'

'Yes, exactly,' said Leela. 'But like I said it didn't make much difference yet…'

'I don't think that's a good idea,' he said, scratching his not-quite-a-beard tuft.

'Because of the funny holes?' asked Albert.

Koriolis frowned again.

'We're not sure what they are,' he said. 'But I think it's best if you stay away from the Crazy Paving for now.'

'What about a second key, to get into the Myriads?' said Albert. 'Do you think it's possible?'

Koriolis ran a finger along the windowsill to collect some dust which he wiped onto a tissue while Albert explained more about the footprints.

'Yes, I see,' said the professor, going to stand behind his desk. 'I'll have to tell Miss Twiss and we'll follow it up. Well done for reporting this. Now we need to get you focused back on your work and reaching your friends. You say you got into Kip's dream?'

'I think so,' said Albert. 'But it faded really quickly.'

'They're probably preoccupied, who knows what they're having to deal with. It could be very…' Koriolis coughed and shuffled some papers. A not-very-encouraging smile struggled with the muscles that pulled his face taut. 'They're busy trying to think of a way to get home, aren't they? Keep persevering.'

Leela nodded her head, feeling all-of-a-sudden tired but not-tired.

'By the way,' said Koriolis, 'I've been working on adapting a Thoughtwave amplifier which could enhance the Dreambomber, if you agree.'

Leela kept nodding.

'Take a break, have some breakfast, and I'll drop it off later.'

They trudged out of Koriolis's study, and returned the Dreambomber to its place in the workshop.

'Grab some fresh clothes and meet back here in thirty?' said Leela.

'You go. I'll stay here and keep dreaming,' Albert replied.

'Don't you want some clean clothes?'

'Can you grab something from my room?' he said. 'Anything will do. And some breakfast?'

Albert sat down in a beanbag and the mowl hopped up on his shoulder to hug his neck.

'Ow-ow-ow! Mowl!' said Albert, trying to release the strong grip of the mowl's talons. 'Your pointy feety bits are really sharp.'

'He's learned that off Pinky,' said Leela wistfully. 'Neck-hugging.'

'Bet he misses her,' said Albert.

He propped the mowl up next to him on the beanbag and stroked one of his black wings pensively.

'I'm having a thought. Are you thinking what I'm thinking?'

'Maaaybe,' said Leela. 'But only if you're thinking that the singular of chickenpox should be chickenpok?'

Albert grinned, looking very pleased with himself.

'Not quite. How about we stick with what we

already know will work? Instead of trying to reach Kip and Timmi directly – at least for now – what if we hijack Pinky's dream and get her to do that sleep-gliding thing again? When they see her doing it, perhaps it will be just enough to remind them of the Dreambomber?'

Leela looked at Albert admiringly and wondered why she hadn't thought of that earlier.

'Albert, you really are as clever as a country,' she said excitedly. 'They might realise we're trying to reach them, and they'll look for us in their dreams, and try to remember what they see.'

Chapter Thirteen

DreaM Lobster

A windswept wasteland stretched out into the vibrant blue distance, scattered with the occasional thorny bush. Kip and Timmi were heading for a nearby outcrop of red rock, and the sharp cutaway of a cave mouth.

As they tramped along, an orange sun broke through the clouds. Timmi stared left and Kip to the right, searching for anything that might give away the gateway to the Myriads.

The sack was lighter now they had eaten some of the supplies and drunk some water, but it still made his back feel extra sweaty. Being a magical source of food, it was Pinky's new favourite sleeping place, and she was there now, sheltering from the daylight.

'I've been thinking,' said Timmi. 'Will Eartha's instructions lead us to the Futurescope? And how will we know what it looks like? What if she forgot to tell us?'

'We'll figure it out,' said Kip. 'She picked us for a reason.'

Timmi swished down a mouthful of water, screwed the lid on the flask and passed it to Kip.

'If we're not careful,' she said, 'we'll stop being able to tell the difference between the dreams in our heads and the Myriads out here.'

'That's not a happy thought. What if we tell each other our dreams every morning? Then we'll definitely stay real and stay ourselves, whatever the Myriads do. You go first.'

'I was doing homework.'

'Seriously? You should take that back to the dream shop – it's rubbish!'

'It was quite nice actually. Just … normal, you know.'

Kip nodded, and passed the flask back. 'I get it.'

'On second thoughts, it wasn't that normal. Leela was trying to get me to eat alphabet soup, only the letters were all wrong. Classic Leela. What was your dream?'

Kip scrunched up his eyes. All of a sudden, it felt very urgent that he should remember it.

'I've got it. You're going to love this. There was this lobster, right. Playing golf. It had a zip down one side and when I opened it up, there were eight prawns inside, all riding bicycles which powered the lobster's golf swing. But this is the best bit: one of the prawns was Albert!'

Timmi laughed so much she wobbled off course.

Why does a stupid dream like that feel so important? Kip thought.

They went quiet for a bit, each lost in their thoughts. Kip watched an eagle flying high overhead, but its path took it past the sun and he had to look away. Remembering the Silent Key, he took it out of your pocket and swept it from side to side like a futuristic metal detector, watching for glimmers of light.

'Is the Silent Key safe enough?' Timmi asked suddenly. 'I mean, make sure you keep your pocket closed up all the time, even when you're sleeping.'

Why do you keep asking that?

'It's not just mine,' said Kip. 'You can take it too, you know.'

He tried to hand it to her, but she pulled back as if she'd been bitten. It felt like she was angry with him, even though she'd asked about the key. It didn't make sense. Then he remembered something Eartha had said.

'What did Eartha mean?' he said. 'Something about mind tricks?'

Timmi began to walk faster and called over her shoulder. 'Nearly there, come on!'

As Kip watched her press ahead, he wondered what was going on. She obviously had a secret. Something that was eating her alive. Something to do with the Silent Key? It was hard to know. *It's OK, we all have problems*, he wanted to say. *Let me help*.

Now they were close up, the outcrop towered over the surrounding scrub. Kip took the sack off his shoulder and leant against the sloping rock near the cave mouth, luxuriating in its shadow.

At least we'll see anything coming from miles around, he thought.

Timmi sat on her haunches and gave the flask a shake. The water inside slapped about as she offered it to him.

'We might have to start rationing.'

The wind picked up and put on its best show of howling and whistling through the cave, as if it had spent millennia hoping for an audience.

'Sounds like we've come to the Myriad of Musical Ghosts,' said Kip.

'Sarcastic Musical Ghosts,' Timmi replied. She stood up, stretched her legs and then rummaged in the drawstring sack before handing Eartha's book to Kip.

'I took a look while you were sleeping in. You should read it too. BRB.'

The moss-green cover was faded in the centre and darker around the edges, where each corner was encased in a triangle of dull, once-silvery metal. Kip turned to the first page and saw a small drawing of an arrow in the margin. It triggered a memory of Incognita's advice as they had fled Eartha's Myriad.

'So these are the shapes we follow through the Crazy Paving?' he said, but Timmi had already wandered off. He flicked through the next pages. 'Hummingbird, starfish … pineapple…?'

Turning to the eleventh poem, he began to read, looking out to the horizon now and then while he digested the words.

The Temples

Hand in hand, they came alone
Mind in mind, in search of home,
From stepping stone to stepping stone,
The conjurors of worlds.

Among the many painted lands,
They happened on a plain of sand,
Where, as the darkling breezes fanned,
The desert mists unfurled.

Twin temples stood, their gates ajar,
Stern strongholds of some mystic tsar,
One golden as the breath of stars,
One black and still as night.

When in the east the sun aligned,
The black shrine's highest height they climbed
And looked down at their feet to find
A treasure rare and bright.

'Er … Kip,' said Timmi. 'Come and look at this!'

There was something in the tone of her voice that made Kip snap out of his thoughts straight away and he was at her side in a few steps. A few metres in from the mouth of the cave, just out of the reach of the sunlight, was the first foothill of a fabulous mountain range of treasure.

Timmi picked up a tiara.

'If the mowl could see this…' she shook her head lightly '…he'd mowlsplode.'

A little voice in Kip's head told him to be careful and he looked around warily.

'That treasure must belong to someone,' he said. 'And they won't want us anywhere near it. We should leave.'

The Scarab Dragon

Kip put the book back in the sack hastily, taking care not to squash Pinky, and set off back towards Arrivals, sweeping the Silent Key in front of him again.

'We should try your search-and-rescue circle,' he said.

But before he'd got very far, a jewel-like scarab beetle landed on top of the key with a whirring of wings. Kip stopped and held it up to observe it better.

'That's more beautiful than any treasure,' said Timmi. 'Just look at the colours!'

And yet there was no time to admire its carapace.

Kip watched, unable to say a word as it began to grow bigger, fast, doubling its size in just a few seconds. He tried to flick it away with a finger but its feet clung to the key resolutely.

'What's it doing?' shrieked Timmi.

She tried to scoop it off, but the beetle didn't budge. Although it was weighing down Kip's hand now, there was no way he was letting go of the key. He looked up, distraught. Timmi had found a twig and was poking at the beetle.

'It sprayed gluey insect stuff at me,' she said, shaking the twig which was now stuck to her hand.

But that was the least of their worries. The beetle's carapace was warping and its legs were swelling out. Hard chitin was shifting and turning to muscle. Kip felt his wrist being pushed up. He grabbed a handful of thick fur that sprang up beneath his hand, and just managed to hold on to an edge of the Silent Key with the other.

'A shapeshifter!' breathed Timmi.

What does it want? thought Kip. And then out loud he said, 'It wants our treasure!'

The shapeshifter scowled at Kip with amber eyes. Its transformation was complete, and before them now stood a kangaroo-like animal with fur the colours of the scarab beetle, and long forearms which grasped its end of the Silent Key. Kip was flung from bruise to bruise as it writhed about.

'Try the Gravity Bracelet,' he yelled.

'I'm already trying,' Timmi yelled back. 'That sticky stuff has gone on the charms. It's not working.'

There was no time to think about that. The shapeshifter was yanking on the key and Kip pulled back with all his might, thankful that his grip was strong from all those Saturday mornings spent at the climbing wall. A tuft of hair came out in the fingers of his other hand as the scarab kangaroo tried to wrench away, and it screamed.

'I can't … let you … take it,' Kip said through gritted teeth.

Too quick for Kip to defend himself, the kangaroo leaned back and jumped with both feet off the floor, landing a powerful kick to Kip's chest. He felt a crack and a sharp pain in his ribcage. The key flew from Kip's fingers and went sailing through the air, before landing right at Timmi's feet with a gentle puff of sandy dust.

'Get it!' he yelled, clutching at his chest.

Kip sensed something was wrong. He lifted his gaze and saw her staring down fearfully at the key, her face frozen in dread. It was exactly the same expression she'd had in the Mindfield room of the art gallery.

The kangaroo reached the key in a single bound, and swiped it up with a mad hoot of joy, preparing to leap away with another push of its rippling hind legs. Timmi roused herself and glared at it furiously.

'That's ours!' she yelled. 'Give it back.'

Just as the shapeshifter jumped, she dived and landed square on its thick tail. But it was already changing and shrinking as it pulled her along with it. Barbed talons grew out of dwindling legs that began to sparkle with scales. A single feather was left in Timmi's hand as an eagle the colour of a scarab beetle soared up into the sky with three beats of its mighty wingspan.

Kip was already unrolling the Skimmi, trying to ignore the sharp pain every time he breathed in.

'I'll fly,' he gasped. 'You lean out and get the key back.'

'No!' Timmi snapped. 'It's not safe.'

Kip couldn't understand why she would say that, but there was no time to argue.

'I'm better at flying anyway.' She stepped on the diamond connectors of the Skimmi and beckoned frantically. 'Give me the sack!'

Timmi made sure the drawstring was done up too tightly for Pinky to get out, and set off so hard and fast that it took Kip's breath away. They caught up with the eagle almost straight away. It wasn't expecting them, which gave Kip a chance to lunge for the key and take hold again. The eagle twisted its neck and screeched in surprise. It reached down and fastened its hooked beak on the key, letting go with its talons, still beating the air with its wings. Kip tried to prise the key away, but the beak was already strong and getting stronger.

'It's changing again!' he warned Timmi.

As its widening wings flexed out, the shapeshifter tried to drag him down off the Skimmi and Kip sank to his knees, trying to make his centre of gravity lower. Racing around and around his mind like a desert dust devil was the thought of what would happen to them if they lost the key. He knew that he couldn't fall himself because of the safety mechanism on the Skimmi, but if the shapeshifter pulled away suddenly, the glass button might plunge to the earth far below. Timmi sensed instinctively what was happening and she kept them cruising lightly alongside their target, tracking its every move.

'Thieving scum!' he shouted. 'You have enough treasure.'

Behind a ballooning body, talons grew as long as scimitars, scales bloomed like armoured flowers. And the next thing he knew, Kip was looking at a dragon the colour of a scarab beetle. It still had a preposterously small eagle's head, beak clamped to the Silent Key. The sulphurous gale from its flapping wings snapped the air, and a murderous growl started low in the shapeshifter's throat, rumbling across into Kip's chest.

Its head hasn't changed yet. It might be a weak point.

That thought gave him courage and he poked at the eagle's eye with his free hand – fury lending him new strength. With a screech, the shapeshifter let go.

'I've got it!' he yelled, curling his fingers around the key. 'GOT IT!'

He felt the Skimmi accelerate away but in that moment there was a crushing pressure around his chest. Looking down, he saw the dragon's talons clamped around him, squeezing tight in an agonising grip. Its other foot had locked on to the side of the Skimmi. The eagle head screeched and, holding Kip's gaze, its fierce pale-yellow eyes began to bulge into amber orbs lined with charcoal black, until a dragon's face looked back. It observed Kip's torment cruelly and in its cold stare he saw an unstoppable desire to conquer and destroy.

I am strong and you are weak, it seemed to say.

Still on his knees, Kip felt himself sag against the steel bars of the talons. Nausea and faintness churned in with the pain and he shut his eyes tightly. Then, out of the blue, his thoughts flashed to something his dad had said to him over the half-term. He'd been talking about running marathons, like he used to in his younger days.

'When you're running long distances – doing anything that requires a lot of stamina and concentration I suppose – the only thing that counts is this moment. Not what you've done to get you here, or the hours ahead of you. This one moment. Are you going to keep going or throw in the towel?'

'There are a lot of moments in a marathon,' Kip had said.

'And each moment is an opportunity not to give up. I used to talk to my body, sort of give it an all-over pat-on-the-back for getting this far. I'd always start out with "Well done, feet." And then, "Keep going, left leg. Well done, right leg. Good job, heart."'

'Well done, hair.'

'Exactly. And then when I'd done the whole body, I'd move on to my brain. "Well done, hippocampus. Well done, amygdala…"'

The scarab dragon squeezed tighter, and Kip felt his breath rasp.

Well done, lungs, he thought.

The shapeshifter growled again. As its bloodcurdling death wish reverberated inside Kip's ribs, it took everything he had to keep going. The talons encircling him seemed invincible; even so, he opened his eyes and tried to break free. Pain shot through his body, and he made himself think around it.

Keep going, hands.

He shifted on his knees and the surface of the Skimmi scraped against his skin. Timmi was yelling at the dragon and whacking it on the nose as hard as she could.

Each moment is an opportunity not to give up.

Telling himself it wasn't useless to try, he strained against the shapeshifter's clutches again, digging his nails into the slightly softer roll of flesh where the talons grew out. The dragon seemed to recoil for a promising second and then set in harder, forcing Kip's face over the side of the Skimmi.

That was when he saw it – sticking out of the rim of the Skimmi like a miraculous gift from the dreaming Universe. A single coral bead like a tiny pumpkin. It didn't matter that the dart must have been there since the sand-gorilla Myriad and that he'd somehow managed to miss it all this time. Here it was now, in this hopeful moment.

The thoughts came all at once now and weren't so much thoughts as a stream of life energy, the rich wellspring of survival. Two of these thoughts were important and stuck in his mind.

The dart is poisoned.

There are no scales in between the talons. It's just bare skin.

Fingers shaking, Kip reached out, forcing himself to move despite the crushing band of pain around him. Somehow, he grabbed the dart, held it tight, and stuck it in the unarmoured flesh of the dragon's foot.

The talons loosened almost immediately and Kip felt a chilling sensation of numbness from his chest down, but he held the Silent Key close to him in triumph.

'Go!' he managed to find the breath to shout. 'GO!'

'Hold on!' shouted Timmi.

The scarab dragon was poisoned, that was for sure. Its hideous screeches filled their ears. But whatever was left on the dart wasn't enough to fell it completely from the sky and it zigzagged after them groggily, tail whipping like a deadly flail.

Kip tried to take a long breath but there was hardly any oxygen coming now and he felt himself spinning. He held the Silent Key tight with one hand and grabbed hold of Timmi's ankle with the other. Deep inside, his heart was letting go, his blood slowing and his brain darkening. From this angle he could see the ground rushing up towards them, coming up too fast to land.

The dragon didn't quite kill me but Timmi will.

It was suddenly all too ridiculous. He laughed out loud but it hurt so much.

And then he realised why Timmi – wonderful, brave Timmi – was nosediving to the ground. There, drawn in enormous lines across the flat desert, were the shapes of the Crazy Paving and they were lighting up like landing strips. She was heading right for the centre of a giant hummingbird, flying so fast that tears streamed from Kip's eyes.

Close behind him came the boulder-splitting cries of the Scarab Dragon.

Chapter Fourteen

Telltale Cricket

Somewhere in the distance was the hum of a lawnmower, muffled by the summer haze weighing down the gardens. Professor Koriolis rapped the side of the table rhythmically with his knuckle as he thought.

'So why do you think it's stopped working?' asked Leela impatiently.

The back panel of the Dreambomber had been removed and the professor was poking around inside, his Candlelight focused into a piercing beam.

'It's hard to say,' he said, standing up. 'It could be that you took it too close to the Crazy Paving…'

Leela looked at the Dreambomber dolefully.

'But it worked fine there,' said Albert.

'There's no sure-fire way to know. And Myriad Waves can be temperamental. You're going to have to be patient.'

'But we don't have time to be patient!' said Leela urgently. 'Kip and Timmi might be in trouble!'

Professor Koriolis pinched the bridge of his nose and sighed.

'I'm assuming you haven't built in a surge protector – no? Well then, if there was a surge of M-Waves there isn't that much we can do. But there is some good news. My Multifarious Interface Theory is holding up very well, and yesterday GENI and I made some leaps forward. We are on the verge of finalising an echo sounder to locate the whereabouts of their Candles in Myriadspace. This should be very soon, perhaps only a few days. Getting them back will be trickier, but all in good time.'

Koriolis patted Leela's head on his way out.

'Don't worry,' he said. 'We'll fix this.'

As the door closed, Albert took a step back as if preparing to dive behind a beanbag. It looked like Leela might explode in a hundred different directions, and he didn't want to be in range.

'Pat, pat,' he said. 'Good Leela.'

'All in good time?' she seethed. '*All in good time*? Doesn't he realise that time is not being good to us?'

She looked at Albert pleadingly.

'I just know they're in trouble. I know it.'

'I feel it too,' he said. 'They need us, and we won't let them down.'

It felt right to hug and that made them both feel

stronger, each of them willing to move time and space itself to get their friends back if only they could find the right way. As they stood, side by side, looking at the innards of the Dreambomber, Albert clicked his fingers.

'Isn't it about time we checked out what's been happening down at the lake? It's been a whole day.'

'Of course,' said Leela. 'At least one of us is thinking straight.'

They flumped down on the beanbags and Albert rummaged around in a mini-fridge as Leela opened her Carousel and scrolled to the camera symbol.

'There's some cheese crackers, a muesli bar and a quarter of a yesterburger,' he said. 'Want some?'

Leela shook her head.

'I don't think you should eat that. It's actually a yester-yester-yesterburger.'

'It's been in the fridge,' Albert said, taking a hesitant bite. 'You know, that was really thoughtful of Iris, whatever else I've said about her.'

'It was,' said Leela absent-mindedly.

'You said we'd call her,' said Albert. 'Maybe we could do with some fresh ideas.'

'After this. Ready?'

Popping the rest of the yester-yester-yesterburger in his mouth, Albert nodded.

'Question GENI, can you help us review some footage of the Crazy Paving?'

GENI's voice answered but it was the automated message again.

'No problem,' said Leela. 'We can do the leg work ourselves.'

She enlarged the playback pane by pulling out its edges with her fingertips.

'Bring it on,' said Albert, wiping a relic of ketchup off his mouth.

'Obviously if we watch the footage in real time it's going to take 24 hours, so I'll put it on fast forward. Shout if you see something!'

But it was still hard going, just hours and hours of not much happening.

By the end of it, they had sunk listlessly back into the beanbags.

'It's like watching a documentary about grass growing,' Leela complained.

Albert shook himself out of the stupor.

'We'll just have to watch it again. Those footprints on the jetty didn't appear by themselves.'

'Maybe whoever has the other key hasn't used the Crazy Paving since yesterday.'

'There must be *something*,' Albert insisted.

So, they watched the recording again. Leela stopped it a few times, thinking she might have spotted someone, but it was just a bird flitting past. They were almost at the end when Albert gestured violently.

'I knew it!' he said.

Leela rewound the recording and played it at normal speed. The grass rustled, the sun shone, a cricket jumped. Nothing happened.

'I can't see it?' she said.

Albert turned to look at her excitedly.

'When we stayed the night down by the lake there was something unusual, but it didn't seem to be important, at least not then. Now though…'

'What?'

'You remember there was a breeze but the rushes by the lake were totally still? Well, when I woke up halfway through the night, the moon had hardly moved.'

Albert waited for Leela to catch on.

'Play it again, and watch the cricket,' he said.

Leela glued her eyes to the footage, not daring to blink. The cricket was the same colour as the grass and the movement was only slight. It flexed its legs as if about to jump, seemed to leave the ground for a split-second and was gone.

'Where does it go?' she said.

'Keep watching,' said Albert.

After about a minute, the cricket appeared again, and did exactly the same thing.

'There. Someone's messing about with Timeyarn,' said Albert, confidently.

Leela considered this for a moment. Timeyarn was made up of threads of Strange Energy that created all sorts of peculiar and powerful effects. Those who knew its secrets could fray and fracture and freestyle time itself. And if anyone knew anything about Timeyarn, it was Albert.

'A Timestitch?' she asked.

'No, not a stitch. A loop. I'd bet my burger on it. Whoever has the second key is using a Timeloop so no one sees them going in and out of the Crazy Paving. They must be switching it on just when they need it, so no one notices. Only they didn't cover their tracks well enough.'

'Let's make double sure before we tell Miss Twiss,' said Leela. 'We should take some readings at the lake – that'd be the first thing she'd do.'

Holes × Holes = More Holes

Outside, a glorious day was waiting – blue skies, a cheery sun and plump white clouds. It would have been the perfect summer's afternoon, if only Kip and Timmi had been here for a Skimmi race to the boathouse.

'So, what sort of reading do we take?' asked Albert.

'The Wave Sensor should give us something to start with,' said Leela, setting her Skimmi down on the jetty.

They both opened up their Carousels and ticked the sensor icons. Veils of energy readings appeared around them, each one displaying waveforms that pulsed in different colours.

'Just need to isolate the Timeyarn...' said Leela, swiping through the veils until she came to a sudden stop. 'Albert! You were right!'

'Wish I'd had one of these when I found that Timeloop on my old school's roof,' grumbled Albert.

Leela looked down at the lakebed.

'What do we do,' she whispered, 'if the other key holder suddenly appears out of the Timeloop? How do we stop them just running back into the Crazy Paving?'

'We need a plan to grab the key...'

'What are you whispering about?' whispered a third voice, close behind them.

Albert and Leela both leapt an inch off the ground and nearly fell off the walkway.

Iris was hovering on her Skimmi not five centimetres away. Painted on its upper surface were the giant gaping jaws of a sabre-toothed tiger, so it looked as if she were standing in its mouth. Her questioning eyes flicked from Albert to Leela and back.

'I've been trying to find you guys for ages. How's it going with the Dreambomber?'

Leela looked across at Albert. Iris was hard work, but it was harder work living with all these secrets.

'We were doing really well,' she said, with a reluctant sigh. 'But now it's stopped working. We don't know why.'

'Oh, that's awful,' said Iris. 'What are you doing here then?'

'We wanted to take some readings of the lake. There's something funny going on.'

Iris raised her eyebrows and followed Leela's gaze to the lakebed.

'It must be something to do with all the strange holes,' she said.

'We found one here yesterday,' agreed Albert. 'But Professor Koriolis wasn't too helpful.'

Iris scoffed.

'What does he know? We need to figure this out for ourselves.' She pointed down at the Crazy Paving. 'It's all connected to that. The holes only started appearing after Kip disappeared. And more of them are showing up all the time. Sometimes you can see them actually multiplying. It's amazing to watch.'

'Holes times holes equals more holes,' said Albert.

He wasn't trying to be funny but Iris's amusement was far worse than her smile. It was like being shot with a laughter machine gun.

'I picked up my library book last night and one was there, in the front cover. And someone had one right in the middle of their bagel this morning.'

'I wouldn't eat one,' said Leela, with a shudder. 'What if it made you empty inside?'

'Or started pulling you inside yourself,' said Albert.

'I heard that GENI's oddjob drones are working on

sealing up the holes with Skycrackle welders,' Iris continued ominously. 'But who knows if they'll be able to hold them off for very long. GENI's got a lot on her mind right now. And if the holes get any bigger...'

'We need to get to Miss Twiss's office,' said Albert to Leela. 'We've got to talk to her about this – and the other thing.'

'There's something else, other than scary holes everywhere?' asked Iris.

Reluctantly, Leela looked at Albert. Iris's dark eyes followed their every move earnestly.

'Iris we're going to trust you,' said Albert. 'But keep it quiet, OK? Someone else has a key to use the Crazy Paving.'

When Iris's upper lip twitched, it was hard to tell if she was going to yell or cry.

'Like the one Kip has?'

'Yes. There was a key missing from the Memoria Technica before we got to it.'

'Miss Twiss is in a meeting,' said Iris. 'I've just come from her office. We should go to Tamara Okpik – the Head of Security.'

Three Skimmies flashed through the air, and three pairs of feet clattered along the path. The door to the Security Centre slid open and a light on the wall flashed as their Candle badges were scanned. The reception area teemed with drones, as well as occasional personnel dressed in grey uniforms with a single white stripe. Tamara came hurrying to meet them. As usual, she was dressed all in black – a black sleeveless jumpsuit and black canvas zip-up boots. Her charcoal-black fringe had been cut short for the summer and her large eyes blazed with a thousand unfinished tasks.

'We've got something to tell you,' Albert almost shouted.

'Things are pretty frantic at the moment,' Tamara said hastily. 'Can it wait?'

'No,' said Iris boldly, and stepped forward. Tamara frowned and folded her arms.

'What is it?'

'Someone has a second key to get into the Crazy Paving,' said Leela.

'And they're using a Timeloop to cover their tracks,' Albert added, 'so no one can see them come and go.'

Tamara's worry lines sank deeper into her forehead as she looked from face to face.

'Are you sure?'

'Sure enough,' said Leela.

'OK,' said Tamara. 'You did the right thing coming to me. We'll look into it, and soon. But right this minute I have to go to an emergency council meeting. I'll get back to you as soon as I have anything.

As they left the Security Centre, Leela kicked at a dandelion and its wispy seedheads eddied upwards and sailed out over the lawn.

'Don't sniff rubbish bins if you have three nostrils,' she said mournfully.

'This just keeps getting worse,' said Iris bleakly. 'Your Dreambomber's broken. And who knows what monsters are in the Myriads with Kip? He might even already be … you know…'

'We don't know anything about anything,' said Albert, firmly putting a stop to any depressing speculation. 'Let's get back to the workshop. Professor Koriolis said we should keep trying to connect.'

Iris hopped into the jaws of the sabre-toothed tiger.

'I can't, sorry. Got to get to class. Catch up with you later though? I want to tell you my idea to help get Kip back.'

'Can't you tell us now?' said Albert.

She shook her head. 'Not yet. I don't want to get your hopes up. I need to check some things first.'

They watched her skimmi in the direction of The Hive, looking back once to wave.

'She's a lunatic,' said Leela.

'I agree,' Albert replied. 'But right now we need all the help we can get.'

They stepped aboard their Skimmies and turned their thoughts towards the Singing Mill.

'Hey,' Leela said, 'want to hear the world's shortest shortest bedtime story?'

'Go on,' said Albert, mistrustfully.

'Once…' said Leela, and accelerated away.

The Mill Room

'Mowwww-ellllll!' called Leela.

Albert looked in the snuggle space between the two beanbags.

'Nope.'

'MOWL!' Leela whistled. 'I'm going to KILL him!' she muttered crossly. 'Should've known he'd nick the Thoughtwave Lenses. Should've kept them locked up.'

'There he is!' yelled Albert.

A black feather poked up from behind a table covered in empty burrito wrappers and apple cores. Albert dived across but the mowl was too fast for him and flap-hopped away, wurbling happily. Leela didn't have any luck either and the mowl scrambled through her legs. Making an unusual *tric-tric-tric* noise, he disappeared out through the open door, clutching the lenses.

'What's that noise?' asked Albert.

'He's laughing,' said Leela, 'or should I say, cackling.'

The mowl's stubby tail disappeared around a corner and, as they turned after him, they saw his roly-poly body duck surprisingly nimbly through an open door. The mill's background whale song was louder here, rising and falling, layer on layer of words in different soft voices that couldn't quite be understood.

Leela went in first, followed by Albert, and they

came into a room full of busy mill machinery. This was no ordinary equipment, however. A collection of tubes, spirals, grooved discs, and tiny cable cars made up a complex marble run that looked very much like extra-terrestrial plumbing. Along this gleaming obstacle course rolled hundreds of iridescent beads.

Beyond the marble run, there was a long window and a balcony. A section of the huge outer wheel on the outside of the building could be seen, paddle dipping down after paddle, after paddle. Every now and then there was a sound like a nut being cracked open.

'So, this is the mill room,' said Albert. 'But what's it milling?'

'Bad thoughts,' said Leela. 'They're terribly crunchy.'

She gazed around the room.

'Where would a mowl play hide-and-seek?'

Her eyes lifted and settled on an observation platform that ran around the top of the room. A black feather was stuck in one of the metal fastenings.

'Up there!' she hissed. 'Follow me!'

Trying not to make any noise, they crept up the ladder and stepped onto the platform. Set against the wall were numerous control boxes and pipes, forming lots of mowl-sized hiding spaces. Silently, Leela pointed to herself and then to the left; then she pointed at Albert and to the right. Albert nodded. But before they could begin, a cannonball of black feathers and orange scales hurtled towards them out of the shadows and thrust the stolen Thoughtwave Lenses into Leela's hands.

'Ch-chark!'

The mowl's eyelids were drawn back, and his orange eyes like headlamps. Summoning all his power and flapping his wings, he tried to drive them back with a second panicked danger call.

'What is it, mowl?' said Leela, very serious all of a sudden.

A little brown finger jabbed frantically and Leela and Albert stared behind him into the shadows. Leela took a few steps forward to see better, until she realised what the mowl was pointing at. There, in the wall, was another hole, the size of a Skimmi. It seethed with energy and there was something hypnotic about it, irresistible, like looking into a whirlpool of unbeing.

'I'm exhausted,' said Leela, suddenly sitting down on the platform.

Albert rubbed his forehead with one hand and nodded.

'Quixars. Hurt. Headache.'

But the mowl was ch-charking constantly now and wouldn't leave them alone. He pecked Leela hard on the hand.

'OW!' she yelled, and then seemed to recover herself. 'We need to go!'

Each step they managed to stumble away from the

hole brought a little energy back. And as they reached the way out they looked up one last time. A mowl feather flounced about in a pocket of warm air produced by the mill machinery. Together they watched in horror as a long, spindly arm grew slowly out from the hole and plucked the feather out of the air.

Chapter Fifteen

The Shapes of Poems

Ice crunched underfoot as someone walked around him. Kip watched his breath spread out like chimney fog, and shivered.

'Kip! Are you alright?' said Timmi's voice. 'Do you remember anything?'

He pushed up from the ground in alarm. She was bending over him, her face tired and worried.

'Does it still hurt?' she asked.

'The shapeshifter?!'

'We got away,' she said. 'Reached the Crazy Paving just in time. But how are you feeling?'

Forgetting he was cold for a moment, Kip put a hand to his ribs, remembering those sharp talons, and hoped more than anything that the space between the Myriads had healed him. It was only when he rolled his shoulders forwards and backwards and took a deep breath that he knew for sure.

'It's OK. I'm fine. Really. It's like new.'

Timmi smiled, and wiped her eyes.

'I knew it would be,' she said. 'I'm sorry. It should have been me … the Silent Key … I couldn't … and then you didn't open your eyes in the Lava-Lamp Limbo and I … I thought you were going to die… If I'd just taken the key when you said, maybe we'd have gotten away sooner…'

'Nothing was your fault,' said Kip.

She looked at him helplessly.

Albert would say something funny right about now, and make everything better, he thought.

'You know that whole thing in the last Myriad?' he said. 'That's basically just like mowl bathtime, isn't it?'

A huge grin dissolved the tight lines pulling at Timmi's eyes and mouth. She busied herself draping a blanket across his shoulders and tried not to shiver herself.

'Your goosebumps have icicles.'

Kip stood up and pulled the warmth of the fleecy material across his chest. It only just covered his shoulders, but it was better than nothing. Seeing Timmi had wrapped both of the blankets from the sack around him, he handed the second one back to her.

'Pinky?'

'She's still in the bag,' said Timmi. 'I hollowed out the last bread roll and she's sleeping in there. Think I've seen departures already, it's really pretty, a blue-and-white-and-purple glacier. The Crazy Paving is made by cracks in the ice. Do you think you're up to it?'

'We've got seven more worlds to go,' said Kip. 'The sooner we get started, the sooner we'll reach the Futurescope. Besides, it's *freezing* here.'

Eartha's neatly drawn signposts in the book of poetry worked faultlessly. For each new Myriad, there was a new poem, and for each new poem, a new shape. Each shape was waiting to be found in the Crazy Paving, ready to take them to the next Myriad in the trail.

Some of these Myriads were wonderful, some terrible, some quite nonsensical. With a little help from Stumpy, Kip copied his earlier notes from the scrap of paper over to some blank pages at the back of the book, and made more drawings and recordings of the places they journeyed through.

Myriad where everything you touch laughs. Sounds great but in reality highly annoying…

Myriad with lamppost in the middle of a snowdrift…

Myriad with windmill-sail trees and creatures made of vines…

By the time they had scraped and bumped their way through a variety of improbable worlds, their legs were scratched, their clothes were torn and dirty, and

Kip's shoes stank to high heaven. At least they had managed to get a quick swim in a warm river in the last Myriad, where Timmi got very excited about being able to clean her fingernails. It also allowed them to carefully dab away the sticky substance left by the scarab beetle on her bracelet, and make sure it was working again.

It hadn't always been easy to find the way out and it felt like they'd been travelling for weeks. The sack had quickly been emptied of food and the flask was drunk dry, but Pinky was good at finding fresh water, and an occasional harvest of wild nuts and berries. They'd found a kind of sweet grapefruit in an orchard too, and raided the stalls in a market town for dry salt-bread and oat biscuits.

'Tell me again why Eartha had to send us through so many Myriads?' said Timmi crossly. 'I want to brush my teeth. Talk about the breath of a thousand and one nights.'

'She knows what she's doing,' said Kip, shielding his eyes against the sun. 'It could be like the ten riddles – she looked into the Futurescope to see the best path to the best outcome.'

'She used the Futurescope to lead us to the Futurescope,' said Timmi. 'That's so Eartha!'

'And we're close now, there's only one poem with a shape left.'

They were walking along a mud track, on either

side of which were fields. Mostly the fields were full of smouldering stumps but here and there were a few islands of a crop that looked like pink wheat.

'I wonder if this is a slash-and-burn farm,' said Timmi.

'Or we landed in more dragon territory?'

Ahead, they could see a high village gate. Behind the fence, which was in need of repair, they could see the tip of a bonfire burning merrily.

'Question GENI,' said Timmi. 'Are we in dragon territory?'

She looked at Kip and shrugged.

'Doesn't cost anything to keep trying.'

There was a fluctuation of noise – hisses and tweets – and then a crackly voice shifted into earshot.

'There is nothing in my databank to suggest that dragons are a living species. Unless you are referring to the Komodo Dragon?'

Tjørngård

'GENI!' yelled Timmi and Kip together.

'It's us, GENI.'

'Kip. And Timmi.'

'GENI, where are we?' said Timmi.

Silence.

'Are you still there?' Kip asked.

'I am analysing your question.'

More silence.

'Antimony Brown?'

Timmi nodded eagerly. 'Yes. Of course. That's me.'

'I do not recognise the name of your companion – Kip, nor your Candle.'

Timmi looked at Kip.

'Maybe there's no you at Quicksmiths in this Myriad?'

'My records show that Antimony Brown is currently in the Buttery. You cannot be there and here. I have therefore computed the possibilities, of which there are many. For example, it's possible that you are an ingenious hacking attempt, disguised as biological human life. The Candle software could be corrupted, or you could have been split into two entities by Strange Energy. But it's overwhelmingly likely that the interference on our communication is from trace M-Waves and that you are Quicksmiths students from another Myriad.'

'Yes! GENI that's exactly what we are,' said Timmi.

'So you're not our GENI from our Myriad?' Kip said.

'I am GENI from *a* Quicksmiths. But not *your* Quicksmiths.'

'How many Quicksmiths are there?'

'I cannot count them,' said GENI. 'I do not have access to this information. The number could be two, or it could be near-infinite.'

'GENI, how come the Candle hasn't worked up 'til now?' Timmi asked.

'There are many variables. But this is my best guess: if the Myriad you visit has a Quicksmiths, and a GENI, and Candles, then your Candle can connect to my long-range Strange Reality Drive, and it will be able to function. We are indeed lucky to be talking now.'

It was a great comfort to hear GENI's voice. She was everything Kip needed right now: strength and confidence and facts. He felt the burden of responsibility drift away, just a little.

'We'd better make the most of it then,' said Kip. 'And by the way, we know for certain that there are such things as dragons. Shapeshifting ones at least.'

'So where are we, GENI?' asked Timmi.

'You are in the Hinterveld, a remote part of Denland.'

'Any idea what this village is called, up ahead?'

'This is a place called Tjørngård.'

'But what happened here?' said Timmi, looking around in dismay as they passed through the village gate.

The bonfire was not a bonfire at all, but the edge of a wooden cart which had caught fire. Most of the thatched buildings lay in ruins. It looked as if some great raging leviathan had torn them in half and thrown their pieces around in a violent rage.

'I cannot see,' said GENI. 'You can describe it to me, or you can activate my sensory input in your Carousel.'

Timmi opened her Carousel and ticked a Touchlight icon that looked like an eye.

'Could you turn for me please,' said GENI.

Timmi swivelled around slowly so that GENI could inspect the scene. Kip turned too, taking in the chaos of broken furniture, farm implements, and clay pots strewn all around.

'This looks like the effects of weaponised Slipstream,' said GENI finally.

'How do you weaponise Slipstream?' asked Kip.

'Any energy can be a weapon in the wrong hands,' she replied.

Torn pictures fluttered at the base of the cart. Families and farmers. Men and women with shaggy overcoats and horns.

'Vikings?' said Kip.

They came to a stable. A horrible, nameless smell filled the air and Timmi covered her mouth and nose with her sleeve.

'Stay here,' said Kip, putting his head around the stable door. Inside were six animals – all dead. They looked a bit like horses with thin necks, short muzzles and black and white cow patches.

'Don't come in,' said Kip, 'there's nothing here.'

No sooner had he said that, than a bedraggled boy ran out, dodged past him, and collided with Timmi.

She and Kip stared at the child, who looked about seven or eight years old. He had two curved horns, one on either side of his head, just like a fancy-dress Viking. Only he wasn't wearing a helmet.

'Hey!' said Timmi, avoiding the sharp points as he tried to head-butt her in the stomach. 'We're friends!'

She stepped back and held her hands up. The boy looked from her to Kip, scowled, and said something unintelligible. Timmi shook her head. After making a strange sign over his chest, he jabbed a finger at the stables.

'GENI,' said Timmi. 'Will your translator work here?'

'Certainly,' said GENI.

The boy watched incredulously as Timmi flicked through the Touchlight symbols and ticked the translator.

'What happened here?' she asked.

Understanding flickered across the boy's face but he made the sign again and seemed afraid. Not taking his eyes off Timmi he reached down for a rock which he held tightly in one hand as if to throw it.

'Woah,' said Kip. 'No need for that.'

'What magic makes your words in my language?' he asked, threateningly.

'It's not magic,' said Timmi. 'It's science. It's a translator, from a computer.'

The boy looked confused.

'Maybe those words don't mean anything in his language,' said Kip.

Timmi tried again.

'It was given to me by a wise woman, a good teacher,' she said. 'It lets me talk to everyone. It's not dangerous, only helpful.'

That seemed to appease the boy's fear, and he let the rock fall.

'What happened here?' asked Kip.

'The Half-Elder came from the Tree of Worlds. And the raiders too. They tore our buildings apart and took our gold.'

'Raiders?' said Kip. 'Like pirates? Myriad Pirates?'

The boy listened to Kip's question and nodded.

'Yes, pirates. An army of pirates. They look deformed, like you. Without horns. They tried to take the Bright Prism.'

'What's the Bright Prism?' asked Timmi.

'It's our village's most prized possession. It has also good-magic and is very powerful.'

'Sounds like one of Eartha's inventions?' said Timmi, looking at Kip. 'She said they were hidden all over the Myriads…'

'Did they take it?' asked Kip.

The Viking child shook his head.

'Our strongest warrior and our greatest mage escaped with it just in time.'

'We need to move on,' said Timmi. 'Is there

anything around here with a pattern?' she asked the boy. He didn't seem to understand.

'Something with lots of different shapes in it?' Kip tried.

'The Tree of Worlds?' The boy raised his eyebrows and nodded his head past the stables, to a second gate in the village fence.

'This tree,' said Timmi, 'does it take you to the Myriads? To other places?'

'The legend says that the Tree brings travellers from other kingdoms. But I never believed it until the raiders came.'

The Myriad Pirates

'Where have all the people gone?' asked Timmi. 'From your village. Shouldn't you be with them?'

'Many are hurt. I came back alone to look for food; the army is still nearby.'

Timmi reached into the sack, then hesitated to look at Kip, shrugging a question. He shrugged back and she gave the boy a couple of oat biscuits. Between spluttered words of thanks, the viking child devoured one greedily before putting the other into his jacket.

'What about your parents?'

The boy turned his face towards some hills in the distance.

'They wait in the high caves. I should return.' He

gestured beyond the stables again. 'Hope you find what you seek.'

They left the village and walked on a short way, keeping an eye out for the Crazy Paving. Up ahead were more smoke clouds and they crept forward on their bellies up a hillside. Over the lip of the hill was a vast encampment – tents stretched as far as they could see. Wells had been dug and deer were being roasted on spits.

'The army hasn't gone very far!' whispered Kip. 'Don't they look a bit familiar to you?'

'Not sure to be honest. I'd have to get a closer look.'

Timmi air-ticked the magnifier symbol on her Carousel and it transformed into a postcard-sized rectangle of Touchlight. A fly landed on Kip's cheek, distracting him, and he waved it away. Meanwhile, Timmi was pulling out the corners of the rectangle with her fingers and positioning it so they could look through at the camp.

'There,' she whispered.

Kip couldn't believe his eyes. Some of them were like identical twins, others were … different. But they were all unquestionably…

'Thag!'

That arrogant, newt-like leer. Those angry red knuckles. Just one of him had been horrible enough at Quicksmiths, back at the start of term. But this was a thousand times more horrible.

'Not just one Pythagoras Grittleshank,' whispered Timmi in mutual horror. 'A whole army of them.'

'How? How can there be so many of them? Are they clones, GENI?'

'Perhaps,' GENI replied. 'But the most likely possibility is that this army has been created with a device called the Myriad Gong.'

'I don't want to find out more,' Kip whispered again. 'Is that the Tree of Worlds over to the left? You see that big one on its own – we just need to crawl a bit further.'

The tree's branches sprouted an abundance of growth, of all shades of green from pistachio to parakeet. Its leaves were formed of slender fronds, and playful sunlight shone through the gaps between them, quivering in a pattern of thin threads on the flat, bare earth at its foot.

'The Crazy Paving,' whispered Kip. He began to wriggle forward on his stomach, keeping his head as low as possible.

'Just a sec,' muttered Timmi, putting her hand on Kip's arm. 'Just let me think a sec. We know where departures is now so … Question GENI: Can you bring us back to Quicksmiths? With the Wormhole Positioning System?'

'Yes that can be done,' GENI replied. 'I will just need a short time to prepare the wormhole for this exact location.'

Timmi turned to Kip, keeping her voice low.

'GENI can bring us back any time. If we go to Quicksmiths, we can get more supplies. And talk to Professor Steampunk and Miss Twiss. Maybe they can even try to get in touch with *our* Quicksmiths…'

'I don't think that will be possible,' said a voice behind them.

As Kip tried to turn around a heavy boot stamped on the base of his spine, preventing him from twisting any more. Pinky's nose appeared at the entrance to the sack.

'*Run*,' he said in the lightest of whispers.

Hoping she would do as he said, he managed to create a diversion by grabbing the leg of whomever was standing on him, one of the Thags he supposed. Savage kicks rained on him. He curled up to protect himself and found himself thinking that the beating was easier to bear than the clutch of the Scarab Dragon. His Candle was snatched away and then, before his assailants had a chance to break any bones, Kip turned back to the ground, feeling sick. But there was some comfort in the sight of Pinky's fluffy tail disappearing stealthily into the undergrowth.

Bye little friend, he thought. *Be safe.* His last impression before a black bag went over his head was of the patterns of light under the Tree of Worlds, just out of reach.

Chapter Sixteen

Emergency Council

Out in the corridor, still running as fast as they could, with the mowl flapping ahead of them, Albert tried to make light of what they'd just seen, but he was sweating and wide-eyed and just as scared as Leela.

'Welcome to our "things that should not exist" series,' he gasped. 'Today: whatever that thing was.'

'Ballmoth,' panted Leela. 'Take us to Miss Twiss!'

The door to the Council Room in Celestial Hall was shut. Through an oblong window, they could see Miss Twiss standing at the head of a large oval table, addressing a few dozen professors and other college staff. Leela knocked and Miss Twiss looked over. She nodded and held up her hand, motioning for them to wait.

Albert rubbed his upper arms vigorously, even though it was another warm day.

'That mill room is in my top five places not to be ever again,' he said.

'You screamed louder than I did,' said Leela, glad to have something to talk about. 'A proper girly scream.'

The door opened and soundbites of conversation leaked out of the council room:

'*...our very existence could be threatened...*'

'*...an aggressive life form, or a deadly virus...*'

'*...there's no choice. The Crazy Paving should be shut down...*'

'What is it?' said Tamara Okpik.

'It's urgent,' said Leela.

'Really urgent,' added Albert.

'We have to talk to Miss Twiss.'

'*...remember we have two students inside the Myriads...*'

Tamara stepped back and held the door open for them. As they walked across the plush red carpet, the conversation petered out and all eyes turned on them. Someone coughed.

'We found another hole,' Leela blurted out.

'There are lots of them,' said Professor Koriolis, straightening the Candle pinned to his lapel. 'One more sighting isn't really for the Emergency Council.'

'But this one's the Mothership Hole,' Leela insisted. 'And an arm came out of it!'

Worried murmurs flared up around the table, interrrupted by Miss Twiss's voice. It echoed inside everyone's heads.

'Are you sure it was an arm?'

'Sure as anything,' said Albert. 'We both saw it.'

The Professor-in-Charge's face remained expressionless as always, although her eyes said she was concerned.

'Where is it?' she asked.

When she had the answer, Miss Twiss turned to Tamara Okpik and it was clear she was thought-speaking with her. Okpik left in a hurry and Twiss addressed the groupmind again.

'Everyone, let's take a break and come back in one hour. Leela and Albert, stay here.'

When the room had emptied, Miss Twiss sat at the table and motioned at two red velvet Airchairs next to her. Interrupting each other and falling over their words, they told Miss Twiss everything they could remember about the swirling fissure in the mill room, the feather falling and the spindly arm. The Professor-in-Charge stared and nodded, and nodded and stared, taking everything in.

'Let me update you on the emergency we are now facing,' she said, once they had finished talking. 'There is indeed a Timeloop at the boathouse, as you discovered recently. It's caused by a clever manipulation of Timeyarn which pulls threads of time back on themselves.'

'I knew it,' mumbled Albert.

'The source of this particular Timeloop is well hidden,' Miss Twiss continued, 'and even GENI has been unable to find it, so far. But that's not the worst of it. As you know, combinations of Strange Energies can sometimes cause interference. This Timeyarn manipulation is interfering with the Crazy Paving and its Myriad Waves, creating instability all around us.'

'That's what's causing the holes?' said Leela.

'Exactly,' said the Professor-in-Charge. 'The fabric of reality is wearing thin and letting scraps of the other Myriads seep through. And, if the holes get big and deep enough, it won't be long before their inhabitants are climbing through too.'

It wasn't a cosy thought.

'The arm,' said Albert, and stopped.

'What about it?'

'It looked a lot like a Prowler's.'

Miss Twiss said nothing, but her skin paled just a little.

'What about the Dreambomber?' she said. 'Are you any closer to reaching Timmi and Kip?'

Leela shook her head, looking at the ground.

'Something's gone wrong,' she said. 'Professor Koriolis is trying to fix it.'

'We'll find them,' said Miss Twiss. 'But for now, pack your things and be ready to leave. Do not return to the mill room.'

'Where are we going?' asked Albert.

'To the Bunker. Now hurry!'

Flying as fast as they could without running red

lights, they headed towards the Singing Mill, and were just landing their Skimmies at the entrance when an alarm like the trumpeting of electric elephants began to sound. GENI's voice spoke over the insistent siren.

'This is not a drill. Evacuation of the college will begin in one hour. Collect essential belongings only and meet at the Garden of Giant Leapfrogs. This is not a drill.'

Bunker

The chatter and gossip in the queue of students was deafening. Mostly everyone had just one bag of essentials but Leela and Albert had the Dreambomber on a Skimmi air-trolley, as well as a toolkit and the mowl's favourite shoebox. He was nestled inside it, grooming his black tummy fur like a lazy otter.

The population of the entire college was all lined up neatly in a queue that snaked around the Garden of Giant Leapfrogs. Two by two, they walked past Bagsworth and the other porters, who tallied the head count.

'I wish Miss Twiss would let us stay,' said Leela, looking in the direction of the Singing Mill. 'I'd rather not see any more of the lurking thing but we shouldn't abandon Timmi and Kip.'

'We're not,' said Albert. 'Miss Twiss will be here

with Professor Koriolis and Tamara Okpik. And GENI of course. And they'll still be trying to reach the Myriads. But if we can get the Dreambomber connected and working again, then that's our best chance. We can do that from somewhere safe.'

'I suppose so,' said Leela, fiddling with the Dreamwave Gauge. 'Like they always say … if you only have bones, make bone soup.'

'Literally no one says that,' said Albert. 'Apart from you. A second ago.'

'Is it true that we're going to the Doomsday Bunker?' someone behind Albert asked.

'I heard it's deep underground, like inside the Earth's mantle.'

A few Skimmies passed overhead and Albert looked up.

'Is that … is there a hole in the *sky*?'

Leela followed his gaze. The hole was about the size of a distant aeroplane. It seemed far off and yet close at the same time, and hard to focus on. A fast-moving cloud passed in front of it and floated away, much smaller. Rumours began to ripple along the snaking queue.

'The holes are going to eat up the sun!'

'The sky's going to fall on our heads!'

The Professor-in-Charge was standing up ahead, talking to the porters. She saw Leela and Albert walk past and gave them a thumbs-up.

'Do your best,' her voice rallied inside their heads. 'Professor Steampunk will help you with anything you need.'

She turned and beckoned to Koriolis, who trotted along after her. His face was stormy as he cast a backwards glance over his shoulder.

A few more forward shuffles brought Albert and Leela to the front of the queue, where they stepped into the blurry shadow play of the wormhole entrance. The sneezesickness it triggered was fierce as always, but short-lived, and was already wearing off as they arrived in a brightly lit, subterranean stone hall.

In a big open space, kitchen helpers were cordoning off an area where Chef Garibaldi was setting up a temporary canteen. The mowl freeped and skipped over to peek inside some large soup tureens. Students were busily placing their bags inside numerous sleeping tunnels that were carved into the thick, rocky walls of the bunker. Big Obi the Head Librarian struggled past with his arms full of books, followed by a couple of drones doing the same.

'Leela! Albert!'

Professor Steampunk was standing by a door halfway along the bunker's far wall. He waved with all four arms and rushed over to meet them.

'Well tickle me pink and call me Bleebleblimp! Is this the famous Dreambomber?' Without waiting for an answer, he took both their bags and Leela's dream machine in one swift motion.

'Allow me! Two admirable Dream Admirals, charting a course where few minds have sailed! Step this way to your quarters…'

Jabbering steampunkishly, the professor led them to a cave-like room, where the air was warm and unexpectedly fresh.

'This is Miss Twiss's emergency meeting room, but we've put some sleeping mats down for you…'

He deposited the two bags in a corner and placed the Dreambomber on a central table. Head bobbing up and down, he circumnavigated the machine with long sidesteps and then stuck his face in very close to it.

'Leela Lee, when you look up genius in the dictionary, I bet you find a little mirror! Now remind me what the problem is?'

Leela turned the green and yellow wheels. The cylinders came up and began to revolve, but the lights were missing.

'We don't know exactly. Professor Koriolis said that it might have been because we used it too close to the Crazy Paving and there was an M-Wave surge.'

'Would you like me to take a look?' Steampunk asked.

'Well, sure. Professor Koriolis already did,' said Leela. 'But it can't hurt.'

'While you're doing that,' said Albert, 'I'm going to find Iris. She had an idea to get Timmi and Kip back and she never told us what it was. Ballmoth, take me to Iris … er … Iris.'

The Ballmoth appeared, but didn't move. There surely couldn't be many people with that name at Quicksmiths.

'Take me to Iris. She's a First Year, new girl, joined a few weeks ago.'

The moth-sized ball of pure white energy bounced just a little on the spot, waiting for more information.

'Professor Steampunk, will the Ballmoth work on just a first name?'

The professor was already unscrewing the back panel of the Dreambomber while Leela laid out the Psychogenic Berets.

'Well, it's better to have a full name,' he said. 'But it'll give you a list of most likely options if you don't.'

'We might have a problem then: I think Iris isn't in the bunker!'

'Iris?'

'The new girl. First Year.'

Steampunk didn't look very happy to hear that. He opened his Carousel, ticked the speech bubble, and said Bagsworth's name. A few seconds passed and a square, moustachioed face appeared in Touchlight.

'We could have a missing student,' said Professor Steampunk.

'A missing student?'

'She might be,' said Albert. 'My Ballmoth won't take me to her. Her name's Iris.'

Even Bagsworth's moustache seemed to frown.

'So, you don't know her last name?' he said.

Leela looked at Albert.

'I... I don't know,' he stuttered. 'She just joined the First Year, but she's not in my class.'

'I can't find an Iris listed here,' said Bagsworth. 'She might use her middle name. We can work around it. What does she look like?'

'She's sort of thin and pale, really intense stare, shortish straight black hair, dark brown eyes, I think.'

'And whose class *is* she in?'

Albert bit his lip. 'I don't know,' he confessed. 'But not Professor's Mo's.'

'Good work, Albert. I'll get the porters to search the Bunker now, and alert Miss Twiss. She can divert some of GENI's drones to do a quick search of the college.'

'Oh, they'll find her, don't worry,' said Steampunk helpfully, after Bagsworth had hung up. 'Nothing and no one can escape a Quicksmiths porter. They're like beachcombing bloodhounds with hypersniffic noses!'

Leadfish

Steampunk peered inside the back of the Dream-bomber.

'Mmmm-hmmm,' he said.

He let out a low, lengthy whistle and turned to the toolbox, cracking his knuckles before selecting a very long, slim pair of tweezers. With his other hands he pulled a pair of goggles out of his pocket, put them on, and adjusted the binocular-like lenses. Sticking his tongue out in concentration, he slowly advanced the hand with the tweezers into the Dreambomber's workings as if he were playing a particularly taxing game of wire buzzer.

'Hmmm-mmmm,' he said, and sucked his teeth. Ever so carefully, he withdrew the tweezers, and Leela and Albert saw something small and glistening caught between their points. Steampunk held it out for them to see. It looked like a grey trilobite, roughly the size of a walnut.

'Suffering supernovas!' he said. 'It's a...'

'A Leadfish?' spluttered Leela. 'How did that get in there?'

'Er, rewind,' said Albert. 'What's a Leadfish?'

'Strange Energy is all around us,' said Steampunk, holding the wriggling thing up in the tweezers so they could see better. 'We need ways of isolating it sometimes, or keeping it at bay. You know those briefcases we keep wormholes in...'

Albert nodded.

'Well, Leadfish are made of the same material. They used to contain real lead, hence the name, but these days they're made of a different element from the Strange Periodic Table...'

'Got it, thanks,' said Albert, politely hastening the professor on. 'What's it doing in the Dreambomber?'

'It's designed to block out a specific Strange Energy,' Steampunk said, dropping the Leadfish into a petri dish he pulled out of a pocket. 'In this case, Thoughtwaves.'

'But it's not part of the machine,' protested Leela.

Professor Steampunk took off his goggles and ran a hand through his downy white hair.

'Then there are two possible scenarios,' he said. 'One: it's on its summer holidays. Two: someone else must have put it there.'

'We haven't let the Dreambomber out of our sight, and no one's been near it, except...'

Professor Steampunk raised his eyebrows.

'He's the only other person who's had access,' said Leela, looking at Albert. 'Could he have put it in when we weren't looking?'

Albert made his thinking face.

'What if he was just saying he had that amplifier so if we caught him messing around with the Dreambomber later on, he'd have an excuse,' he said.

'But why would he want to stop us reaching Timmi and Kip? That's just...'

'Who exactly are we talking about?' asked Professor

Steampunk, his raised eyebrows hovering just on the edge of a frown.

Both Leela and Albert were reluctant to make any sort of accusation, but Steampunk tweezered it patiently out of them. And he was the one who said aloud the word they were both thinking.

'Sabotage! We must tell Miss Twiss immediately.'

But there was no answer when he called.

'I'll send a message,' he said, leaving the room, 'for now, you just concentrate on getting this droolingly dreamy device back up and running.'

Leela hastily screwed the back panel on and turned the wheels again, flooding the room with spinning lights.

'How are we going to get to sleep?' she said worriedly. 'I'm still wide awake after that freakout in the mill room.'

'Don't you worry about that!' said Albert. 'Get comfy, I'll be back in five minutes.'

Leela was just getting the mowl settled in his shoebox when Albert returned. And he wasn't alone.

'Reinforcements are here!' proclaimed Badger, swooping into the room.

Penny stepped in after him. 'I brought my special book-shaped pillow.'

'Let's put some zzz in the sleep bank!' said Maya, dropping an armful of rolled-up sleeping mats.

Em was last in the door. Ready for bedtime, her

skin art had transformed into fluffy clouds floating among gently turning stars and crescent moons. Captivated, the mowl waddle-flapped over and admired the animation for only a few seconds before his furry head nodded down and he rolled over on his side, fast asleep.

'This is the plan,' said Leela. 'First we'll get to Pinky to make her sleep-fly. And then we'll try the others.'

Albert was already in his beret and snapping on an eye mask.

'Aye aye, cap'n,' he said. 'Full dream ahead.'

Chapter Seventeen

Outlaws

Kip woke up with a start, and a moment later, someone slapped him hard across the face.

'Oh sorry,' said an unpleasant voice. 'Did I wake you up?'

Knowing it would probably be pointless to attempt to move, Kip tried nonetheless. As expected, his arms and legs wouldn't budge.

'Kip!' said Timmi. A hand touched his and he realised he was sitting on a chair, tied up back-to-back with her. A thick rope looped tightly around his body several times.

Where did they get two chairs from? he wondered fleetingly. *Everything in the village looked broken.*

But there were more urgent things to think about.

'Timmi, are you OK?'

'Don't worry,' said the voice of their kidnapper. 'We're feminists, so we gave her a good slapping first.'

'I'm fine,' said Timmi defiantly.

With deliberate attentiveness, Kip took in his surroundings. First: they had been moved away from the encampment near the hill. There were trees around, but this was a pine forest and the Tree of Worlds was nowhere to be seen. Second: two Thags stepped around the chair to leer over him. One of them had red hair, the wisps of a feeble beard and a metal, cybernetic eye; the other one had strange lacy gills instead of ears, and a broccoli-like lump instead of a nose. Kip had seen enough action films about alternative realities to guess what this meant.

Thags from different Myriads.

'Where are we?' he asked.

'Why do you need to know?' said Cyber-Thag.

'We're somewhere where that monstrous harpy that calls itself a supercomputer can't find you,' said Fish-Thag.

'Shhhhh, shrimp-breath,' said Cyber-Thag. 'Don't tell him anything.'

The drawstring bag and Kip's Skimmi were leaning against the end of a log. A third Thag, with a bowling ball head and very short legs, was going through their things. He was running a scanner over Eartha's book of poetry, presumably to look for wormholes and other Strange Energy, flicking through to make sure nothing was hidden inside.

'Get this, lads,' said Bowling-Ball-Head-Thag,

turning back to the others gleefully. 'It's a book of *poetry*.'

Fish-Thag and Cyber-Thag roared with laughter and clutched each other in malicious delight. Bowling-Ball-Head-Thag threw the book at Kip; it was a good aim and struck him just above the right eye. The pain was sharp and fiery and Kip felt a trickle of blood along his eyebrow.

'Who's in charge?' he asked.

'Wouldn't you like to know?' said Fish-Thag.

'Is it you?' asked Cyber-Thag, with a shocked face.

'Is it me?' sneered Bowling-Ball-Head-Thag.

That inspired a cacophony of Thag laughter. It was all too much to bear. Kip closed his eyes and wished for the longest moment that he was back in his and Albert's attic room at Quicksmiths or in his bedroom at home. He would have given anything to hear his dad go around the flat, opening up the windows in the morning; the complaining squeak of the shower taps being turned; the shaky rumble of the old pipes. For some reason, a memory strayed into his head, a memory of when he was much younger, with his sister Suzanna, sliding along on pillowcases to help clean the wooden floor of their bedroom corridor at the old house by the sea.

'Am I paying you to crack jokes?' said a new voice, an even-more-horrible voice that hurled itself through the air and crushed itself into Kip's ears.

Before he'd even opened his eyes, he knew it was Thag from their Myriad. Kip had never considered for a moment that they'd meet again after the college had voted to send the brutish sixth-former packing. But now here they were, and Thag held all the aces. Reluctantly, Kip forced up his gaze and faced his old foe.

A hand in a studded black glove held up the Silent Key. The light twinkled in its inner dimensions, taunting Kip: *I'm not far, I'm not far, come and find me, the Crazy Paving.*

'This is mine now,' said Thag, putting it in his pocket. He grimaced nastily. 'As are you. No Miss Twiss to save you. My rules.'

Winding him up isn't going to help. Maybe I can flatter him.

'Well, looks like you've won,' said Kip, shaking his head as if in disbelief. 'You've beaten us.'

'Oh, have I?' mocked Thag, and then leaned closer. 'I haven't *beaten* you at all yet.'

Leaving them with that frightening thought, Thag mustered the others, who all seemed to obey him readily, stomping away while Fish-Thag was left behind to keep guard.

Secret

The captives whispered as softly as they could, while

Fish-Thag sat with his back against a nearby tree and whittled a piece of wood with a flick knife.

'What are we going to do now?' Timmi murmured first. 'They have the Silent Key. They have everything.'

'I can hear you,' said Fish-Thag.

No point in telling them any plans we think of, thought Kip. *We'll have to wait for our moment. They're going to slip up, get sidetracked.*

The daylight was sinking slowly, Kip noticed, and the moon was already rising in the paling sky.

Maybe the guard will get sleepy during the night.

Fish-Thag stopped whittling, gurgled with cruel laughter, and tried to stab the knife into some small woodland creature that was scampering past. Kip thought of Pinky's tail disappearing into the underbrush not so long ago, and his heart felt the heaviness of unseen chains.

Be safe furball, he thought. *Stay far away from here.*

'Timmi, I know this has been really hard,' he said. 'This whole thing.'

'It's not exactly been a cakewalk,' said Timmi.

'But, well, I feel like you have a problem that you're not telling me.'

Timmi squeezed one of Kip's fingers.

'He can hear us,' she hissed.

'I know, but I don't care. Now is the only time we have to talk. We don't know what will happen next. There might not be another "now".'

'Kissy, kissy,' said Fish-Thag.

Behind him, Kip felt Timmi move around restlessly, and he waited for her to feel calm again before he went on.

'It's been ever since you looked in the Mindfield, in the second Myriad. You've been acting like my dad does when he's trying not to tell me bad news about my mum.'

Timmi sighed as if she'd made her mind up about something.

'You're right. It did start with the Mindfield. Kind of. It's like the headset woke something horrible up. And now it won't leave me alone.'

Fish-Thag laughed again and muttered to himself.

'Oh, this is just classic.'

'Ignore him,' whispered Kip, as softly as he could. 'It's just you and me.'

He felt the ropes pinch as Timmi nodded behind him, and she squeezed his finger again.

'I looked into the Mindfield,' said Kip. 'I saw bad things too.'

'Everyone's different, maybe it just didn't affect you the same way,' Timmi said unhappily. 'I didn't just see bad things; it's given me bad *thoughts*.'

'We all have bad thoughts,' replied Kip.

'Not like this,' insisted Timmi. 'I think I'm cursed.'

'There's no magic. There's only Strange Energy. How can there be a curse on you?'

'Who knows what weird stuff has happened to us in the Myriads, scrambling up our Thoughtwaves?'

After that, she didn't speak. Kip waited. And then took a deep breath. This was going to be hard, very hard, especially with that Thag guard listening. But he had to get to the bottom of whatever was troubling Timmi and help his friend.

Now it's your turn to be a Nevergiverupperer, he thought. *Like Albert.*

'In the Mindfield,' he started. 'My mum's there, and my sister, Suzie. Everything's just like it used to be, except I'm me now, not me from seven years ago. But then the earth starts to fall apart and the quake takes Suzie first – the nothingness inside it pulls her away from me, I watch her falling and falling. And then it's just me and mum left – she's hanging on to my hand, only I can save her, and I'm holding on to her and it seems like everything's going to be OK. And then…'

Fish-Thag slammed his knife into the trunk of the tree.

'…then she just falls. I can't hold on. She just falls…'

'What a train wreck,' jeered Fish-Thag.

Timmi seemed to come back to life after that.

'You'll never do that,' she said. 'You'd never let go of your mum. It's different for me.'

'Maybe I can help if you tell me what you saw,' he said.

'All right. You can't let me touch the Silent Key. If I do, something really bad is going to happen.'

It was the last thing Kip expected to hear.

'What do you mean?'

'The Mindfield showed me taking the Silent Key. And something terrible happened.'

'Something terrible, like what?'

'There was a horrible disaster. Everyone died.'

'But why? And how?'

Fish-Thag laughed and his gills wheezed like a dusty accordion.

'It's me,' said Timmi, trying to ignore the interruption. 'I make it happen. That's why I keep checking to see that you've got the key, in case the curse has made me go mad, and I can't remember what I'm doing. I need to see it to know it's safe, but I don't want to look at it in case the curse makes me take it and we both die – or worse, you die and I don't.'

Kip tried his best to understand what Timmi was getting at. It all seemed so illogical, but her fear was disturbingly convincing.

'The Silent Key can just stay in my pocket,' he said. 'You don't have to have anything to do with it.'

'But I do, don't you see? Something's trying to make me take it. And the same thing is telling me that the worst things will happen if I do. I'm afraid I won't be able to control the thought and that I'm going to do what it's telling me.'

The tears tugged at her voice.

Maybe everything is just getting to her, he thought. *We've been away from home a long time.*

But there was nothing more he could do or say to console her. So close to him and yet out of reach, she sniffed quietly, her back turned to his, as night fell.

Up, Up and Away

Camp Thag was lit up with cooking fires and glowsticks that marked out the pathways between tents. At the first hint of nightfall it got busier. Thags of all shapes and sizes came and went. One had a head shaped like a hammerhead shark's; another had lizard skin and T-Rex arms; one or two wore special bubble helmets that hid their faces.

Helpings of roasted meat and potatoes were passed around, which the Thags made sure to wave under their captives' noses. Two bowls of tepid sludge were delivered for Kip and Timmi, but Fish-Thag threw the contents in their laps where they couldn't reach it.

After dinner, the Alpha Thag from Timmi and Kip's Myriad stood before his army. He was still wearing that pair of black elbow-high gauntlets with metal spikes on the arms and studs on the knuckles. Like a braying beast, Alpha Thag called out to the crowd.

'What shall I pulverise with my Slipstream Gloves?'

'Tree!' bleated a Goat-Thag.

'Big rock!' yelled Bowling-Ball-Head-Thag.

'Them two gobwombles – the hostages!'

An army-sized burst of loathsome laughter bellowed out, shaking Kip to his core. Thag nodded and strutted and ripped a stout pine into pieces, followed by a rock that he crushed to powder in one hand. There was some scattered clapping from the assembled thaggery.

That's what tore apart that poor boy's village, thought Kip.

While the guard was amused by Thag's exploits, Kip picked at the cable around his wrists but it was made of hard plastic and there was nothing to undo. As he tried to loosen it anyway, he felt the cold of something metallic against his fingers. It could be connected to the cable, or it could be…

It could be our ticket out of here, he thought, trying to rein in his hopefulness just in case he was wrong.

Eventually, a chrome-skinned Thag came to take over guard duty and the camp died down as the rest of the army who weren't at their posts went to sleep. The minutes and hours passed. Kip kept up his vigil, silent and unmoving, until he saw Chrome-Thag's head loll to one side.

'Timmi,' he whispered.

It wasn't easy to squeeze her finger, but he managed it after a few attempts.

'Timmi!'

'What?'

'I think we've got a chance to escape.'

'What are you talking about?'

'We have to go now.'

'How?'

'Did they take the Gravity Bracelet?' Kip whispered.

Timmi's fingers went into hyperactive mode, bending and straining as she tried to feel for her invention.

'I think it's still here!' she whispered finally.

The long minutes dragged on while she tried to activate it. Without blinking, Kip watched Chrome-Thag, searching for any twitch or sign of wakefulness. Then Timmi let out a tight sigh of exasperation.

'I can't reach the charms, not the way my hands are tied,' she whispered. 'Can you try? It's on my left hand.'

Kip curled the fingers of his right hand inwards. He could just reach, with some difficulty.

'Which one? And how do I make it work?'

Timmi went quiet.

'Which one? Timmi?'

'I'm thinking … the ladybird! You just pull the chain until you feel it click and then twist in any direction.'

It was almost impossible to guess what the charms were, from touch alone, with his hands tied behind his back. But Kip was surprised to learn what he was capable of when his very life depended on it. He had to stop twice when his fingers cramped up, but eventually he managed to identify the ladybird by its rounded shape – all the other animals had pointy beaks or legs that stuck out and grazed his fingertips. Kip was starting to sweat from the concentration and he realised he was clamping his jaw tight. He stopped and relaxed and tried again, this time catching the charm between his two forefingers.

Please help us, gravity ladybird, he thought as he pulled and twisted the chain. Nothing was happening and Kip tried to grab the charm again, but then he felt something, a lightness in his chest.

Is it working?

As that thought faded it became clear beyond a doubt. They were lifting, lifting, inch by inch above the ground, still tied to the chairs. Timmi squeezed his finger but he only dared whisper to her when they were above the treetops and the lights of the glow sticks were like matches below them.

'Leela was right when she said that's the best thing you've ever invented. You're like a modern-day Eartha.'

Kip couldn't see, but he was sure Timmi's face must be glowing in the darkness.

'I'm not really, but that's sweet, thanks Kip,' she said. 'Hey, aren't you, me and Pinky going to have some great stories when we get home?'

'Pinky! I told her to hide. We're going to have to find that village again, she'll be waiting there...'

But as they looked down at the receding scenery below, something didn't quite add up. Timmi spoke first.

'I can't see the village. Everything looks totally different.'

'GENI didn't send help, did she?' said Kip, feeling his heart sink. 'She would have known roughly where we were, even if they destroyed our Candles. The only way for the Thags to have known for sure she couldn't find us...'

'We're in another Myriad! They must have brought us here after they knocked us out.'

Even if they managed to sneak back into Camp Thag and steal back the Silent Key, Kip didn't know how to retrace their steps in the Crazy Paving to find Pinky. Would it be possible to capture a Thag and make him talk, find out more about how all this worked...

'What if they have Skimmies?' he forced himself to return to the immediate danger.

Kip's neck was beginning to ache from twisting to hear Timmi's words. He turned the other way, and Timmi copied him.

'They might do, but I didn't see any,' she said.

Hope those Slipstream Gloves of Thag's don't have a long range, Kip thought, but didn't say anything out loud.

'Going up was still the only way we could get away from them,' said Timmi. 'They might not think to search the sky when they're looking for us, at least not at first. Besides, this Myriad seems to have really low clouds which will keep us hidden.'

That was true, but it also meant they'd have to guess what was happening below. The next question was almost too horrible to contemplate, but Kip couldn't push it away.

'What happens when the Gravity Foam effects wear off in ten minutes?'

'Five minutes,' corrected Timmi. 'Don't freak out, OK? When it wears off, we'll fall back down.'

Kip tried to see how far up they were already. The misty edges of a cloud were beginning to envelop them.

'You'll have to keep reactivating the ladybird, then we'll keep floating. We'll count the seconds. Actually, we should try it again now, as we don't know how much time has passed already.'

That was not the answer Kip had been hoping for.

'What if I lose my grip? It's not that easy.'

'You won't lose your grip,' said Timmi.

They'd escaped, things should be easy now, it was only fair. But the Myriads weren't fair, they were simply dreams. Kip concentrated his hardest and felt for the ladybird charm again.

It worked, and it worked once more. Had they

been in their own Myriad, they might have been buffeted by strong winds as they climbed, but the sky stayed hospitably calm. But then just as Kip started to feel they were over the worst of it, he realised they had another problem on their hands. They had begun to get so high that his breathing was becoming shallower.

'Timmi…' he said, fighting off a growing dizziness.

It was getting harder to talk, and harder to hear. Kip strained his neck to the side as far as he could.

'I know,' Timmi said weakly. 'I feel it too. I don't know what to do.'

'Should I stop twisting the charm?'

If they floated any higher, they might pass out altogether from lack of oxygen. But if he let the Gravity Foam effect of the bracelet lapse, he might lose his shaky grip of the charm as they fell out of the sky. Then they would just keep on falling.

Timmi went quiet, she must have been thinking again, and the next thing Kip knew was that his pulse was being taken. He couldn't understand why she would do that but he was too tired and breathless to say anything. In his groggy state he felt the chair descending – fast but at an angle, not in a vertical plummet – and a terrible fear came over him that Alpha Thag had found them.

With all his strength, he managed to take in a deeper breath and a rush of oxygen helped him straighten up, for his neck had drooped over to one side. They were closer to the ground now – he could see a moonlit pond below them, but no sign of Camp Thag.

'Is there someone there?' he asked, knowing the answer.

Timmi replied.

'Someone's pulling us down! But I can't see who it is!'

'Shhhh!' said a voice.

They carried on earthwards like passengers on a peculiar sky sleigh. Eventually, the chairs touched down and Kip felt a steady hand preventing them from lifting up again. A dim blue light arose in front of him, illuminating two bewitching moons in a face of delicate chainmail links.

'Incognita!'

She put a finger to her lips.

'I've landed us some distance from the camp, but they could have scouts around. We should still be careful.'

She took their pulses again, and the subtle chainmail of her face rearranged itself into a relieved expression.

'How did you find us?' whispered Timmi.

'Eartha sent me. She knew this place, this time is important. So here I am.'

Seeing that the chairs had now fully returned to the earth, she stepped off Kip's Skimmi and tapped at her wrist. Her left hand hinged back and a sturdy scissor attachment extended from the socket.

'Stay still!'

With careful snips, Incognita sliced through the rope and the cable ties that secured them. Soon Kip and Timmi were freed and they stood up gratefully, rubbing their sore hands and shaking their feet.

'How did you get my Skimmi?' Kip asked, and noticed then that she was carrying the drawstring sack too.

'My attachments can be most useful,' Incognita replied. 'I am in fact an excellent pickpocket.'

Proving her point, her right hand did a high-speed swivel, detached itself from her arm, and leapt on to the ground. Standing vertical, fingers pointing upwards, it tottered about on two short mechanical legs.

'I have all your things, the book and the key too…'

'That's incredible,' said Timmi, throwing her arms around Incognita's neck, who stopped talking in surprise. 'You're incredible! So where do we go now?'

'We have to go back,' said Kip wildly, remembering Pinky. 'We have to find a way back to the last Myriad…'

Incognita opened the drawstrings of the sack so Kip could look inside. Pinky lay sleeping happily in her hollowed-out bread roll.

'You found her! You *are* incredible!'

'She was waiting at the Crazy Paving as I passed through.'

Pinky squeaked but didn't wake up, so Kip took her carefully, put her in the big side pocket of his cargo shorts and did up the Velcro.

'We must move quickly,' said Incognita. 'They will be discovering their loss very soon, and the Crazy Paving is close to their encampment.'

She retrieved her hand and set off into the pine forest. They followed in her footsteps, trying not to step on fallen twigs, but it was impossible in the darkness.

'I think I need a shower,' said Kip. 'Flies keep landing on me.'

'Um yee-hees,' Timmi replied. 'We're going to have to burn those shoes when we get back. At least twice.'

'I have fresh clothes for you, you can change soon. But in a short time, we must stop talking,' said Incognita. 'Not even whispering.'

'Wait,' murmured Timmi. 'If the Thags brought us to a new Myriad, then have we lost the trail in Eartha's book?'

'All this has been taken into account. We simply follow the final signpost Eartha drew for us – the shape next to the tenth poem.'

The muscles in Kip's shoulders slackened and he realised they had been hunched tight for a long time. Help had come. Incognita was surefooted and keen-eyed, and she knew things he did not. It was just as if his dad were here, or Professor Mo, or even Eartha herself.

'Can't you take us home next,' Kip said. 'So we can let everyone know we're OK and then we'll come back?'

Incognita shook her head. 'I cannot do that. We must follow the shapes of the poems exactly.'

'But you must know the password?' said Timmi.

'I do not. You still have to discover it, the two of you, and the twelfth poem will help you. That's the best way for all of us.'

Kip's own breathing was the loudest thing he'd ever heard, as they crept past Camp Thag and held hands at the edge of the Crazy Paving. In a step and a flash they were back in the rollercoaster ride of Myriad Waves, and heading for the next world.

Chapter Eighteen

The Golden Temple

A magnificent golden building rose out of the desert sands. Its sides were made of giant steps: six colossal storeys scaled by a long, steep stairway, climbing to a crowning temple at the very top. Kip recognised the style from his history lessons but couldn't quite remember the word for it at first.

'Zig-something.'

'Ziggurat,' Timmi said quietly. 'It's a ziggurat.'

Down its stepped sides spilled clusters of vivid flowers and climbing plants. At the base of the dazzling structure was a wide plaza of fountains and networks of clay canals that ended in delightful water gardens. Despite all this abundance, the air was blisteringly hot and heavy with dust and it felt like it hadn't rained here for many years.

'Where does all that water come from?' Kip wondered. 'Out here in the middle of the desert.'

'And who looks after the gardens?'

Kip pulled the book out of the sack and looked at the eleventh poem again.

'If that's the golden temple, where's the black one?'

'Nothing else in sight,' said Timmi, scanning the sands around them. 'The ziggurat looks really old. Thousands of years. Maybe there's another one buried somewhere in the sand? Or it could be behind one of the bigger dunes?'

A fly landed on Kip's face. He tried to blow it away. 'Buzz off!' he hissed. 'I don't smell that bad.'

'You don't exactly smell like roses,' laughed Timmi.

Warning Kip and Timmi to stay low, Incognita took the Skimmi and investigated the grounds. Once she had returned, declaring that there wasn't a soul in sight, they walked cautiously on towards the burnished temple.

At the outskirts of the plaza, the sand gave way to hard clay and their footsteps crunched loudly as they crept along the central avenue past the inky water gardens.

'What do you think that is?' said Kip, his voice coming out in a whisper.

Up ahead, blocking one of the white clay pathways that snaked among the lily ponds and groves of almond trees, was an imposing four-metre-high stone head. They gathered at its base and looked up at the unseeing eyes that stared out towards the empty desert.

'It is not alone,' Incognita said.

Kip glanced across the gardens to see more of the grey, weathered effigies jutting out above the trees at intervals.

'This is the right place,' she added.

'What do you mean?' asked Timmi.

'Eartha told me that the Futurescope was guarded by a tribe of temple giants.'

'The Futurescope is somewhere here?' Kip asked, not quite believing they were finally close.

'Yes,' said Incognita. 'And we should move on.' She gazed up at the colours of the sunset clinging to the top of the darkening dune. 'The desert can get cold at night.'

Sleep-flying

Incognita took out a torch attachment, fixed it to her arm, and led the way past the giant head. As they came closer to the ziggurat, the torchlight rolled along the lines of carvings in the sides of the massive golden blocks.

Shimmering symbols stretched out into the gathering night beyond the torchlight, and the trio of travellers stood in silence contemplating the ziggurat's unknown past. Kip couldn't read the glyphs of these ancient sagas, but they called to mind heroes battling monsters, eyes looking down on the underworld, and forces that looked remarkably like Strange Energy.

'We should see if there's a way inside the building,' said Timmi.

But in the whole length and breadth of the ziggurat, there was not so much as a window.

'Do you think there's any food around here?' Timmi said, once they had arrived back where they'd started.

Kip was suddenly ravenous and clutched at the growl forming in his stomach.

'I believe there is,' said Incognita, 'and I packed some milk and barley bread as well. There's a sandy patch up ahead. We can make camp and I'll see what the gardens have to offer.'

Kip and Timmi sank side by side down onto the soft sand while Incognita built and lit a fire in less than five minutes. Grateful for the warmth, they sat sharing milk from a flask, listening to the dry brushing to-and-fro of the palm leaves in the breeze, and staring up at the unfamiliar desert stars distorted by the plumes of smoke.

'Is there more good or more bad in the Myriads?' asked Timmi softly.

'Neither,' Kip replied. 'Most life is just life. Trying to survive, it's not good or bad.'

'But what about all the humans? And there must be lots of intelligent life forms other than us.'

'My dad told me that most people are good,' he said. 'That's what makes it so easy for the bad ones.'

'Like Thag,' said Timmi.

'Like Thag.'

'But what if you're not trying to be bad?' Timmi scraped at a stain on her shirt sleeve and Kip watched her for a while.

'Are you thinking about the Mindfield?'

She nodded and kept scratching at the stain.

What if it's called the Crazy Paving for a reason? thought Kip. *We have no idea what effect M-Waves might have on people. They could be Mad Waves, not Myriad Waves. What if she's right about the curse?*

He searched for some outward sign, something to show him Timmi had changed. But she just seemed a bit withdrawn and sad.

If the Crazy Paving's made her crazy, am I in some kind of danger?

He shoved away that thought. This girl, his friend, sitting next to him had saved his life – more than once – and no matter how hard things got, even if the Myriads were eating at their minds, he was going to see it through and get them home.

'Hey, look at Pinky!' said Timmi.

The exhausted flying squirrel was asleep between them, in a dip of the sand. Her limbs twitched, and her paws curled and twitched again, before she flattened herself out, spreading her arms and legs.

'She's sleep-flying,' Kip murmured.

They watched her for a while, as she nibbled comically at some imagined squirrelish delight.

'Kip,' said Timmi. 'What if...'

Somehow, he knew what she was going to say next.

'…what if they're trying to reach us, through the Dreambomber!'

Forgetting their hunger and their worries, they lay back on the soft sand. It had been a long time since they had rested for more than a couple of hours. The air rocked with the crisscross chitchat of scattered cicadas, and Kip was asleep before you could say "ziggurat".

After a few blank moments, he was flying high above terrain full of rock pools, feeling the wind on his face. When he swooped in a bit closer, he saw that each pool contained an entire civilisation. A bird flapped up leisurely to join him.

'Kep, kep!' the bird cried.

Kip looked over. Were they ribbons in its feathers? Another bird pulled up alongside, and two more.

'Kep, kep!' they all cried.

Kip frowned. The birds' faces weren't exactly human but they were familiar.

'Do I know you?' he asked.

'Kip!' said the ribbon bird.

'Follow us!' said a bird with a tufty bun on its head.

Intrigued, Kip followed the birds to land beside one of the rock pools. They flapped their wings and span about, and one by one disappeared, leaving him alone at the poolside. Attached to the rock were two green shoots, one with a black starburst flower and one with indigo eyespots. The shoots waggled root-like fingers and began to grow at a bewildering speed.

'I think it's worked!' the starburst plant said.

It was nearly as tall as Kip now and he stepped back in alarm as it leapt out of the water.

'Is it them?' asked the eyespot plant, clambering out afterwards. 'Are they OK?'

'Kip, can you hear us?' said the first dream plant.

And without having to ask, Kip knew it was Albert and he gave his dream-plant-best-friend an almighty hug. Everything started spinning and Albert grabbed Kip's arms.

'Careful,' he said. 'Don't want to bust up the dream just as we've found you!'

'It's taken us ages,' said the second plant, looking a lot more like Leela now. 'So much has happened ... but where's Timmi?'

She was sitting by one of the rock pools, playing with an aquatic Pinky, who was flapping through the water doing her best furry manta ray impersonation.

'Timmi!' they all yelled.

In a daze, she looked up.

'Timmi, it's us,' said Kip. 'You were right, Albert and Leela came to find us in the Dreambomber.'

They sat down in a circle and the rock pools faded away into the background.

'We've got so much to tell you,' Kip said.

'Us too,' said Albert. 'But you start.'

There had been so many worlds, so many marvels. Before Kip could find the words for his racing thoughts, Timmi spoke.

'We met Eartha Quicksmith.'

'No way!' said Leela.

'For real?' said Albert at the same time.

'Real. And way,' said Kip. 'She's in a Myriad where the Universe is dreaming her backwards, where she's really slowly getting younger…'

'WHAT?' said Albert. 'You are NOT allowed to have Timeyarn adventures without me! I'm freaking out here.'

'We all knew you'd say that,' Kip laughed.

'Did you at least get me a Timeyarn takeaway?'

'Better,' said Kip. 'We've got Eartha's best android, Incognita.'

'Hmph,' said Albert. 'I suppose that's pretty cool.'

'Wait 'til you meet her,' said Timmi. 'So when we were at Eartha's house, she gave us a book of poetry with clues in it to help us find the Futurescope. And, get this: she wanted everyone to think that she burned all her inventions. But she hid them in the Myriads.'

'No-no way-way!' said Leela.

'Way-way,' said Kip.

'So is the Futurescope the invention she saw ending the world?' Leela asked.

Kip had to think for a second.

'She didn't say.'

'You would not believe the things we've seen,' Timmi continued, 'most of the Myriads basically tried to kill us or eat us. I was poisoned, and Kip nearly got crushed to death by a shapeshifter-dragony-thing.'

'We saw a Prowler too,' said Kip. 'At Eartha's house, but she told us to run or we'd all die.'

Turtles bobbed their heads out of a rock pool. They were wearing shower caps.

'Then we got captured by a Thag army…' said Timmi.

'A *what*?' said Albert.

'A Thag Grittleshank army. Different Thags from different Myriads. And our Thag from Quicksmiths was their leader.'

'If he's in the Myriads,' said Leela, 'it must mean he has the second key.'

'That's Very Not Good,' Albert said. 'Very Not Good At All.'

'Agreed,' said Leela. 'So you were captured by the Thag army, and you escaped?'

'Incognita saved us,' said Timmi. 'She's here right now while we're asleep, looking for food.'

'I'm glad she's looking after you,' said Leela.

'Me too,' said Timmi. 'Well, I think that's everything.' She looked at Kip, who shook his head. 'Yup, we're done. Your turn.'

'Well,' said Leela, 'everything went pear-shaped at Quicksmiths…'

'Hole-shaped,' interrupted Albert.

'Everything went all-over-the-place shaped, and we got evacuated from the college. Miss Twiss is there with Tamara Okpik trying to get you back. Professor Koriolis sabotaged the Dreambomber but we don't know why yet.'

'We saw footprints on the jetty, after you disappeared,' Albert continued.

'So was that Thag?' asked Kip, a little confused.

'But how did he get into Quicksmiths?' said Timmi. 'GENI would never let him back.'

'Leave it with us,' said Leela. 'We'll try and find out more. Albert already worked out that there's a Timeloop at the boathouse. It's covering up the area around the Crazy Paving, so we can't see everything that's going on. GENI hasn't been able to undo it yet…'

'But why did you get evacuated?' asked Kip.

'The Timeloop's interfering with all the Myriad Waves,' said Albert. 'And these weird holes started appearing around the college, which are letting the Myriads leak into our world…'

'We found a giant hole in the Mill Room – the Mothership Hole. While we were watching, an arm came out, a long spindly arm.'

'We think it was a Prowler. And Iris has gone missing – Bagsworth is looking for her.'

'Did the Prowler take her?' Kip asked, afraid of the answer.

'That's just one more thing we don't know for sure,' said Albert.

'There's a lot we don't know,' concluded Leela with a sigh.

Hearing everything described out loud was like listening to an adventure boast-off, but it had all really happened and suddenly things felt overwhelming. A Thag-faced flying fish jumped out of a rock pool. Kip flinched and felt the dream beginning to shift.

'Kip's spinning out,' said Leela.

His friends' faces started to blur and the rock pools spilled out all their contents until Kip was swimming and spinning, spinning and swimming, losing control.

'Kip,' said Albert's voice. 'Remember Deep Thinking. Remember being in the moment, like Professor Mo taught us.'

Kip thought about taking a full breath deep down into his stomach, even though he didn't need to breathe in the dream, and things started to settle.

'Just think of us, where we're sitting by the rock pools. I'm holding out my hand.'

Kip reached out and Albert's hand took his and pulled him back into the dream.

'Thanks, Albert,' he said once he was firmly back in the circle. 'I thought you were really rubbish at Deep Thinking?'

'Leela taught me some cheat moves,' Albert said. 'And I was a *very* annoying student. Look, before anyone spins out again, what's our plan to get you both back?'

'We can't yet,' said Kip. 'We promised Eartha we'd find the Futurescope. Once we have that, we need to work out the password for the Silent Key to come home.'

'So that's what the letter wheels are for!' said Albert.

'Yes, and one of Eartha's poems will help us figure it out,' Timmi said.

'I heart poems!' said Leela. 'Can we help?'

'Just be here when we need you,' said Kip.

'But how will you know when we're asleep?' Timmi asked.

'We're taking shifts,' said Leela, 'so one of us will always be looking out for you. The others are helping too – Badger and Maya, and Penny and Em. Just think of this place when you go to sleep and we'll meet you here, when you're ready.'

Chapter Nineteen

The Black Temple

A hand shook Kip's shoulder. He raised himself up quickly on one elbow. It was still dark, but he felt rested and wondered if the nights were extra-long in this Myriad.

'They found us!' he said, sitting up fully. 'Albert and Leela.'

As Timmi moved, moonlight flashed briefly off the seahorse charm on her bracelet.

'I think I've figured out the eleventh poem.'

She held out Eartha's book of verse.

'How?'

'I woke up, and everything felt quixary after the dream, and my brain was churning things over, and when I read the poem again, it just seemed to click.'

Kip blinked. Incognita was sitting with her back against a palm tree, where she'd kept guard as they'd slept. The toothed sphere in her chest whirred softly in a mechanical sigh.

'What time is it?'

'Time to do what we came here for,' said Timmi.

'We'll take Pinky too,' said Kip.

But Pinky refused to leave and squeaked grouchily, digging into the sand when Kip tried to pick her up.

'Fine,' he said. 'You stay here and sleep off your Crazy Paving jet lag. Stay! We'll be back soon.'

A few handfuls of nuts and dates and a short Skimmi ride later, and they were standing on the roof of the shrine at the very top of the ziggurat. The unfamiliar constellations faded star by star as the sky turned its face away from night.

'Are you watching, Incognita?' said Timmi.

'I am,' the android replied. 'As soon as I think it's time, I'll tell you.'

Timmi sat down at the brink of the temple's roof and swung her legs.

'So, are you going to explain everything?' asked Kip, sitting down next to her.

She opened the book, turned to the eleventh poem, and held a finger to the text.

'There's a golden temple and a black temple, right?'

'Right.'

'And we haven't found the black temple?'

'Right.'

'But it's not missing.' She tapped the page with her finger. 'We weren't looking at the right time.'

Kip scanned down to the bottom of the page and read the last verse.

When in the east the sun aligned,
The black shrine's highest height they climbed
And looked down at their feet to find
A treasure rare and bright.

'The sun rises in the east. At least, it does in our Myriad. Does it align with something in the ziggurat? A window at the top?'

'No,' said Timmi. 'We haven't actually climbed the temple yet.'

Kip looked around in exasperation.

'Of course we have! Stop being so mysterious!'

'Now!' said Incognita, peering intensely down at the plaza far below.

At the foot of the ziggurat, six giant storeys down, the first fingers of dawn light were trailing through dark pools, and shadows were beginning to form beneath the canopies of the hanging gardens. Timmi pulled down the brim of her cap and stepped aboard the Skimmi.

'Coming? We're going to climb the black temple.'

Hungering for an answer, Kip jumped on behind Timmi and Incognita followed, the Skimmi widening to accommodate them all. Following directions from the android, Timmi headed for a treeless section of the water garden, where they landed on a bare island in the centre of a lotus pool.

'There you go!' she said.

Expecting a big reveal, Kip saw only an unexciting patch of earth.

'The black temple is the shadow of the golden ziggurat,' Timmi explained. 'Its twin. Right now, when the shadow's at its longest, when it first appears and the sun is low, we're at its "highest height".'

As the early morning sun inched higher in the sky, Kip watched the tip of the ziggurat's shadow gradually shrink away from the patch of earth, retreating a few centimetres across the surface of the island. He'd never really watched a shadow before and wondered if they always moved this fast.

'Antimony Brown,' he said. 'You are the Riddliest Riddler in all the Myriads.'

Incognita had begun to dig with a shovel attachment on her arm. They stood by, hardly able to endure the itching suspense, until there was a clunk as the spade hit something hard.

'Is that it?' squeaked Timmi, dancing around the discarded piles of sandy soil.

After a bit more digging, Incognita hauled something up. But the Aeon Light radiating from the unearthed object was so brilliant that Kip couldn't look at it.

'What is it?' he asked.

'Can't you see?' said Timmi.

'Squirls,' he said, shading his eyes, although that didn't help at all. 'They're too bright.'

'It's an old metal box.'

There was a creak as the lid lifted and Timmi held up the contents. After a few seconds, the squirls ebbed away just enough for Kip to look at the artefact that fitted neatly in her hand: a collapsible brass telescope.

'This is it then?' Timmi murmured. 'The Futurescope.'

She handed it to Kip and as he took it, his hand dropped with the weight of it.

'Why is it so heavy?' he asked.

Incognita tapped the side of the telescope.

'When Eartha homunculised her inventions – made them smaller – she translated mass into Strange Energy, which meant the weight could be reduced accordingly.'

'Like the Gravity Bracelet,' murmured Timmi.

'Precisely. But the Futurescope is special, and it could not be completely disguised.'

It was hard to coax the telescopic tubes out, but eventually Kip succeeded in extending them fully. As he held it up to his eye, he noticed that there were corkscrew marks in the wood, as if an attachment were missing, but that didn't stop him looking through. The Futurescope magnified the world a touch, but little else.

'How does it work?' he wondered aloud.

'Wait, there's something else in the box,' said Timmi.

She handed him something that felt like a small, chipped stone, and Kip had to squint through bright squirls again. It was a piece of quartz, pale blue with an amber wave just to the left of centre. In amazement, he forgot about the Futurescope.

'What does it mean?' breathed Timmi.

Kip was just as baffled. He pulled at the cord around his neck to lift out the forked pale-blue icicle pendant that was always tucked under his T-shirt. It was almost identical to the crystal they had just unearthed.

'My mum gave me this. But the second piece must be from Eartha if it's in here…'

He held up the blue-and-amber quartz from the box.

'Do you recognise it, Incognita?' he asked.

'I have never seen it before,' she replied. 'But Eartha told me you had one like it.'

However much they questioned Incognita, it seemed she knew no more than this. Kip tried looking at the two pieces of quartz through the Futurescope, but nothing happened. When he inspected them more closely, he saw that the edges fitted each other perfectly. They merged with a satisfying clink to form one single piece, like two long-lost lodestones brought together again by some strange force. He took one last look and slipped the newly combined pendant under the neck of his T-shirt.

'Shall I take the Futurescope?' said Incognita. 'For safekeeping.'

She flipped open her wrist and placed the brass telescope inside before closing the hinge.

'I've been meaning to ask how you have space for all those hand tools,' Kip said. 'And now it turns out you have room for a Futurescope as well!'

'Space isn't always what it seems,' said Incognita mysteriously. 'You should know that by now, Kip.'

Ozymandias

While they'd been talking, a fly had landed on the upturned lid of the now empty box and was rubbing its legs. Timmi rolled her eyes and laughed.

'Pinky's going to get jealous of all these pet flies you know.'

It crawled around boldly. Kip knew it wasn't the scarab beetle, couldn't possibly be, but even so, he had to shake off the bad feeling that came with that reminder as he batted the fly away.

'It's time to go,' he said. 'Let's find the Crazy Paving.'

Kip took the Silent Key out of his pocket and they flew low over the gardens, looking for the lights that signified departures.

'There!' shouted Timmi. 'I saw something, under those trees.'

Incognita landed the Skimmi on a clay path dotted with desert rose petals. The sound of nearby fountains grew louder, burbling comfortingly. Following the shivers of light, they came to a large pond surrounded by date palms. At its centre, on a sandy island, was another of the giant stone heads.

The surface of the pond was completely covered in water-lily pads and, as the Silent Key came close, the outlines of the lily pads began to glow brighter. Two jewelled dragonflies skittered above the rich green quilt, in which each shape was embroidered with celestial gold.

'There it is,' said Kip.

Although he was expecting to feel relieved, there was instead a thin trickle of sadness that the adventure was coming to an end.

'We should return to camp for Pinky and the rest of our things,' said Incognita. 'And then all that remains is for you to find your way back to Quicksmiths.'

'Time to read the twelfth poem,' said Timmi.

She flicked through the pages, and gave a murmur of surprise.

'Oh!' she said. 'How did I miss this? The eleventh poem: it's not finished.'

His heart picking up a beat, Kip looked over her

shoulder to see some extra verses at the top of the next page. But as he read them silently, the sweet feeling of elation turned sour.

They thought their journey's end was nigh,
But watching was an evil eye,
For in pursuit there was a spy:
A creeping enemy.

The desert guardians stood near –
They'd thirsted for four hundred years;
One hope could wake them with its tears:
The charger of the sea.

Kip looked up from the page sharply. Nothing had changed; everything was calm. But before they could begin to decipher the poem, Incognita let out a rusty howl of alarm. Timmi held one hand over her mouth in horror as a creature stepped between them and the Skimmi. Kip's eyes refused to accept what they saw at first, until he realised he was not going to be able to blink it away.

A horrifying swarm of centipedes writhed together, creating a form of human size and shape. Within its rough face were two eyes, two black masses of crawling flies.

'The poem!' Incognita screeched.

A black wave of centipedes surged up against Eartha's android with startling speed, pushing her backwards forcefully and slamming her into a tree trunk. Incognita was shaken but managed nonetheless to plunge her arm deep into the centre of the centipedes. The swarm stopped as if locked in place, and Kip thought for a moment that they might be saved. But as Incognita thrust her arm further in, a small grey crustacean – shaped like a shrunken trilobite – was carried aloft by the centipedes, and wriggled up to her shoulder. Kip's cry of warning rang out too late: the squirming thing was already worming around the glass pane in her chest.

'Incognita!' he yelled.

Her free arm twitched, and then a leg. She shook her head over one shoulder as if trying to dislodge something from her ear and then looked at Kip in confusion, eyes clouded. With an unintelligible noise, she marched away clumsily.

The poem, thought Kip. *There must be something in the poem to help us.*

But all he could remember in his fear and confusion was the last line.

The charger of the sea.

It didn't make sense. They didn't have phones on them, and an old temple surely wouldn't have electricity. For a second Kip wished bitterly that Eartha had told them plainly what they should do, instead of speaking in riddles. But the poems were their secret language – a necessary way of keeping her master plan out of the wrong hands.

'No!' shouted Timmi. 'No, no, NO!'

The centipedes were flowing towards her now and she shrank back against a tree, dropping the book.

'Over here!' Kip yelled, waving his arms, trying to buy some time. 'I have the Silent Key!'

The whirling human form turned and a thick tentacle of centipedes reached out towards him. With no idea what else to do, Kip tried lunging into the swarm like Incognita had done, but the centipedes just crawled repellently over his skin. The horror of it stirred something in his mind, some deep activation of survival mode. A distant recollection, the scrap of a lesson at his old school, broke the dark surface of his unconscious mind, and he knew instantly what the last line of the poem meant.

"Charger" is an old word for horse.

Hadn't Eartha looked at a charm on Timmi's invention? Hadn't she said something, all those Myriads ago?

'Timmi,' he yelled. 'The bracelet! Use the seahorse!'

By now the tentacle was fully wrapped around him and his struggle with the centipedes took all his might. Another tentacle reached out for Timmi, but not before she'd twisted the seahorse charm of the Gravity Bracelet.

In response to its silvery heartbeat, a mist of water

rose up from the lily pond and rippled in the air for a few moments. Then there was an angry yelp from Timmi as the centipedes ripped the bracelet from her hand, and a fine spray of droplets spattered down around the Crazy Paving and on the stone head.

Kip waited for a miracle to happen; but it didn't come.

'I see you've met Ozymandias,' said a voice Kip recognised only too well.

Alpha Thag was walking down the path towards them. He was accompanied by a tall man with commanding eyes, who wore jeans, a white shirt and rimless glasses. His face was round and pale, like Thag's.

Thag's dad? thought Kip.

'Julius Grittleshank,' said the tall man, answering the question in Kip's eyes. 'Of the Grittleshank Collective.'

'Make this *thing* let us go!' snapped Timmi.

'That won't be possible I'm afraid,' said Julius. 'Not just yet. Ozymandias, take care not to hurt them too much. They're just children. And they're useful.'

The squirming flies that made up Ozymandias's eyes all turned and looked at Kip as one.

'Yes, Julius,' said a voice that came from deep within the swarm, and the tentacle holding Kip relaxed slightly.

'You sound like GENI, only evil,' Timmi gasped.

'That's because Ozymandias is a Strange Supercomputer,' said Thag. 'And a million times better than that she-gargoyle you have at Quicksmiths...'

'You two have handled the Myriads with style,' Julius cut him off. 'Perhaps we could offer you a place...'

Julius stopped when he saw Kip's hate-filled glare. 'Well, no. Perhaps not.'

'What have you done to Incognita?' said Kip.

'It's just a Leadfish,' said Julius. 'We'll recover your servant later. I look forward to taking it apart and seeing what makes it tick...'

We can't let that happen, thought Kip.

At that moment, a feeling slithered along his spine, and he knew it wasn't anything to do with the centipedes, or Julius, or even Thag. It was something else, something even worse, coming this way.

'She's hardly a threat to us though,' said another voice.

Oh, please no...

Thag and Julius Grittleshank stepped aside to let someone else down the path. This familiar stranger walked with a cane and suffered from an affliction that divided him almost exactly down the centre. The right half of his face was youthful, with a healthy crop of strawberry-blond hair. The other half was gaunt and wizened.

Kip's horrified stare was met by an uneven gaze –

one brilliant blue eye and one glazed cataract. He hadn't seen Gorvak since the day of the accident and he felt a headrush of hot anger followed by guilt and more anger.

It wasn't your fault, he said to himself. *Gorvak tried to grab the Grandfather Clock. Gorvak did this to himself, and he could have easily done just the same to you.*

'Why are you here?' said Timmi, her words only just audible. 'I thought you hated Thag.'

The Grittleshanks and Ozymandias all seemed to find that amusing. Gorvak looked at Thag and grinned. He grinned back, greasily.

'Oh, you know. Family's family,' Gorvak said.

'*Family*?' said Kip.

'You'll be delighted to hear that I'm not just a descendent of Eartha, but also of Sir Solomon Grittleshank. That's right, they had a lovely little secret baby who was my fourteenth great-grandfather.'

'You two were working together all along, to find the Ark?'

'Not exactly,' said Thag, punching Gorvak a little too hard on the arm.

'Call it a friendly rivalry,' Gorvak replied with a wan smile that instantly faded. He gave Thag a snide look and faced Julius.

'We shouldn't make the mistake that Thag made when he had them before. Everything gets taken.'

Julius nodded and Ozymandias's centipede limbs

seized the book and the Silent Key. When the tentacle tugged at the cord around Kip's neck, and tried to take the quartz his mum had given him and the second piece he'd just found, Kip tugged back. He held on so tight that the circulation seemed to stop in his fingers. In the end, Ozymandias prised it away anyway.

Before Kip could say anything he felt someone speak behind him, so close that the breath tickled his neck.

'Hello partner.'

'Iris?' croaked Timmi in disbelief.

'Iris Grittleshank, reporting in,' she announced, looking at Julius.

'Daughter dear, you're a credit to the family,' he replied, lips drawing upwards in a thin smile.

'You're not a new student at Quicksmiths,' Kip said, his words catching up with his thoughts. 'You're not a student at all.'

'Clap. Clap. Clap,' said Iris.

The feeling of being played was horrible. Now Kip was really looking he saw that Iris's smile was very similar to Thag's – too wide, splitting her face.

'I promised myself I'd never get conned again,' he said, furiously. 'I thought I knew better.'

'Someone who thinks they can't be conned is the perfect mark,' said Iris.

She handed two books to Julius.

'I got them. It was really easy once they called the evacuation, just like Mother said.'

Kip recognised the tattered cover of one of them. It was his Book of Squirls and, along with it, Eartha's Book of Aeon Light.

Julius gave Iris a pat on the back and she beamed with pride and took a glowing glass button from her pocket.

'How did you get that?' spluttered Kip.

'The Ark of Ideas told me,' Gorvak boasted, stealing Iris's answer away. 'It was disguised as a key of the Memoria Technica. Just like the one you found later.'

'You stole it!' Timmi said, hardly able to get the words out past her anger.

'Stealing is a strong word,' said Gorvak. 'And that would make you thieves too. I just took advantage of being the first in the study.'

'Shame you didn't take both of them,' said Thag smugly. 'Then we wouldn't have had all this mess.'

'The Ark didn't tell me there were two,' retorted Gorvak coolly. 'Although you could've always taken it yourself if you hadn't managed to get kicked out of Quicksmiths.'

'How can a whole army use one Silent Key?' said Timmi. 'Do you all hold hands? And how did you get all these people through the Crazy Paving without anyone seeing?'

Kip watched Iris sidle up to Timmi and pinch her hard without Julius seeing.

'We're not stupid,' she said. 'We don't tell just anyone our secrets.'

'While you were enjoying your holiday, Kip, we've been on a little scavenger hunt,' Gorvak boasted some more. That mangy black parrot told me where all of the old girl's inventions were hidden, and *I* remember everything I hear – an audiophonic memory can be quite useful at times. Eartha's not that clever if she made a record of everything and left it lying around for us to find.'

'Mr Grittleshank, did you make the Timeloop?' said Kip to Julius. 'It's tearing the Myriads and they're leaking into Quicksmiths. You still have time to undo it before the whole college breaks apart.'

'I can't authorise that,' said Julius. 'Adelaide Twiss has been interfering with our affairs too much of late. Now she's expelled Pythagoras, things would get much easier for me if Quicksmiths were to shut down. Now, enough playing catch-up, children. We need to finish searching the compound and get out of this godforsaken place. Thag, Iris, come with me. Gorvak, Ozymandias, keep an eye on our guests.'

'Oh, gladly,' said Gorvak.

Casually, he raised an aged left arm to sweep away the thin powder-white hair that had fallen over the withered side of his forehead and glared at Kip while

Julius led Iris and a reluctant Thag away from the lily pond. Gorvak looked down at the wrinkled claw of his left hand meaningfully, and then back up at his prisoner.

'I think we have a score to settle, you and I.'

'Leave him alone,' Timmi cried out.

'Ozymandias has been working on an antidote for me. We're not quite there yet, but the research has thrown up some interesting things.'

Gorvak trailed the fingers of his good hand in a nearby fountain. He seemed to take great delight in turning his teenage side away to reveal the wizened half of his face more fully.

'You see, we've been able to build a machine very similar to Eartha's Grandfather Clock. It's bigger though. Big enough for a whole person to fit inside.'

He turned back and flicked his fingers in Kip's face.

'Once we get you back to HQ, I'm going to lower you in very slowly, feet first. It's going to hurt a lot. So much more than this.' He gestured coldly to the haggard left side of this body.

The threats weren't idle. It was clear in those chilling eyes that Gorvak meant every word. And Kip knew that however he might try to reason, it would only make things worse. He felt more lost than he'd ever been in any of the Myriads.

But then he noticed a small and subtle movement in the background. Behind Gorvak, the stone guardian was stirring. Just as the final verse of the eleventh poem had promised, it was awakening, some unseen mechanism activated by the stray water drops falling on its dusty brow. Its eyelids slowly lifted, and its mouth opened silently.

Timmi, you legend! Kip thought.

'This is all a dream, isn't it?' he said, keeping his voice level. 'Sooner or later, it will end.'

'And what then?' replied Gorvak lazily. 'Do you really think our Myriad is special? What if it isn't? What happens if the Universe wakes up before you do? Where do you go when the dream ends?'

Battle of the Ziggurat

There was a muted shout and Gorvak turned his face in its direction. At exactly that moment, a flaming arrow flew out of the stone head's mouth and grazed his ear. The awakened guardian began to hum with energy and its eyes crackled. Gorvak whirled around, his expression unreadable, his eyes both fierce and blank. He took a step towards his prisoners but, realising he was in danger, he thought better of it, and hobbled away into a thick knot of trees.

Kip shouted at Timmi to get down as the great stone head swivelled and two rays of energy streamed from its eyes. But the rays passed straight through them, and only seemed to affect the centipedes, making them hiss and writhe. Ozymandias scattered, letting go of his hostages and the stolen items, and reformed himself in a tight coil around the mighty guardian.

'This way!' hissed Kip.

'Wait!' Timmi said.

She knelt down and snatched up the book of poetry and the bracelet, throwing Kip's pendant forward to him. Her hand hovered above the Silent Key and she gave Kip a look so anguished he was beside her in moments, grabbing it on the run.

Once they were out of the lily pond grove, they could see the immense Thag army had converged on the ziggurat and a battle was now raging in full force around them. All through the gardens the stone heads had awakened. Their eyes blazed, slicing through the legion of pirates, and volleys of arrows flew relentlessly from their open mouths. The air churned and sizzled with Strange Energy. Jets of Skycrackle flickered out from pirate cannons, burning everything they touched in a deadly rainbow of superheated plasma, and sending huge chunks of stone hurtling through the air.

Kip's stomach went cold inside, as if someone had poured in iced water.

It's just Skycrackle, he thought. *It's just Skycrackle*.

Even though he knew the Strange Energy plasma wasn't the same as lightning, it still awakened an old fear. He'd thought, he'd hoped, all that was behind him. But the fear was too deep, too primal, and he was out in the open here, vulnerable, just like that time long ago when his mum had been struck down.

Kip stayed frozen on the spot, the Skycrackle reflecting all around him, until Timmi pulled at his arm, dragging him down into a dry canal beside a row of lush ferns. From here, they watched for a while in silence, as the Thags and the stone guardians struggled for supremacy. Alpha Thag was easy to spot, as he uprooted handfuls of almond trees and tore them in half with his Slipstream Gloves, sending showers of soil flying. Gorvak and the other Grittleshanks were nowhere to be seen.

'Pssst,' said Timmi. 'There's Incognita.'

The android didn't hear them call or see them beckoning and stayed walking clumsily on the spot.

'They've broken her,' Kip said angrily. 'They break everything.'

'We have to help her!' begged Timmi. 'And she has the Futurescope too.'

They didn't get very far through the fierce fighting and quickly retreated to the canal. Twice more they tried to breach the battle to reach Incognita, and twice they were forced back, until they had to accept it was too dangerous to do anything but hide.

Many horrible hours passed, and the sun crawled painstakingly through an inflamed sky. Although it was hard to work out exactly who was winning, eventually it began to look as if the stone heads might be gaining an advantage.

'Look!' said Timmi, pointing out the Grittleshanks, who seemed to be fighting their way back towards the Crazy Paving.

'Where are the children?' Kip heard Julius shout. 'We can't leave them here.'

His glasses had been bent and his shirt torn. Looking around methodically, he surveyed the gardens around Incognita and then by an unfortunate stroke of unluck, looked straight through the ferns and directly at Kip.

'Follow your sister,' he barked at Thag, and darted out across the devastated greenery.

'We can't stay here!' hissed Timmi.

Are we safer with him or in a combat zone?

But there was no time for further thought. Timmi had begun to run away in a low crouch along the dry canal, and Kip stumbled after her. Catching his breath, he paused and risked sticking his head up for a quick look. Timmi stopped beside him and together they watched, too stunned to speak. Two arrows had pierced Julius Grittleshank's chest, and he had sunk to his knees. His eyes locked on to Kip's for the briefest of moments before another shower of arrows thudded around him and Julius fell forward lifeless on his face.

Alpha Thag was already sprinting across the battlefield, skidding to his knees beside his father's body. His roar of grief and anger was unbearable and Kip wanted to look away but had to keep watching. Close behind, Gorvak calmly checked Julius's pulse, while he rifled through the dead man's jacket.

Over the noise of the Skycrackle and the cries of war, Thag's howled words sought Kip out.

'I'll rip you apart, Bramley! You did this to my dad. My DAD!'

Guessing at his father's intended destination, Thag's eyes swept wildly across the scene and quickly spotted Kip looking over the lip of the canal. His black-gloved hand reached out and, despite the distance between them, Kip felt himself rising into the air. Slipstream shimmered and wrinkled around him, and a turbulent force wrenched his arms until it felt like they were going to snap. Just as Kip was on the verge of passing out, an arrow struck Thag, knocking him backwards into Gorvak. The Slipstream dropped away, Kip crashed back heavily to the ground, and everything blurred…

'Kip!'

His eyes opened. How long had he been out? A minute? An hour? Flaming arrows still rained down on the gardens. Thag was gone, and so was Gorvak. It was Timmi calling from behind a block of blackened granite. She was standing on Kip's Skimmi. Her long hair had been almost completely burned away – perhaps from a stray spark, there was no time to ask. All that was left behind was a short layer that stuck up like the soft fibres of a shaving brush. Pinky's whiskers poked out from her cupped hands and the little flying squirrel squeaked joyfully as Kip staggered over.

'Hang on,' said Timmi. 'We're getting out of here.'

The Skimmi blasted up from the battle zone, hovered for a moment, and sped out at a right angle over the dunes.

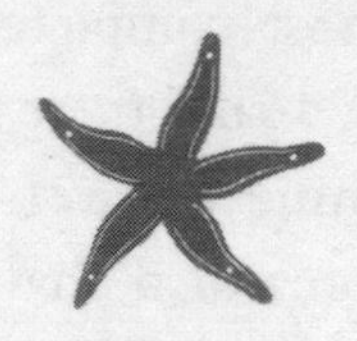

Chapter Twenty

The Twelfth Poem

Desert winds brought only silence over the sandscape, and carried only whispers onwards.

'How will we know when it's safe to go back?' Timmi murmured.

They were huddled out of sight, under a rocky overhang. Sensing the severity of the situation, Pinky stayed quiet, hugging Kip's finger and not asking for food or water even though she must have been ravenous. The three of them peered out through a screen of thorny trees. It was a reasonably good hiding place, at least.

Kip took the Silent Key out of his pocket and gave it a long look.

'Whatever happens, we still need to find out the password,' he muttered.

'Eartha said we'd know what it is when we need it,' Timmi replied.

She waited for Kip to put the key away again, before shifting closer with the book, which now had singe marks on its cover. Together, they turned to the twelfth poem.

After the Battle

From boiling pond and burning tree
The weary travellers did flee;
Uneasily they read the poem
And sought the road to lead them home.

Four minds, four hearts, four friends grew near
All dreamed as one to face one fear;
At last they knew, when all is done
A shared dream is a stronger one.

Refreshed, the sleepers did awake
And stood beside the lily lake;
Each friend began to solve the test
That held the answer to their quest.

As they had dreamed, so they conferred
Together to make up the word,
And solve the final mystery:
The secret of the Silent Key.

'See!' said Timmi. 'That last verse must be about the password.'

'A shared dream?' said Kip. 'Sounds like we're going to need Albert and Leela.'

'They said they'd take shifts at sleeping, didn't they? So, we should find them straight away.'

At Timmi's suggestion, they stared at the poem together for a few minutes, memorising it as best as they could, and then rested their heads back on the sand. The desert held them softly, calming their still-racing hearts and hushing away the fierce world with warm breezes.

'Don't forget your Deep Thinking,' Timmi whispered.

Kip drifted in half-wakefulness for a while, until he fell asleep properly and found himself standing in a familiar place – full of rock pools. Timmi, Albert and Leela were already sat cross-legged, waiting for him to join the circle.

'Timmi told us everything,' said Albert.

'I think we should all focus on the Silent Key,' said Leela. 'Let's deepthink it here in the dream. With all of us together, we should be able to figure out what to do.'

Everyone stared at the empty space in the middle of the circle: Leela looking vaguely lost, Albert with knitted brows, Timmi with eyes half open.

'I can see it!' said Kip softly, not breaking his concentration.

The glass button materialised weakly and dissolved. They tried again, but the same thing happened.

'There's something else,' said Albert. 'In the background.'

Kip saw the shape of it wavering in the air and recognised it at once.

'It's the VR headset,' he said. 'From the art gallery.'

Timmi looked away fearfully.

'Timmi,' he said gently. 'You have to think of the key with the rest of us or it won't work.'

'I'm trying,' she sobbed, 'but that horrible thought keeps coming back.'

'What's wrong?' asked Leela, patting Timmi's knee.

'Timmi had a bad experience in one of the Myriads,' Kip explained. 'We looked in a VR headset and something called the Mindfield showed us things we're scared of. It shook us both up, and it's stayed inside Timmi's head.'

'I'm cursed,' she mumbled. 'If I touch the key something bad happens.'

Kip looked around the circle, trying to work out how they could get past this.

'Would it help if I looked at the Mindfield as well?' offered Albert. 'I warn you though, it won't be pretty. I'm actually terrified of clowns.'

Timmi bit back tears and smiled.

'I'm serious!'

'I'll look too,' said Leela. 'For the record, I'm scared of being lonely.'

'Lightning,' said Kip. 'And not getting my mum back.'

'But it's unbearable,' said Timmi. 'No one should look.'

‘I say we think it here right now and we’ll all have a go,’ said Leela firmly. ‘Then you won’t be on your own.’

There was no point in arguing with her and they tried again, holding hands at her insistence. Kip thought back to the gallery, and the headset resting on the table. This time it appeared fully, solid, hanging in the space between them.

How to Face Your Fear

‘Who’s going first?’ said Leela.

‘Just a sec,’ said Kip. ‘There’s something about this in Eartha’s poem.’

He screwed up his eyes tight, trying to remember.

‘This is just a guess,’ he said, ‘but I think we should all look at the same time.’

‘How do we do that?’ said Timmi. ‘There’s only one headset.’

‘Let’s just dream up some more,’ Leela suggested.

It didn’t take long before three extra visors had materialised next to the first.

‘I can’t believe I’m saying this,’ said Kip, ‘but we’re about to go inside a virtual reality, inside our dream, inside the Universe’s dream.’

‘Head … exploding…’ said Albert.

Kip smiled encouragingly as he gave the word, and all four of them put on their visor at the same time. Observing the wavy lines rumple and reform, he had that strange feeling that only comes in dreams, of being all at once the audience, the director and the actor...

As if there had never been anything else, Kip felt his feet flying, thudding against the ground. It wasn't only him running, it was all of them. And something was following them, something bad.

Sometimes you just know things in dreams, and Kip knew this: all four of them were together in one person, with one shared set of feet, and one pair of eyes, and one body. The thoughts came as thick and fast and ragged as their breath, and it was hard to tell which thought was his and which was someone else's.

Don't slow down.
We have to get away!
The key, can't touch the key.
Don't think about the key.

Deep inside, Kip felt a sense of foreboding like a leech draining his ability to think clearly, drinking all his other thoughts dry and leaving him dark and afraid. He knew Leela was feeling this too, and Albert, all as one mind, all drowning in Timmi's fear.

They came to a door in the end of a gloomy corridor and their fingers closed around the handle. The door opened. They ran through. It slammed behind them.

Another door!
It's bolted.

Quick undo it, quick!
Go through, keep going!
Lock the door behind you!

Fingers fumbled and a single heart pounded with the fear of four souls.

Who are we running from?
They have the key.

There was an overwhelming urge – a dreadful magnetic attraction – to turn and grab the key. But pushing against that was a sense of impending disaster – repellent enough to keep their feet flying over the ground.

It's trying to make me take it. Can't touch the key. You'll all die.

The fear was absorbing them into itself. A sudden dream-knowledge came to Kip: the longer they ran, the harder it would be to stop, until they became trapped here, fleeing forever. With a supreme effort, he tried to come to a standstill, but their feet still struck the floor relentlessly.

We have to stop. What did Eartha say? When we look through each other's eyes, only then we can trust each other. Trust me.

Kip tried to break the run again, and this time with

Albert and Leela's help he felt their feet beneath him slowing, slowing, easing to a stop. Behind them, the following footsteps came to a halt too.

We have to turn around.
No!
We're all together, we'll be OK.
But what if I'm right?
Eartha told you about a trick of the mind – I think she meant this.
We'll look after each other, I promise.

Kip was already turning around, and Albert and Leela were helping him, and Timmi had no choice but to turn with them. Through one set of dream eyes, four friends faced Timmi's tormentor.

But, but it's me. How can I be chasing myself?

A ghoulish Timmi stood before them, twice the size of their friend, snarling like a wild animal. Her hair snaked wildly – long hair from before the battle – and her eyes bulged. She sidled towards them and held out a hand. In it the Silent Key glowed.

NO!

Kip resisted the urge they all felt to turn and run again. Albert and Leela joined in and their feet stayed firm. With certainty now, Kip knew what they had to do, and the others began to understand too.

Timmi, don't you see?
We have to face your fear.
It's in the poem.
You're kind to all of us, now it's time to be kind to yourself.

Together they forced their hand forward, reaching out towards the ghoulish Timmi. She growled and snapped and brandished the key at them. One in four made them take a step back, but three in four stepped forward again. Ghoul-Timmi whimpered and her eyes began to look more human.

Kip's arms were wrapping around the ghoul, but it wasn't just his arms, it was Leela's and Albert's too. And Timmi herself. Ghoul-Timmi sighed blissfully – shrinking down in size and looking more like real Timmi by the second – and held out the key again, this time as a peace offering.

Four friends held their breath as one hand closed around the Silent Key. Time seemed to stop. Then Ghoul-Timmi was gone as if she had never been.

Kip took off the VR headset, and so did the others. They all shared a long, incredulous stare, and it sunk in that they were back in their own dream bodies.

'That felt real enough for me,' said Albert. 'Can we do the clowns another time?'

'It was, and we should,' said Leela. 'By the way, I think we all did a pretty good job in there. And, do you know what? It's made me realise something: superhero pants are just ordinary pants on the outside.'

And then they were laughing and crying happy tears, and hugging each other, and agreeing how outstandingly weird that had been.

'You're not cursed at all!' said Albert. 'You took the key and nothing bad has happened.'

'It was all a trick of the mind,' said Kip. 'Just like Eartha told us.'

'Thank you,' said Timmi, the sadness melting from her jade-green eyes. 'Thank you.'

'We got you,' Leela replied. 'Always. Now we just need to work out the password for the Silent Key, so you can come home.'

'What else did the poem say?' Albert asked.

Kip screwed up his eyes and then remembered he was dreaming. All he had to do was think about the book – and sure enough it appeared in his hand, opened at the twelfth poem.

'The first two verses are about a dream – this dream I suppose,' said Kip. 'Looks like the last two are about waking up.'

Refreshed the sleepers did awake
And stood beside the lily lake;
Each friend began to solve the test
That held the answer to their quest.

As they had dreamed, so they conferred
Together to make up the word,
And solve the final mystery:
The secret of the Silent Key.

'How are we going to solve the test together *after* we've woken up,' said Albert. 'That's confusing.'

But his voice was already drifting further away, and the rock pools were spinning into nothingness.

A Word to the Wise

Kip's eyes flickered open and let the starry desert sky in.

We need to get to the Crazy Paving.

As if that wasn't going to be hard enough, they would have to find Incognita and the Futurescope as well, if the Grittleshanks hadn't stolen her away.

He sat up. The desert night was chilly, but it wasn't just the cold that made him shiver. A figure was standing beyond the natural screen of thorn trees, looking into their shelter, its eyes glistening in the darkness. To Kip's relief, a familiar voice spoke and sent his worries scuttling away into the sands.

'Timmi, I have brought an ointment for the burns on your face and neck – it will help to soothe the pain.'

Timmi jumped up and clasped Incognita tight, and Kip threw his arms around them both. The android's chainmail skin was icy and smooth but her rolling heart was warm, he knew. She stepped back an inch, and then patted their backs with stiff hands.

'We thought you were broken,' said Timmi. 'But we couldn't reach you through all the fighting.'

'The Grittleshanks' device stopped my Spherical Cog from working correctly, and I could not think,' she said. 'But my hand is separate from my core. It was able to remove the obstruction.'

'Are they all gone?' asked Timmi hesitantly. 'The Thags?'

'Yes,' said Incognita grimly. 'They have been driven away. It is safe to return to the ziggurat now.'

'And the Futurescope?' Kip almost didn't dare ask. 'Is it safe?'

Incognita unhinged her wrist and showed them the telescope, safely hidden away inside her forearm. Kip touched it with his fingertips. The brass was cold and real and he uttered a silent thanks.

'Do you now know the password to take us to Quicksmiths?' the android asked.

'You're coming too?' said Kip in surprise.

'I must see that you are returned safely.'

'We still haven't worked it out.' He turned to Timmi. 'The dream didn't end like I was expecting it to.'

'I know,' she said. 'It doesn't matter. I have an idea. Let's get after it.'

They all boarded the SkiMi and Incognita flew them back to the ziggurat, its once perfect steps now ragged and uneven. The pathways were littered with enormous lumps of stone that had fallen from the cracked guardians, and only a handful of the great heads remained intact.

'Did Eartha build this whole place?' Kip wondered aloud. 'Or did she just add the heads?'

'That I do not know,' said Incognita. 'Her plan for the Futurescope was put in place long before I was born.'

She set the Skimmi down in a trampled flowerbed near the water-lily pond. The almond groves all around had been almost completely flattened, leaving only spiny stumps of trunks rising up out of the dirt.

As they began to pick their way through the rubble towards the Crazy Paving, Pinky leapt from Kip's shoulder. She scratched at the edge of something pink among the clods of earth and broken stems.

'Hey, your baseball cap!' said Kip.

He bent to pick it up, dusted it off, and handed it to Timmi, with Pinky still clinging to the cap's peak. As the cap changed hands, Pinky scampered up Timmi's arm and nuzzled her ear. Timmi laughed and ran her fingers through her short, spiked hair, burned away in battle. There was something new about her, Kip thought, a quiet confidence just under the surface, as if her self-doubt had been scorched away too.

'Thanks, but nah,' she said. 'I don't need to hide under this anymore.'

In spite of the widespread devastation, the Crazy Paving pond had been kept safe by the stone guardian on its island. The leafy edges of the lily pads lit up as the Silent Key came close and Kip took it out of his pocket.

'Do you know the answer?' he asked, handing it to Timmi.

She smiled at him knowingly, hesitated, and then her fingers closed around the glass button.

'Let's look at the poem again.' She opened the book. 'First: it says here we have to make up the word together.'

'But a made-up word could be anything,' said Kip.

'Depends on how you read it. Second: Albert and Leela aren't here, but the poem says each of us begins to solve the test.'

'*Begin* is a strange word,' said Incognita. 'You are at the end now.'

'Exactly,' said Timmi. 'There are four letters in the password, and four friends in the poem.'

A word with four letters. Four friends. Each begins…

Kip looked at Timmi with a new kind of awe: it could only be one thing.

'Our initials? Timmi, Albert, Leela, Kip? TALK? That's the password?'

'Let's see if we're right,' said Timmi.

Kip watched intently as she turned the wheels one after the other to form the secret word that he hoped would take them home. As the last letter slotted into place, Incognita spoke.

'The gateway changes.'

Before them, the hundreds of different-shaped lily pads in the pool were merging together, leaf by leaf. At last, only one giant lily pad remained trembling over the water, inviting them to step aboard.

Chapter Twenty-One

Rage

The Lava-Lamp Limbo spat the three of them out on to a green lawn that smelled of summertime. Timmi spread her arms wide and tried to hug the grass.

'Are we really, truly home?' she asked, looking at all the familiar places with tears in her eyes.

There was no mistaking the sugar-white pillars of the Quicksmiths Library, glittering in the sunshine.

'Home sweet home,' Kip replied.

But something was missing: it was deathly quiet.

'Where is everyone?' he asked.

'The evacuation, remember?' Timmi replied. 'They must all still be in the Bunker. But they said Miss Twiss stayed behind.'

She opened her Carousel and flicked to the speech bubble.

'Miss Twiss,' she called, 'GENI! We're back! We're home! We're at the Library.'

In a few minutes, the Professor-in-Charge came soaring through the midday sky.

'Thank the stars you're back,' her voice spoke in their minds before she had set the Skimmi down. 'Are you hurt?'

'We're OK,' said Kip.

'And who is this?'

'Miss Twiss, this is Incognita,' said Timmi. 'Incognita, this is the Professor-in-Charge of Quicksmiths.'

Incognita stepped forward and bowed.

'Honoured to meet you,' said the android.

'Incognita has been looking after us,' said Timmi. 'She saved our lives.'

'Then you are welcome here, always,' said Miss Twiss, taking the android's hand.

'Have all the holes been fixed now?' asked Kip.

'How did you … ah the Dreambomber! Things took a turn for the worse after the evacuation but it all seems to be under control now.'

'What happened?' Timmi asked.

'I was taking some readings at the Singing Mill, when a Prowler pushed through the opening in the wall, emitting a Strange Energy I didn't recognise. I tried to speak to it but it didn't respond, and I found myself too weak to move as it came closer. But then at the last minute, it seemed to heed some call and withdrew back into the fissure.'

'We saw one too,' said Timmi. 'At Eartha's house.'

'We must record all these details, and soon,' said Miss Twiss. 'But first, how long has it been since you ate and drank?'

'Ages,' said Kip. 'A day and a night. I think.'

'Then let's continue our stories in the Buttery.'

There was no hot food, but Miss Twiss found them some milkshakes from the fridge, a heap of savoury scones, and some bowls of fruit. The wholesome smell of oranges brought Pinky out from Kip's pocket; she ate between yawns, with her eyes nearly closed, before returning to bed. All the while, in between bolted mouthfuls, Kip and Timmi's questions exploded out and they answered more in turn.

'You mean to say that Julius Grittleshank is dead?' said Miss Twiss.

'It was awful,' said Timmi.

'The loss of life should never be celebrated, but it was lucky for you in a way. You wouldn't have been treated well had you remained their captives.'

Kip thought back to the Thag Camp, and to Gorvak's threats, and knew Miss Twiss was right.

'We met Eartha too,' he said.

The Professor-in-Charge interlaced her fingers, and her eyes sparkled gladly with just a hint of envy.

'Extraordinary,' she said. 'Extra-extra-ordinary. Luck shone on you in the Myriads.'

'She told us to find the Futurescope and we did. Incognita, show Miss Twiss!'

The Professor-in-Charge took the ancient brass telescope from Eartha's android and, just as Kip had done, she held it up to her eye and looked for hidden marvels.

'Well, well, well!' said her voice in his head. 'You've made some staggering discoveries in your short time at Quicksmiths … but finding this … this is going to change everything.'

Timmi smiled proudly at the rare compliment, and Kip felt himself doing the same.

'But you also say the Grittleshanks have been stealing Eartha's concealed inventions from the Myriads?' Miss Twiss's voice said, in a darker tone. 'This is disturbing news.'

'It isn't great,' agreed Kip. 'Although Eartha wasn't worried about those so much. She said it's the Futurescope that counts.' He took the telescope back from Miss Twiss's extended hands. 'But I can't get it to work properly.'

'It looks as if the eyepiece is missing,' said Miss Twiss, pointing at the marks in the wood.

As he collapsed its tubes back together, Kip couldn't help feeling a biting disappointment.

'Can we make a new one?'

'Only time will tell,' said the Professor-in-Charge. 'The important thing is that you did as Eartha asked, against all odds.'

'Something's bothering me,' said Timmi. 'Why did Iris take Kip's book?'

'It's not clear what the Grittleshanks hope to achieve from this theft,' said Miss Twiss, 'but whatever it is, we can be sure that it's not a noble intention.'

'It must be something to do with the squirls, right?' said Kip. 'They took Eartha's book too.'

'Does that mean we won't ever be able to understand Aeon Light properly?' Timmi asked.

'Oh, I wouldn't say that,' said Miss Twiss. 'We may have lost the books, but now we have the Futurescope.'

Miss Twiss's Candle beeped and a speech bubble floated up. She reached out to tick the Touchlight, and Tamara Okpik's face appeared.

'Adelaide,' she said. 'The holes we've been sealing up seem to be staying closed now, as long as we keep the drones actively stabilising them. GENI's still weak, but it's good progress. What do you want me to do with Koriolis?'

'Him!' said Kip. 'He sabotaged Leela's Dreambomber!'

'Was he trying to kill us?' asked Timmi angrily.

'That's not quite what happened,' said Miss Twiss's voice inside their heads, 'although it might have been the end result, had we not intervened. He was so determined to be the hero, to make his Myriad masterpiece work successfully, that he didn't want to be upstaged by Leela.'

'He was *jealous*?' said Kip, not quite believing his ears.

'He was jealous,' Miss Twiss confirmed. 'And that jealousy consumed his sense of right and wrong.' She turned back to Tamara. 'Keep Alexios in the holding cell.'

'Will do,' Tamara said. 'Things are pretty busy over here, I could do with an extra pair of hands...'

'I have an idea,' said Miss Twiss, looking at Incognita, 'perhaps we could call on the good nature of our guest?'

Incognita readily agreed to help, and once she had set off for the Security Centre, Miss Twiss ushered Kip and Timmi to her office in Celestial Hall.

'If it's all right with you,' she said, 'I'll lock the Futurescope away for now.'

Glad to switch off for a bit, Kip and Timmi sat down at a table, watching as the Professor-in-Charge put the brass telescope into a safe disguised as an ornamental fireplace.

'Why don't you get some orange juice while I check the diagnostics from GENI? With any luck we can bring the evacuees home soon.'

Miss Twiss called up an array of Touchlight panels, which floated like ghostly parchments in the air around her. A hail of numbers, words and mathematical formulas streamed across them.

Kip sipped his juice and leaned back in the Airchair. It felt good to rest completely, and the office was warm and peaceful. His eyes were just beginning to flutter shut when a trumpeting alarm pulsed urgently through the walls of the room in short, sharp blasts. Miss Twiss stood abruptly and changed the content of the monitors to viewpoints around the college. One of these showed a lot of activity – too much activity, like cockroaches seething from an open drain.

With a stab of outrage Kip realised that the battle wasn't over: the Thags had come to Quicksmiths.

'We must hide!' said Miss Twiss. 'The Bunker has been sealed for safety, and it will take too long to reopen the wormhole. There may just be enough time to get to Atlas House.'

Speeding through the timeworn corridors on Skimmies, they took the corners at breakneck speed, Timmi only just managing to keep up with the remarkably agile Professor-In-Charge. The entrance to the Hall of Maps sprang open before them and Miss Twiss headed straight for the Great Globe.

'Can you secure the globe once we're inside?' she said. 'I'll try to contact Tamara Okpik.'

Hunting around inside the doorway, Kip and Timmi found a metal hook that was holding the entrance open. When they unlatched it, the wooden steps folded up with a wheeze and the Africa door hissed shut behind them. Miss Twiss already had another pane of Touchlight open, and in it Kip could see hundreds of Thags pouring into Clock Tower Courtyard.

'What do they want?' whispered Timmi. 'Why are they here?'

'Miss Twiss, we should warn Incognita,' said Kip.

The Professor-in-Charge turned to them, her eyes skimming over Kip, and it occurred to him that she might be conducting several conversations at once.

'I can't reach her,' she said.

'How can the Thags get past GENI?' said Timmi. 'She always keeps us safe.'

'Her defensive drone network has been reassigned to stop the Myriads from leaking into Quicksmiths. Even though she is a Strange Supercomputer, GENI has her limits. She cannot seal up the holes while securing the perimeters, and the Grittleshanks know it.'

The speech bubble icons in each of their Carousels flashed and Alpha Thag's voice burst through sharply, too loudly.

'Bramley!' he yelled. 'I'm coming for you!'

The rage spilled over in his voice – the rage of a child who'd lost his father, and the fury of a young man without a leader.

Miss Twiss held a finger to her lips.

'He doesn't know we're here,' she said, inside Kip's mind.

Images flickered in the Touchlight as it tracked Thag stalking the empty corridors of Celestial Hall. At the Buttery, he smashed several tables into firewood with a black-gloved fist. In Miss Twiss's office, he ripped her bookcase from the wall and stamped out in a storm of torn pages. Back outside, in Confucius Courtyard, as he was just about to tear the old oak from the earth, he stopped to listen to something, an earpiece perhaps, and smirked nastily.

'Sounds like we've got a tin can to recycle,' he said, stomping out of the courtyard.

A group of moon-faced, punk-haired Thags were gathered around the Security Centre door, waiting for him. Without touching a thing, Alpha Thag smashed in the door, reached inside, and dragged out Incognita. The force of the Slipstream Gloves kept her a few feet off the ground, dangling from the neck. Her arms twisted and turned, trying to catch hold of Thag, but he kept her well out of reach.

'Kip Bramley! If you turn yourself in, I'll let your robot slave go.'

Miss Twiss shook her head.

'He's not to be trusted,' she said.

'I'll give you … too late!'

They watched in horror as Thag pulled at thin air with his black-gloved hands. Several metres away, the chainmail of Incognita's neck stretched and creaked for a short moment before shredding like rags, spilling out a cascade of tiny wheels. Thag tossed her limp body to the ground, and kept her severed head hanging in the Slipstream with one bearclaw hand.

'You're next, Bramley. But first I'm going to make you watch me eat that flying rodent of yours. Alive.'

Kip had never heard such violence in a voice, not even in a film, and it chilled him to the bone. He looked down at his shaking fists – he'd punched a tree once and it had really hurt. That was the extent of his combat experience. But if he was going to have to fight, he would fight, and he would fight well.

'What's that?' whispered Timmi, peering into the Touchlight.

Unseen by Thag, something at floor level – a terrified garden creature perhaps – was hurrying away from the scene. Kip's heart stopped until he checked his pocket for Pinky and found her still there. He looked back at the screen but whatever it was had gone.

'What do we do now?' he asked.

'I'm going to speak with GENI and Tamara,' Miss Twiss said, gravely. 'To see what our options are.'

'We could check around the study, see if there's anything we can use to defend ourselves,' Timmi said.

'Excellent,' the Professor-in-Charge replied. 'Bring whatever you can find to me.'

Hoping to discover something at least as powerful as Eartha's Grandfather Clock, Kip sprang over to the desk and began ripping open drawers. Over to his left, Timmi was rifling through wooden chests.

When the faint knock on the door came none of

them were in the least bit prepared for the shock. Miss Twiss put a finger to her lips again and scrolled along the pane of Touchlight until she could see the outside of the Great Globe. Then, still expressionless as always, she walked swiftly to the door and opened it just a crack.

There was an uneasy wait while the steps unfolded, and then something scrambled up and hopped into the study. Miss Twiss shut the door again firmly, while the others watched the new arrival. From the way it moved, Kip knew it was the creature they'd seen scuttling away from the Security Centre. And then he realised it wasn't a living thing at all.

'Incognita's hand!'

'And it's carrying something!' said Timmi.

Its matchstick-sized mechanical legs brought it scurrying with a slight wobble towards Kip.

'She must have detached it before Thag got to her,' he said.

Their strange, disembodied visitor presented its delivery at Kip's feet, and waited. If the hand had had a tail, it would have been wagging now.

Kip picked up a brass disc about the same size as the hand itself. A mallet was clipped to the back, and the front of the disc was polished smooth. Some words were engraved there:

Blood must be drawn before you can play me.

‘The Myriad Gong!’ said Miss Twiss, stepping closer.

‘That’s the Myriad Gong?’ said Timmi. ‘GENI told us about it. Ages ago. In the Viking Myriad. Remember, Kip? She said Thag used it to make his army.’

The Professor-in-Charge examined it hastily.

‘Yes, it’s believed that whoever plays the gong can summon counterparts, linked selves from the Myriads.’

‘Incognita must have swiped it from Thag,’ said Kip. ‘She tried to save us, even though she couldn’t save herself…’

After everything that had happened in the other worlds, this was the closest Kip had come to breaking down. Unable to get any more words out, he bought some time by staring hard at the gong.

‘If we can get it to work, maybe we can find a way to send them back to where they came from?’ said Timmi. ‘It can’t be that difficult if Thag can use it.’

‘That would be the least violent option,’ said Miss Twiss. ‘But I expect Thag would need to play it himself to reverse the effects. An easier use of the gong would be to bring an opposing army here to help us.’

‘But what does that mean, “blood must be drawn”?’ said Timmi unhappily. ‘There’s already been enough blood lost.’

Before anyone could reply, there was clattering and shouting outside in the Hall of Maps.

'They're here,' Miss Twiss said. 'Kip, can you find a way to activate the gong?'

Taking Eartha's artefact from the Professor-in-Charge, Kip nodded with more certainly than he felt.

'Timmi, come with me. We need to buy Kip some time. The entrance is narrow so we have a good chance of holding them off if they manage to open the door. Help me lift those wooden chests to block the way in...'

Blood is Drawn

Thinking ahead, Kip took Pinky out of his pocket, pulled a couple of thick books off the bookcase and lifted her up to the shelf with a whispered promise.

'Stay! I'll come and get you when it's safe.'

He pushed the books back in halfway to make a hiding space for her at the back, and then half-pulled a few more out so they wouldn't look out of place. It was too much of a risk that Thag would get to her if he was caught again.

Moving swiftly to Eartha's old desk, he swept a workspace clear and put down the gong. It wasn't easy to unclip the mallet from the brass disc, but Kip managed to prise it free. He re-read the words of the engraving, blackened by the centuries.

Blood must be drawn before you can play me.

Does it need a genetic sample? he thought.

There was another question – almost as difficult. Who would play the gong? As he ran through the options, his head swam with doubts.

One: Miss Twiss.

She's clever but old. Thag wouldn't hesitate to hurt her.

Two: Timmi.

Could hundreds of her defeat the Thags? Maybe they'll arrive carrying inventions, but that's not something we can rely on.

Three: himself.

Am I any match for all those Thags either?

Aside from all of that, the Miss Twisses or Timmis or even the Kips from the other Myriads might not want to fight someone else's battle, and even if they did some of them would end up being hurt or perhaps killed. It didn't seem right.

I'll deal with that later, he thought. *First, I need to get this working.*

The study shook as someone, perhaps several people, began to hammer on the surface of the Great Globe.

Kip forced himself to concentrate on the mallet, which had a ball at one end and a blunt point at the other. He tentatively struck the gong with the spherical end. It didn't make a sound, so he tried again, bending closer to hear better.

'First the Silent Key,' he muttered, 'and now a Silent Gong.'

The onslaught of blows on the outside of the Great Globe moved around indiscriminately, probing for weakness. Thag's muffled voice could be heard outside.

'What's the question to open the globe? Someone find out for me. Get hold of Shrivelly-Chops.'

'No pressure,' Timmi's words darted from the direction of the door. 'But how are you getting on?'

'Just keep him out,' Kip replied.

Deep in his brain, clusters of quixars churned, stirred perhaps by unseen Myriad Waves coming from the gong.

Do I have to give it my blood?

His thoughts were drawn to the mallet held in his fingers and he pressed its point against the back of his hand. But it wasn't sharp enough to break the surface of his skin.

It has to be something else.

If he'd learned anything over the last few months it was that Eartha was a Sideways Thinker. She expertly hid things in plain sight, things that often had a second purpose…

Blood must be drawn.

Kip swivelled the gong around, looking from all angles, searching for a sign. Then, making sure to be thorough, he inspected the mallet again, finally coming to hold it like a pencil so the point faced the disc. As he brushed the tip over the polished surface, a faint red line was left behind.

It's a pen!

'Where is the Study of Secrets?' boomed Thag's voice outside.

Kip didn't dare look away from the gong as the Africa door hissed and flew open, flooding the study with sounds of clashing, grunts and cries. And he began to write.

B ... L ... O ... O ... D

The letters looked as if they had been scrawled with a red-hot poker. As they lingered, Kip's mind reached for the next problem. There was no time to consider the options again. He would have to play the gong himself, so he turned the mallet around and held it ready to strike.

'GENI,' Miss Twiss's voice sounded in Kip's head. 'Call GENI.'

It was obvious, and perfect. Kip responded without needing to think.

'Question GENI,' he said. 'Can you come here, in your body?'

When her voice replied, it was weak and faltering.

'Yes, Kip. But it would take too much energy. My drones would power down and I would no longer be able to keep the holes sealed up. I would be too weak to help you.'

'That won't matter,' said Kip. 'If this works, it'll make you strong again. Please, come here.'

GENI materialised before him and Kip's heart leapt to see her. But her eyelids were half-shut, and her shoulders stooped with lethargy.

'Quick!' said Kip. 'Play the gong!'

He pressed the mallet into GENI's listless hands and helped her to hit the polished face of the brass disc. This time a peaceful chime rang out, the kind that might call pilgrims to meditate in a mountain sanctuary.

Please work, please work, please work.

Biting fingers clamped on Kip's shoulder and whirled him around. There was a brief impression of a wrathful sneer, and a fist slammed into his face.

Small but Deadly

One eye blinked open. The other one didn't seem to work too well. Kip found himself lying face down, one cheek against a wooden plank. Feet scuffled around him and he pulled his hands in.

'Kip,' said Miss Twiss's voice insistently. 'Get under the desk!'

He shuffled quickly into the confined space, and peered out past the chair, trying to work out what was going on.

Timmi and Miss Twiss were huddled in an alcove at

the side of the bookcase. Thags were spilling through the doorway and Incognita's mechanical hand was nipping at their heels. Everywhere else Kip looked, GENI's counterparts were lifting up off the floor like angels. Some were children, some were as old as the hills; some were male, some female, some neither, or both, like GENI; some were of one race, some of another; some were of all races, or none. But they were all unmistakably GENI, with deep, calm, wise eyes.

Kip looked for his GENI and found her. She was standing upright now, seeming to draw energy from her family. Out of their midst, she looked straight at him and smiled.

'You think those gruesome *things* can help you?' barked Alpha Thag, lunging in the original GENI's direction. 'Where's Ozymandias?'

'He's back at HQ,' shouted a Thag with snail eyes, who was already trapped against a cabinet. 'Gorvak recalled him.'

Alpha Thag bellowed with rage. Before he could shout out another order, the GENIs crowded around him, pushing him backwards towards the door, into a reversing clump of Myriad Thags.

Miss Twiss's voice spoke to the groupmind, challenging Thag.

'You're outnumbered Pythagoras, and outpowered. Withdraw your army.'

Thag let out a yowl of boiling frustration and

clawed the air with his black-gloved hands. Several GENIs reacted fast to protect those in their care, blocking the path of destruction. Looking around the chair, Kip saw their forms wavering, and falling apart, and feared that the Slipstream Gloves might be too powerful even for GENI and her Myriad family.

But, as he watched, the defenders of Quicksmiths pulsed brightly in perfect synchronisation, and came together into a single nebula formed of thousands of energy moths.

'You think a few Mothballs will stop me?' jeered Thag.

'You can't rip apart a cloud, Pythagoras,' said the GENIs with one voice.

Flurries of silver-veined Mothballs swept around the study mercilessly, flying at the Myriad Thags from all directions, and Kip saw that they were different from the ones he was used to. Razor-sharp wings sliced and jabbed at Alpha Thag, causing him to yelp in pain, driving him back, along with the rest of his kind, out of the Great Globe.

Still clutching the gong, Kip went to stand at the open Africa door with Timmi and Miss Twiss. Out in the Hall of Maps, the great cloud of Mothballs drove the Myriad Thags before it as if they were a herd of swearing sheep. Occasionally, one of them turned and tried to fight, and fell in a hail of small but deadly wings.

They watched in Miss Twiss's Touchlight panel as

the invading army was driven back from the ancient halls and high-tech chambers of Quicksmiths – down the grand staircases, along rickety corridors and through space-age vaults – towards the boathouse and the Crazy Paving. Elbowing each other and jostling for space, the Myriad Pirates poured onto the lakebed, disappearing in flash after flash after flash, and the infestation was swept clean almost as speedily as it had arrived.

'Won't they be able to come back?' asked Kip.

Miss Twiss shook her head.

'GENI tells me they have been escorted to a very unpleasant place indeed. She also took back the stolen key, along with the Grittleshank devices that enabled Thag and his army to share the key's power and move freely from our reality to the Myriads. They can no longer terrorise any of the other worlds.'

When Kip went to collect Pinky from her hiding place on the bookshelf, her tiny body was shivering. He held her close, so she could feel his heart beating.

'He's gone now,' he said soothingly, as much to himself as to her.

As they left the Hall of Maps, Tamara Okpik came running up. Her cheeks were flushed and her eyes shining.

'I saw everything from the top of the Clock Tower,' she said. 'It was incredible. A home win!'

During the short walk to the Security Centre, the

host of Myriad GENIs whisked around the college grounds, sealing holes shut, recharging drones and repairing the damage left by the marauding Thags.

'I wish they could all stay,' said the Professor-in-Charge ruefully. 'Imagine what we could achieve!'

Kip and Timmi looked at her hopefully but she shook her head.

'They must return, balance must be maintained.'

When the Security Centre was in sight, Timmi made a soft, strangled sound and Kip squeezed her hand. It was unbearable to see Incognita's miraculous body thrown carelessly in the herb garden. The glass pane of her chest was cracked and the marvellous Spherical Cog inside was exposed. Close by, an Oddjob Drone was carefully collecting up the tiny wheels that had spilled from the android's torso.

'Oh, Incognita,' Timmi whispered.

'Thank you for keeping us safe,' murmured Kip. 'We'll never forget you.'

'Androids can be surprisingly resilient,' said Miss Twiss. 'There may be life in her yet. Instruction GENI: take Incognita to the laboratories.'

They watched in silence as their GENI appeared and stooped to gather the broken parts in her arms. A single Mothball kissed Incognita's forehead with its wings, and GENI was gone.

'The prison's empty,' said Tamara, emerging from the gape of the shattered doorway.

They all turned to her in disbelief.

'Professor Koriolis escaped?' said Timmi.

'I'm not sure how,' said Tamara, with a sharp nod and a frown. 'Perhaps he was driven away with the Thags.'

She turned to Miss Twiss.

'I don't like loose ends, Adelaide.'

'A loose end can pull the rug from under our feet,' agreed the Professor-in-Charge. 'But there is little to be done, other than search the grounds in case he's still hiding here.'

Miss Twiss looked around the college. There was not a blade of grass out of place on the neat lawn, not a hole in sight, neither in the land nor in the sky. A blackbird trilled somewhere, heralding the early evening.

'Instruction GENI,' she said, 'I think it's time to send your counterparts home.'

Kip wondered what his GENI might be thinking.

I'd be sad if I suddenly had all this family, and then had to send them away. She's a computer. But she's made of Strange Energy. Maybe she has feelings.

After a few seconds GENI returned, along with another human form which took shape in the air beside her.

'My sister has a request,' the original GENI said to the Professor-in-Charge. 'A crisis approaches in her Myriad and she believes the gong may save many lives.'

Miss Twiss nodded and her voice sounded in all their minds.

'It is not our place to withhold such a great gift. Take it, with our hopes that it may change your world.'

GENI's sister took the gong from Kip and held it out so that GENI might easily strike it. Their Myriad family appeared around them, standing and hovering, some holding hands, like generations of ghosts gathered for a reunion. As GENI closed her unreadable eyes, so did they, perhaps saying a silent goodbye, and then she hit the gong lightly and gave the mallet to her sister.

In receding waves of energy, the Myriad GENIs washed away, until all that remained were the first evening stars in the dusk.

Chapter Twenty-Two

The Last Proverb

'I'm going to hug you so hard your eyes squish out like one of those squishy stress balls.'

True to her promise, Leela squashed all the air out of Timmi's lungs, and then Kip's, and then went back to Timmi. Albert tried to pick Pinky up, but the mowl put his little fat arms around her jealously and wurbled.

'Fine by me,' said Albert, scooping them both up. 'Two for the price of one!'

The mowl lirriped and, sitting on his tummy, Pinky tried to copy him, but all that came out was a happy squeak.

'Thanks for not giving up on us,' said Kip. 'It was touch and go for a bit in there.'

Albert gave Kip his best best-friend grin. 'We would never give up on you. Not for all the burgers in all the Myriads.'

They walked side by side along the winding path between the sunflower-yellow First Year Block and the black stone walls of Celestial Hall.

'Are you feeling better now?' Leela asked Timmi.

Timmi tried to twirl a piece of her phantom hair around her fingers, and remembered it had mostly burned away. She smiled sheepishly and spoke with that same quiet confidence Kip had seen in her at the ziggurat.

'Much better, thanks,' she said. 'I spoke to Miss Twiss about it. She said that when I took the VR headset off, the Mindfield went on affecting me – and not Kip – because the wiring in my brain is different. So once the Mindfield thoughts were planted they got stuck in a sort of loop – like an earworm, I suppose, you know a song that just keeps playing in your head. Over time it wears you down, because it doesn't have an off button.'

'So, was it all in your mind?' Leela said.

'Yes and no. Imagine a projector playing a film. All the parts in Kip's projector brain work together as they should, so he can watch a whole film smoothly – there'll be scary scenes or violent scenes but they come and go in the right order like they should. My projector brain has parts that miscommunicate, so I might see one scene pop up again and again at weird times and places, until it starts to take over the plot of the film.'

'I wish I'd known before,' said Kip.

'That makes two of us,' said Timmi.

'But it's gone forever now, right?' asked Albert.

'I'll always be made this way, so it might come back – maybe in a different form. The Mindfield woke something up.'

Leela said what they were all thinking. 'But we stopped it, in the dream!'

'That's still important,' said Timmi. 'You taught me how to deal with it. Miss Twiss said that facing it head on, finding a way to laugh together, that takes away its power.'

'You'd do the same for us,' said Leela.

Timmi didn't need to say thanks, but she did anyway.

'If we were only friends for the easy stuff,' said Kip, 'then we wouldn't be friends at all.'

'Trudat,' said Albert.

'The good news is that getting brain-stuck is actually more common than you'd think,' Timmi said. 'There are even a few other people at Quicksmiths with the same thing. And Miss Twiss said the Singing Mill helps to smooth out their thoughts. So I'll be just fine.'

Pinky sprang to her feet and launched herself from Albert into Timmi's arms, with the mowl a few hop-waddles behind. He climbed over Pinky and tried to slurp the inside of Timmi's nostril with his long, orange tongue.

'What about them Grittleshanks, huh?' said Leela.

'Thag will hate you even more now,' said Albert, looking at Kip.

'Thag *and* Gorvak want revenge,' Kip replied. 'Lucky me.'

'Thag should want revenge on me too,' said Timmi. 'I was just as much to blame, when Julius died. Although really, neither of us were to blame at all.'

'He won't see it that way,' said Kip sadly, but he was glad Timmi had said that all the same.

He shrugged off the gnawing dread, the deep-down instinct that he wouldn't be safe from Gorvak or Thag ever again. But they were far away now, and Quicksmiths was a stronghold where he was protected for the moment at least.

'But what have the Prowlers got to do with everything?' Leela asked. 'Did they come from the Myriads?'

Kip's thoughts went to the menacing figure they'd seen creeping over Eartha's roof.

She must be OK. She has to be.

'We still don't know what they want,' he said.

While they all pondered that, the path kinked itself around a corner and Celestial Hall came into view.

'Hey,' said Albert. 'Chef Garibaldi's planning a celebration feast. Did I tell you that already?'

'Five times,' said Timmi. 'Six if you count that last time.'

'I do believe there's a saying for exactly this situation,' said Leela.

Everyone groaned as she bounced ahead of the group and turned to face them in a philosophical pose.

'Never bring beard crumbs to a barber's banquet.'

From all around the college, people were gravitating towards the Buttery, hanging on trails of delicious smells. The mowl gallop-waddled ahead, running back every few steps to try and hurry everyone up. As they entered one of the low crooked doors that led into Celestial Hall, they saw four figures waiting.

'It's true! You're back!' said Em. The henna artwork on her arms and hands shook itself into a flicker of bursting party poppers.

'Thanks to all of you,' said Timmi. 'You guys found us.'

'We're just glad we could help,' Maya said. 'That Dreambomber's out of this world!'

'Did you really meet Eartha?' asked Penny.

Kip nodded.

'She was everything you imagine. And, although she's this big important person, she was just like one of us. I wish we could have brought her here to meet you all.'

'Can't wait to hear all your stories,' said Badger. 'There better be some weird stuff or I'll be very disappointed.'

'Oh, don't you worry,' said Kip. 'We've seen shedloads of weirdness, right Timmi?'

Timmi nodded.

'Enough to fill a Museum of Weird.'

As they all trooped into the Buttery, a thought hit Kip and lit him up on the inside.

'Hey Leela, can I borrow the Dreambomber later?'

Not the Last Dream

Kip turned in early after the feast, and collected the Dreambomber. The rest of Team Glowflyer would be at movie night for a while, watching *The Return of The Returninator II: The Returning.*

Feeling more excited than he'd felt in all the Myriads, Kip connected up the Psychogenic Beret and set the cylinders of the Dreambomber in motion. He lay back on the lower bunk, closed his eyes, and spiralled into a liquid daydream…

The sun was shining on the old house by the sea. Kip still remembered every detail – the diamond of glass in the front door, the worn carpet on the stairs, the leaf-pattern curtains in the lounge. By the bay window was the mahogany beachcombing cabinet, full of salvaged treasure.

There was an old but familiar sound – the front door opening – and Kip ran into the hallway, eager and yet full of uncertainty. This moment was everything. And there she was, wearing her favourite jeans and one of Theo's shirts, her hair pulled together in a messy half-bun-half-ponytail.

'Who's that?' she said, blinking in the bright sunshine, and Kip's heart fell.

'It's me, Mum, Kip!'

The lost look in her eyes swirled and came into focus.

'My Kip!' said his mum, wrapping him in her arms and kissing the top of his head.

'I knew I'd find you in here,' Kip said happily, holding on to her tightly. 'I *knew*!'

'But you're all grown up!' said Rose, gripping his shoulders.

How did Kip begin to explain the Dreambomber?

'We're inside your mind,' he tried. 'I just wanted to talk to you so much.'

'But we talk all the time,' she saw Kip's face and looked worried, 'don't we?'

'No, Mum,' said Kip. 'You were in an accident. You're in a care home. And … well, you don't recognise me most of the time now.'

Rose Bramley's face collapsed. She put her hand to her heart and sat on the sofa, pulling Kip down beside her.

'Never. It can't be possible.'

'That doesn't matter,' said Kip, 'we're talking now, aren't we?'

She spoke slowly, as if realising something for the first time.

'I sense her now, Kip. The me out there, the damaged me. If I were a book, then it's like some pages have been torn out. Sometimes I can make out one or two words, but the rest is gone. I can't piece me back together.'

'In here, things are different,' said Kip brightly. 'And now we'll be able to talk whenever we like.'

'But you need me!' his mum protested. 'What kind of a mother am I? And I'm missing out on you growing up. I have to get better!'

'I'm working on it,' said Kip. 'It might help if you can tell me more about the accident … the lightning.'

Outside, a dove cooed reassuringly, while Kip's mum leaned forward and stared at the carpet. She put a hand to her temple briefly and then sat up straight.

'I was visited by an old friend that day … what was his name? I never saw him though, he only left me a note.'

'What did it say?' asked Kip.

'I don't remember,' said his mum, biting her bottom lip.

'What about this?' said Kip, holding up the piece of quartz that hung around his neck.

Rose took it hesitantly, her eyes questioning.

'You spoke a few months ago,' he tried again, 'you said this was important.'

She was trying hard, her face tensed, but after a while her shoulders drooped and she shook her head. Then her eyes widened as something came back to her.

'We were by the old lighthouse. There was someone walking at the edge of the cliff, but they were in the air.'

Could be a Skimmi, thought Kip.

'And the storm?' he asked.

'No, there was no storm,' she replied, confused. 'It was a lovely calm day, blue skies. But then…'

The curtain billowed up in a breeze from the open window and the sunbeams crowded in, catching in Rose's hair.

'Time seemed to stop … and the light was … broken? And you…'

She wrapped her arms around Kip again.

'I saw you, lifted up in the air, just a small mite of a thing, hanging there, out of reach, next to the old lighthouse.'

Kip nodded. It sounded as if there were a lot more going on here than he'd ever suspected.

'What does it all mean?' said Rose.

'I don't know yet. But we'll figure it out together.'

He grabbed his mum's hand and pulled her towards the cabinet.

'Remember this?' he said, opening the glass front.

Rose laughed delightedly and picked out a shell,

and the tangled brown tendrils of a mermaid's purse, and then a pink sea-polished stone.

'Oh, your dad loved this one, didn't he? Look, he connected up the marks to make a smiley face!'

That's a thought.

'Just give me a sec,' he said.

While Rose pored over the sea treasure in the cabinet, Kip closed his eyes and focused his Deep Thinking, searching for his sister Suzanna in his mind, trying to conjure her here too. But all he found was a blurry outline, just a hollow memory. Saddened but not yet discouraged, he shifted his thoughts instead to his dad – the smell of freshly baked bread, kung-fu film nights, climbing weekends and games of Find-the-Raisin with Pinky.

The front doorbell rang.

'I think you should get it,' he said.

His mum smoothed down her hands on her jeans and walked with a light step into the corridor. The door creaked open and there was a pause that hung like the tick of a long clock, followed by muffled sounds of surprise, of lost-and-found love, and good-old-days regained. Kip gave his mum and dad some space, waiting patiently by the cabinet, until he thought it was time to go out.

'Kip!' said his dad, through tears of happiness. 'C'mere!'

Theo pulled them both outside into the warm

sunshine and whirled them around in a tight circle, the tulips and cherry plum trees and yellow-and-blue sky blurring into one, the three of them together again, holding on for dear life to the safety and warmth that only dwells deep in the roots of family. Kip started to lose his grip on the dream and he slowed them down to a gradual stop.

'Hey Dad,' he said. 'What's your favourite word?'

'Picnic!' said Rose and Theo at the same time and laughed like teenagers.

'That's perfect,' said Kip, and just like that he was holding a basket covered in chequered cloth.

Theo Bramley looked down at the cosy blanket that had appeared in his own hands.

'If this a dream,' he said, 'I never want it to end.'

'The end doesn't have to be the end, Dad,' said Kip. 'I see plenty more dreams in our future.'

Author's note

Have you ever had a thought that make you feel upset or sad? Turns out you're not alone. Everyone has these thoughts from time to time – they rise quickly and fall away like waves, and they are perfectly normal, part of being human.

However some people become stuck with the idea of a fearful, horrible and unwanted thought, and struggle to stop thinking about it. Getting brain-stuck in this way usually means that you are experiencing 'obsessive thoughts", sometimes called intrusive thoughts. The author Edgar Allen Poe talks about this type of thought in one of his short stories, and that is one of the reasons why I chose a quotation from him to start this book.

Many people who struggle with obsessive thoughts – like Timmi – think they are the only person in the world to have this problem, and they feel very frightened. They usually suffer in silence, and they tend to be very sensitive and caring people.

Because it is frightening, sometimes we can find these thoughts difficult to talk about. It can be hard for others to understand what is happening, or know how we are feeling, because no one can see inside our heads.

Thoughts like these are often part of Obsessive Compulsive Disorder (OCD), although they do occur in other conditions. The most recent studies suggest that some form of OCD occurs in approximately 1 in 200 children.

What can we do?

As parents, guardians and teachers: be alert. Inform yourself of the symptoms and signs of intrusive thoughts – they can be harder to recognise if they are purely internal and do not trigger any visible compulsions. Know where professional advice can be found: a good starting point is a charity called Nip in the Bud, as well as OCD-UK and OCD Action. Two excellent self-help books I can recommend are *Overcoming OCD*, Veal and Wilson (2021) and the slightly older *The Imp of the Mind*, Lee Baer (2002).

As friends and family: be kind. If you know someone who might have intrusive thoughts, you can help them more than you think. Kip, Albert and Leela are there for Timmi in her moment of need, even though she sometimes tries to push them away because she is afraid.

As yourself: be brave. Talking about intrusive thoughts can be difficult, and you should only do so when you are with someone you trust. Help is never far away. Sometimes schools have therapists you can talk to about how you are feeling. Charities like Childline can also be a good place to start talking about your feelings and experiences. Therapists are trained in treating intrusive thoughts, just like a doctor is trained in treating a broken leg or a stomach upset. And when you learn how to manage your fear, like Timmi, you will find that its power will gradually fade.

Look after yourselves.

Joris

Thank you to OCD-UK and OCD Action for reviewing this note.

Acknowledgements

Thanks to:

Arts Council England, without whom this book could not have been written.

The Books Council of Wales who work wonders getting books in the hands of children.

All the lovely Fireflies, especially my patient and wise editors Penny and Leonie; Robin for his ceaseless encouragement; and marketers and all-round cheerleaders, Meg and Amy.

Roland Clare who gave up his time for an invaluable early edit, and made many astute suggestions, including the ingenious answer to the password.

Liam, who is always a reassuring voice of both reason and madness and a never-ending fountain of ideas.

Charlie & Kai, the original Albert!

Everyone who has otherwise contributed to the production of this book including the wonderful Anne

Glenn (book cover), Jackie Maxfield (illustrations) and Elaine Sharples (typesetter).

Bounce Sales and Marketing who do such great work getting our books out to the world.

My agent Anne Clark, and foreign rights agent Margot Edwards, who constantly champion their authors.

My friends and family who have supported me in so many different ways, especially Rebecca Hughes, John Stead, Zelda Rhiando, Molly Pocket, Aunty Dorothy, all my cousins, Susan Jones, Dan, Jessica & Luke.

My Zimbabwean WhatsApp group, in particular Irene Rusike, Flora Chigwedere, Annette Daly, Nikki Travlos, Shakira Khan, and Shameela Sirdar.

Tuqan Tuqan for thoughts on henna.

All the tireless booksellers and bloggers who inspire us all with your love of books.

All the educators, librarians, parents and guardians who make reading special for children wherever they may live.

All the authors who I have met (mostly) virtually over the last few years, and whose friendship has kept me going, and especially Kieran Larwood who revealed the book cover (and endorsed *Ten Riddles* along with Dan Walker), and Jennifer Killick and

Gavin Hetherington who helped to launch my first book.

All the readers everywhere who are transported to myriad worlds every day. An extra special mention for Quicksmiths fans Zara, Neve, Penny Maddy, Clara, Ellie, Charlotte, Georgie, Alex, Edie, Freya, Delilah, Fenella, Leila, Lizzy, Sarah, Amelie, Noemi, Nahla, Ash, Milan, Ryland, Harry, Alfie, Kester, Douglas, David, Buddy, Teddy, Oliver, Ozzy, Josiah, Lucas, Lawrence, Jaiveer, Zack, Oluwanimilo, Will, Jasper … and ALL the booklovers I've met at schools, or online, or who've left an anonymous review or message, whose names I don't know!

If I have accidentally missed anyone out, please forgive my forgetful brain.